Praise for

'In *Confidence*, Ben Richards lo[...]
compassion and heartlessnes[...]
for a gratifyingly long time, m[...]
about them. Almost everything possesses duality . . . Richards'
handling of these opposites and the well-paced narrative,
with its regular arrival of fresh developments, make *Confidence*
readable and enjoyable' *Times Literary Supplement*

'The novel is the perfect showcase for Richards' formidable
talents, matching the political bite he has often displayed in his
novels with the knack of creating sharp, fast-paced narratives . . .
Ambitious and timely modern morality tale' *Mirror*

'London is full of good-enough actresses, most of them should
really get another job. In Ben Richards' dirty city fable of one
such girl, a second-rate actress becomes a first-rate liar through
her Faustian pact with a nasty Welsh devil. Generously going
against type in a modern morality tale, Ben Richards offers a
tantalising possibility that, in the end, truth and hope might
just win through' Stella Duffy

'One part *Brighton Rock's* Pinkie, one part *Catch Me If You Can's*
Frank Abagnale Jr, one part Howard Marks (that's the Welsh
part), Evan is the thinking girl's modern Mephisto' *Guardian*

'London-based and contemporary to its core . . . a gutful of
"no-don't-do-it" moments, but funny gay best friend Mark
offers some light relief. Richards' philosophical musings on
Blair, leftie liberals, morals and more are thought-provoking'
Eve

'[Richards'] screenwriting expertise is exuberantly to the fore in
Confidence, which reads so much like a superior television
drama that it may even become one. Stylish, well paced and
up to the minute . . . A slick crime drama' *Independent*

Ben Richards is the author of five previous novels, the most recent of which, *The Mermaid and the Drunks*, was a Richard and Judy Summer Read in 2004. He now writes extensively for television, including the hit BBC drama *Spooks*.

By Ben Richards

Confidence
The Mermaid and the Drunks
A Sweetheart Deal
Don't Step on the Lines
The Silver River
Throwing the House Out of the Window

Confidence

BEN RICHARDS

PHOENIX

A PHOENIX PAPERBACK

First published in Great Britain in 2006
by Weidenfeld & Nicolson
This paperback edition published in 2007
by Phoenix,
an imprint of Orion Books Ltd,
Orion House, 5 Upper St Martin's Lane,
London WC2H 9EA

1 3 5 7 9 10 8 6 4 2

A CIP catalogue record for this book
is available from the British Library.

ISBN 978-0-7538-2162-6

Typeset at The Spartan Press Ltd,
Lymington, Hants

Printed and bound in Great Britain by
Clays Ltd, St Ives plc

The Orion Publishing Group's policy is to use papers that
are natural, renewable and recyclable products and
made from wood grown in sustainable forests. The logging
and manufacturing processes are expected to conform to
the environmental regulations of the country of origin.

www.orionbooks.co.uk

For Faith

PART ONE

Terrapins

The early-morning sun is warming the water on the lake as a blue-shorted jogger clutching an iPod in one hand outpaces the red buses crawling up the road parallel to the London park, running past a middle-aged man from one of the expensive terraces overlooking the park who is walking his dog.

The dog is called Rab and his owner – a lecturer in social history – is composing a paper in his head about the nature of selection and class bias in the contemporary British education system. He turns and whistles back to the dog, which comes running with such enthusiasm that it is almost laughing as it is running and it looks as if its front legs might actually rise higher than its head, such is its determination to arrive at its goal. The man turns away from the dog and continues walking, but Rab does not arrive at his heels, and so he turns back to see that the dog has suddenly stopped to sniff the feet of a red-headed girl sitting on one of the benches. She is quite tall and dressed simply in a long skirt made from a light and frothy material with silver thread running through it and a plain black vest. Sometimes she glances at her shoulder as if checking to see that her vulnerable skin is not being burned by the morning sun. One of her long legs is crossed, and he can see the bright red of her nail varnish as she jigs a black flip-flop on the end of her foot. The lecturer sighs slightly and for an instant he wonders what an attractive girl like that – perhaps a little younger than his daughter Lucy – is doing sitting alone by the lake at this early hour. Then he feels slightly impatient with himself for thinking it. Why shouldn't she sit here just staring at the water?

Why should he be thinking about her in that way? Perhaps she has a good reason, people have all kinds of worries and sorrows, perhaps she just wanted a little time to think, nothing wrong with that. Still, she should be careful. There are people . . . he feels the flash of irritation with himself again, something a little like shame . . . all right, but she should be careful, that's all. At this time of the morning there are all kinds of strange people in the park, especially in these quieter bits by the lake with the bushes just behind them. He whistles his dog a second time and it bounds towards him again – a little cylinder of energy, all packed muscle on its little legs, and the girl turns to watch it, smiling at its singular exuberance. The lecturer walks on and doesn't look back at the red-haired girl or wonder any longer about her well-being or the nature of the internal drama that has impelled her to come and sit by the lake. He has just seen his neighbour walking her boxer and he thinks he really might say something about the satellite dish that she has just had installed in what he considers far too prominent a position on the front of her property.

Kerenza Penhaligon watches Mr Dressed-Exclusively-By-Marks-and-Spencer disappearing with his funny little dog, smiles again and turns back to the lake. Right in front of her bench is the log where sometimes terrapins sit and sun themselves, but they are not there today, although a squadron of ducklings are puttering about. They are so tiny and helpless, she imagines some sharp-toothed predator gliding towards or, worse, underneath them; a pike perhaps attracted by the morse code of those fragile legs disturbing the water. Dot Dot Dot Dash Dash Dash – snap me up for breakfast.

She's been sitting here for about half an hour because she woke up at about half-past four in the morning worrying about credit card bills and direct debits (four due in the next couple of days, no funds with which to pay them, four charges for unpaid direct debits) and the rent which is due to her housemate, Anna. For a while, she lay watching the digital clock change and the tail of her cat Smut – high on top of the suitcase – twitching as she dreamed. In the end she had got so pissed off with lying awake letting the same information kaleidoscope in her mind that she had got up and walked down Green Lanes to buy a paper. The early-morning sun had been shining so brightly – and unexpectedly – that she had stepped into the park and walked to the lake to try and brush out her fatigue and worry.

'It's just money,' she thinks as she sees a young girl pushing a pram with a kid she has seen in the park before. The kid has cerebral palsy, flaps his arms chaotically. But this thought doesn't console her much. She doesn't have cerebral palsy, it's true, but that enables her to worry about other things. The girl pushing the pram stops at the spot where the terrapins normally are, then turns and shrugs at Kerenza.

'They're not here?' She is very young, her accent sounds Eastern European, unlikely to be the child's mother, some hired help. Kerenza shakes her head but points out the ducklings. The girl kneels down to the pram and shows the ducklings to the boy, who lolls his head and flaps his arms. Kerenza gets up and heads for the park exit, walks back down Green Lanes – past the Ockabasis and Turkish coffee shops – towards her own house. On her way back she sees the man with the dog again, but he is on the other side of the road and does not notice her.

'Hey, Ren.' Anna is pushing down the plunger on the cafetière as she pads into the kitchen followed by Smut. 'Sleep well?' Kerenza sits down at the kitchen table, lets the cat jump onto her lap, reaches for a piece of cold toast, takes a bite, throws it back onto the table. Smut stands with front paws on table and back paws on lap, sniffs the toast and looks outraged from toast to owner and back again.

'I'll take that as a no, then.'

Kerenza studies her friend, who is scratching the back of her leg with one foot. She has known Anna since their first day at school together, when Anna had come up to her and said simply, you're going to be my best friend, and Kerenza had said, oh all right, and Anna had nodded, and they have managed to stay best friends even when Anna went off to university and Kerenza was at drama school. Now Anna has a job lecturing on international law and human rights, a funny Croatian husband she married so that he could get a passport and a purse that contains money and credit cards which aren't maxed out even though she doesn't earn so much. She is one of those people who just seems to manage her affairs well, who chooses her best friend decisively at eleven years old, has her paperwork in box-files and fills in forms on time. She doesn't have an iPod or a Palm or a Blackberry, her mobile is so old it's fashionable, although she does not know or care about that. She also owns their house, which was left to her by an aunt. It is an old and comfortable house; a great willow in the garden overhangs a bench where Anna often reads her books on human rights abuses and violations of international law, and Kerenza some-times watches her from her own bedroom window, envying the quiet certainties of her life. Anna charges Kerenza a ridiculously low rent for the spare room, and Kerenza sometimes thinks that, without the house and without her best friend, life would be a complete disaster.

'I can't pay the rent this month.'

'OK.'

'You can evict me if you like.'

'Don't be stupid. When do you think you can pay?'

'I don't know.'

'Whenever.'

Anna sits down, cradling her cup of coffee.

Kerenza says, 'You going in to your department today?'

Anna shakes her head.

'Got some stuff to do here. You want to go and see a film this week? We can go to the Rio: it's further than you think.'

Kerenza laughs at the name they use for the cinema in Dalston. They always set off for it on foot and always end up grumbling about the distance.

'I haven't . . .'

'I'll get the tickets. I just don't want to go on my own.'

6

Kerenza nods and peers out of the window to the road. There is no traffic and a yellow-jacketed policeman is making exaggerated circling gestures to oncoming cars, urging them to turn around.

'What's going on out there?'

Kerenza shrugs. 'Shooting? Accident?'

'Go and have a look. Go on.'

Kerenza goes obediently to the front door, opens it, stands on the step, with the grey wind brushing around her bare ankles. She makes a mental note to do her toenails that morning. A little further down the road a police Land Rover stands enclosed by blue and white tape in the road. A maroon van is parked at an odd angle and policemen are making notes.

'What happened?' she asks the Turkish café owner who is standing nearby with his arms folded, also watching. Everyone watching has their arms folded.

'Woman was trying to cross the road. She saw a car coming and stepped back but that van was coming on the inside lane. Split her head right open. Dead.'

Kerenza turns her gaze on the instrument of death. A maroon van with a sticker in the window. The sticker says McGeery Motors. There is something both forlorn and sinister about the stationary vehicle. Behind the scene, a pair of greenfinches are skeering between the branches of the trees. A couple of kids holding chocolate bars pause and stare at the scene outside the newsagent's. The boards for the local paper outside the shop say 'Rapist forced scissors down my throat'. The police take notes. Smut sticks her head around her ankles and Kerenza shoos her back inside, although Smut doesn't like it outside and only ever leaves the house crawling nervously on her belly and staring at the sky as if it might come crashing down on her. Bit of a scaredy-cat when she's not on top of the wardrobe. The postman arrives, staring also at the scene, shaking his head. He hands Kerenza their letters and she turns back into the house.

'Accident,' she tells Anna when she returns. 'Woman was hit outside the dry cleaners.'

7

'That's awful. Is she . . . I mean . . .'

'Dead. Apparently.'

'Oh.'

'What's the post?'

Mostly white envelopes, mostly full of vague threat.

'Kerenza – boring, Kerenza – boring, Anna – college, Kerenza – irritating, Anna – Homerton Hospital . . . what are you going there for?'

'Oh, just some stupid check-up,' Anna says. 'That'll be my appointment.'

'What for?'

'Just some gynae thing.'

She starts to read the paper, licking her finger as she turns pages. It's the *Guardian*, so the headline is not about the scissor-wielding rapist but a claim by the head of MI5 concerning the inevitability of further terror attacks on the UK. None of this matters any longer to the woman who stepped backwards into her death. It was an understandable thing to do, Kerenza thinks, she can visualise herself doing the same, just hopping back out of range of the car seen, not thinking about the other traffic unseen. While Kerenza was sitting in the park looking for the terrapins the woman was still alive, maybe picking up her keys hurriedly from the kitchen table, kissing somebody goodbye.

She wonders again how old the woman was. Young? Impatient? Late for work? Was she middle-class, educated, with a nice sensitive husband at home? Was she a drunk clutching a can of super-strength lager? Would that make it less tragic? Kerenza has to admit that the answer to this question is not as straightforward as she would like to think. She turns and walks back to her bedroom.

In the garden outside her window, a brightly coloured paper windmill propelled by the morning breeze spins in a flowerbox, small and irrelevant under the London sky. The little windmill makes her feel an almost overwhelming sense of despair and then anger at her despair because she hasn't just had her skull split open by the McGeery Motors van, she's not being herded with rifle butts onto a cattle truck, it is just that her chosen career is not going very well and that the careers of others are. Why then is she so miserable that she feels as if the air is entering her lungs and choking her?

For a magic moment, a few years ago after she played Cordelia in a fêted production of *King Lear* that propelled the director to Hollywood, it had seemed that she was about to cross the moat into the castle, but somehow she got waylaid, detained just before the drawbridge while charlatans like her drama-school contemporary Olivia Scott wave their handkerchiefs blithely from the battlements. It is vulgar and unattractive – she knows – to hate Olivia quite so vehemently, to feel like weeping when she hears of the new part she has just been offered, to experience nausea at the sight of the fawning profiles. But her hatred is now a hard cyst inside her because she knows – with equal certainty – that Olivia's success is so out of proportion to her feeble talent. She clenches her teeth as she sees photos of Olivia with her new boyfriend from a serious and earnest pop band. She digs her nails into her hands as Olivia – who has neither a political nor a literary bone in her body – is asked what she thinks about the latest international crisis, the downgrading of cannabis, her most hilarious *faux pas*, her favourite TV programme or her summer reading suggestions.

And what did you expect? cry the mocking voices in her head. *Justice of some sort? Didn't your mad old dad have a few words on this topic, something about plating sin with gold?*

If she had had a fall from grace that was dramatic it might have been better, but now it seems that all the promise and hope and bright confidence of a few years ago has simply oozed slowly away, and she has been powerless to prevent it; nobody pays her the slightest bit of attention any longer, and she can't understand why. What has she done? What has she failed to do? What is wrong with her? She cannot even really identify a turning point, one moment her Cordelia was receiving accolades and people were predicting a glittering future, her agent was fizzing, and then expectation and waiting and then nothing, just a gradual waning of interest, a slow, painful puncture that she can neither locate, nor fix, nor understand. And perhaps, in spite of the pettiness of her rage at the success of Olivia, this lack of an answer lies at the heart of her misery; she just doesn't know. Stories of overnight success require, if they are to have any dramatic impact, the possibility of failure. Some of those eating cold baked beans, packing shelves and fighting to find the coins for the electricity meter while they pursue their dream have to *continue* doing so otherwise there would be nothing interesting about the stories of the luckier few. But who is bothered by the dashed expectations and unrenewed contracts, who really cares about the kid packing away his football boots after being told he is no longer needed by the club that once promised him glory, the actor waiting for the phone to ring?

Sad Fucking Losers

Dear Mark,

Thank you very much for sending me your script 'Sad Fucking Losers', which I greatly enjoyed reading. I am afraid, however, that with my list being rather full at the moment this is not the kind of project I feel I would be able to represent.

While there was a lot that I liked in your depiction of failure, I wondered whether anybody would be interested in so much self-pity? In addition, I feel that you sometimes have a tendency to underplay things. It's not in bad taste for stuff to happen!!! The dialogue was very funny and sometimes made me laugh out loud, but there was perhaps a little too much of it and scenes cannot live on gags alone! I am not in the least squeamish, but it did also push the boundaries of taste from time to time. You would never get the scene with the ferret past a commissioning editor.

My fundamental question, however, is: why do I care about these characters?

You are, however, a talented writer and I would be interested in hearing of any other projects you have.

Emily Holt

Kerenza puts the letter down and shrugs at Mark.

'She's got a point,' she announces.

Mark scowls. 'Everybody likes watching people worse off than themselves.'

Mark adores television. He reads the *Guardian* media overnights every day to follow the ratings of particular programmes.

He is always particularly cheerful when a programme which is supposed to be successful goes into freefall.

'Who's Emily Holt?' Kerenza asks.

'Superagent. If I can get her then I'm halfway there. She's wrong about the ferret, though – it was an *inspired* idea.'

Kerenza nods politely. Mark's acting career had suffered a similar fate to her own after he appeared as the love interest in a widely promoted, disastrously received paranormal rom-com show about his tricky affair with a girl who turned out to be dead. Mark's obsession with ratings started when *Shiver* managed to shed over a million viewers in the first two weeks. This haemorrhage was accompanied by critical derision as the critics scented blood and gleefully lined up to see who could be the most clever in ripping it to shreds, kicking Mark in particular – 'It's a rom-com without the com and – in the case of Mark Pendleton – very little rom.' He had not been offered anything since apart from an advert for gravy granules. Now he has decided to become a writer instead.

'Emily Holt will get my work. I bet those are just the comments of some reader at her agency. Everybody wants Emily.'

Kerenza zones out, calculating that she has at least twenty minutes before Mark will notice that she hasn't said anything. Mark has two topics of conversation – his work-life and his love-life. Neither is going well, especially since Mark started hacking into his ex-boyfriend's e-mail account – something which Mark admits is wrong but claims has become an addiction. The danger of this course of action, of course, consists in reading treacherous and unflattering descriptions, and Mark has still not quite recovered from being referred to as a hysterical drama queen obsessed with a world which – if it has any sense – will continue to keep the door firmly bolted against him. But still – glutton for punishment – he persists in reading the poisoned barbs of an ex-lover.

Kerenza is glad, of course, that his script has been rejected and tries to work out if there is a single German word which means *Terrifying-fear-that-one-of-your-partners-in-failure-will-sud-denly-become-successful-and-leave-you-behind.*

Goedehapsbrungshaft. Meklenbrukegrasse.

She glances around the bar, which is in Shoreditch. Kerenza had sworn never to come back here but has made an exception because it is sunny and daytime. At night, she feels too old for it and finds the shoddy little streets too disturbing. She worries about the hedonistic young girls staggering down the street and the predatory feel of some of the men stalking in the shadows, as if they are waiting for one of them to become separated from the flock. She feels contempt mixed with a degree of irritatingly nostalgic envy for the mobile conversations outside pubs planning the stages of the night. But she also knows that it ends up – always ends up – in the company of the lost and the lonely filled with nauseous self-loathing.

'I'm not frightened of drama. I'm a fucking dramatist!'

At the table behind them somebody sniggers.

A man enters the bar with a bucket of roses. Kerenza glances at the bar staff to see if they will throw him out, but he begins to move around the tables, trying to sell his roses to people who will never buy them. The man offers a rose to a man who is sitting alone. He is reading *Hangover Square* by Patrick Hamilton, a book which Kerenza likes. He holds his hand up in polite refusal and as he looks up from his book he meets Kerenza's gaze. He is stocky with dark eyebrows, simply but stylishly dressed, wearing a black cashmere jumper and jeans. Kerenza keeps her gaze on him for a second longer than she should, and he smiles before returning to his book. The smile is a curious mixture of confident and contemptuous. She notices a tiny scar on his cheek.

Rose man offers a flower to a couple, who also refuse. Kerenza tries to work out where he might be from – he is very dark and small, maybe somewhere like Uzbekistan. She remembers a drunken conversation in a bar with a 'producer' who wanted her to star in a porno movie as an asylum seeker who would do literally *anything* to get her indefinite leave to remain in the country. He had frowned and lightly lifted one of her red curls and suggested that she might have to wear a headscarf but that was OK because the more Muslim she looked when she got done and deported by five duplicitous immigration officers the better. Kerenza had been so drunk that she had taken his card. A feeling of nausea rises from the memory like smoke – curls around the people lifting beer glasses to their mouths, the cigarette packets, the babble about superagents, the man holding out his roses with that smile. Where does he live, the rose man, perhaps he goes home at night to his olive-eyed, curly-haired kid, he's somebody's dad selling roses in bars, the woman stepping backwards into a van with a sticker saying McGeery's Motors, somebody's getting that news right now, their life changing forever, as they sink down, hand clasped to mouth.

Is that why she no longer gets decent parts? Red hair and pale skin. Nobody likes a ginge. Why not? Something to do with barely suppressed anti-Celt feeling? Who decided that red hair was to become the target of such mirth and mockery? Kerenza has always liked the soft red curls she inherited from her Cornish mother, in spite of jibes from drunken men who seem to think that it gives them automatic licence to make vulgar speculations about the colour of her pubic hair. People think she's pretty, they often tell her so, they say she looks a bit like the girl in *Will and Grace*. Her boyfriends would sometimes say that she was sexy in a *different* kind of way, which she supposed they intended as a compliment.

'Drama? If it's done well enough you can get drama from two characters just talking.'

'Somebody should fall over as well,' Kerenza says. 'I love it when people fall over.'

'It's hard to go wrong with somebody falling over,' Mark agrees and then throw up his hands in the kind of exaggerated despair that has always endeared him to Kerenza.

'But if they won't make *Sad Fucking Losers* then where are we? Back with another cop show?'

Kerenza shakes her head. She genuinely doesn't know, because the only TV she watches now is docusoaps; she can't bear to watch drama any longer and be reminded of her own lowly status. She's not interested in *Big Brother*-type programmes with reality constructs but loves the ones about people doing their jobs, particularly if they involve airports. She could watch late, indignant passengers swearing at check-in staff for hours, silently urging the check-in staff to hold firm and not let the stupid feckless passengers on the plane. Last night Anna had come in alarmed at the sound of her yelling. *Should have turned up on time, you muppet.*

Two men walk into the bar. They crackle with purpose as they look around, focus their attention on a table. The man reading *Hangover Square* sees them and smiles calmly. He puts his book down and wipes his mouth as they approach his table.

'Anyway, that's enough about me. How's your love-life?'

The answer to this question would not have taken very long had Kerenza had time to answer it. Kerenza's last boyfriend Carl had been a TV director. Talented, yes, but with all the moral fibre of a greedy kid in a sweet factory. She had been prepared to tolerate a certain degree of misbehaviour but had drawn the line at his misdemeanours with the runner on his last show, who was a lemur-eyed twenty-one-year-old in cowboy boots and short denim skirt called Katy. So fucking predictable, so lazy, how brilliant would it have been if he had spurned sexy-but-stupid's advances because he was in love with his girlfriend. Oh, she had lashed him with her tongue for that one – asked him what he thought it was about a balding, B-list director with an expanding waist-line and a drink problem that had first attracted a pretty girl fifteen years his junior. She remembers his face going moon-like with hurt and how it had made her despise him even more.

In any case, she does not get the time to answer Mark's question because one of the new arrivals has taken out a plastic bottle and poured the liquid it contains over the head of *Hangover Square*-reader. The other has taken out a cigarette lighter. He is wearing a camouflage jacket, his ring is heart-shaped and made of little coloured fragments like a mosaic. Kerenza thinks: there is a story to that ring, but I will never know it.

'Give us the money.'

A smell of petrol. People in the bar can see what is going on. Mark turns his head as well.

'Give us the fucking money or you're burning.'

The Uzbek flower seller stands with his bucket of cheap roses, frozen in his gesture of offering one to a very skinny fashion-girl in pinstripe trousers and trainers. For an instant he looks oddly gallant.

The petrol is obviously stinging the eyes of *Hangover Square*-reader. But he still has the same confident, almost infuriating smile. His smile is not doing him any favours with the man holding the cigarette lighter.

'Wipe that fucking smile off your face, Evan, or I'll burn you anyway.'

Finger caressing the wheel of the lighter. Kerenza realises – almost gratefully – that she does not want Evan to be set on fire: nature – and perhaps nurture – has set limits to her desire to see others suffer with her.

Kettenspurgenshaft.

'I don't have your money,' Evan says calmly. His voice is from the Welsh valleys. Kerenza knows this because she once studied for a part in a film about the miners' strike that was eventually given – to her utter fury – to Sophie Collingwood-Hunter, a girl whose father was on the board of HSBC bank.

'Where is it?'

'Well, I spent it on food, some books, CDs and a holiday in Sicily with a girl I wanted to impress. Taormina – I can really recommend it.'

The two assailants glance at each other. It would obviously be easier if Evan were stammering pleas and excuses. He moves his copy of *Hangover Square* out of the little pool of petrol that has poured from his forehead onto the table in front of him.

'Well then . . .' the one with the lighter says.

And Kerenza knows in that instant that he is going to do it. That, boxed into a corner, he can see no option but to allow his finger to stroke the wheel. She takes her mobile out of her pocket and stands up.

'OK, I'm an undercover police officer.'

The whole bar turns to look at her.

'Based at Shoreditch police station, which I can call by pressing one button on this phone. So walk away and let me get on with watching idiots going in and out of the bogs.'

The bar staff glance horrified at each other. Kerenza laughs.

'Yeah, you should look nervous. There's turning a blind eye and there's collusion. I'll be talking to *you* later.'

Then turning back to the men with the lighter.

'You still here?'

One of them approaches her.

'Where's your warrant card then, ginger?'

She juts out her lip, grateful for the small part she last had as a rookie cop. Natalie O'Brien, ganged up on by colleagues, taking bets as to who can get her knickers down in the locker room. Natalie has to stand up for herself and gains posthumous respect by facing down some drug dealers who torture and shoot her at the end of Act One. Natalie's voice was streetwise Cally Road white girl, and Kerenza slides into it effortlessly.

'Listen, you two-bob muppet, I'm giving you ten seconds to get out of here or I'll press one key on this phone and have CO19 down. And those boys are extremely trigger-happy these days, so don't go crying to the Police Complaints Commission if they mistake that lighter for a lethal weapon.'

Even Evan has now turned to look at the man with the lighter, as if curious to see what he will do now. The answer arrives in a missile of spit in his face.

'Get me that money in a week or you're dead.'

He casts Kerenza a look of contempt, gestures to his companion, and they turn and walk out of the bar. Evan takes the napkin from under his coffee and wipes his face. Then he picks up his book and starts to read again. Kerenza stares at him.

'Think nothing of it.'

He puts the book down and meets her gaze fully. When he is old his eyebrows will be bushy, have a life of their own. His shoulders are satisfyingly broad, as if made to hew coal or prop up the scrum.

'One: I hate cops. Two: why should I thank you for doing your job?'

This is a little too much for Mark, who turns around and leans over his alcove.

'She's not a cop, you stupid Welsh prick.'

Evan ignores Mark.

'Aren't you?'

Kerenza shakes her head, smiles at the bar staff, whose faces flicker between relief and irritation.

'She's an actor,' Mark says. 'And she just saved your life, so I think you should say "thank you" rather than sitting posing with your book.'

Evan gives an amused shrug.

'I'm not posing,' he says. 'I'm reading.'

'It's OK,' Kerenza says and sits down while he returns to his book.

'Do you like it?' Kerenza suddenly asks. '*Hangover Square*?'

'I love the girl. Netta Longdon.'

She bursts out laughing and then realises that he isn't joking.

'Why are you laughing?' He is half-smiling.

'Isn't she meant to be the villain?'

'I think she's cool. And it must be a right pain having that big lump pleading with you all the time, waking you up when you've got a hangover and dragging you out of your bath: "Oh, Netta, dear, won't you be nice to me? Come away with me, Netta." Fuck off, you boring stalker, or I'll get an injunction.'

Kerenza laughs. She knows he is striking a pose to amuse her. He laughs as well.

'You're a good actor. I believed you there.'

'Evidently.'

They consider each other for a moment. And Kerenza is

unwilling just to leave it there; his mannered pose has something appealing about it, it lacks cynical artifice. And he did not abandon his calm when he was facing considerable danger. Behind them she sees the man with the plastic bucket of roses leaving the bar.

She says, 'You didn't even buy me a rose,' and he raises a thick eyebrow.

'You don't look like the kind of girl who would want a rose.'

What kind of girl do I look like? Kerenza wonders as she sits back down opposite Mark. A redhead girl in her early thirties who has no idea where her life is going? A girl with no money who wakes up the middle of the night worrying about direct debits? A girl with such a severe case of peer-envy that it borders on psychosis, who can feel physically sick with envy and injustice. How does Mark see her, or the rose man, or Evan, who is getting up to leave and whose life she may have just saved?

'Can I borrow your mobile?'

A faint smell of petrol. Evan is standing in front of them buttoning his jacket now to leave.

'You haven't got a mobile?'

He shakes his head.

'I wouldn't normally ask, but it's very important.'

'Listen, mate . . .' Mark shifts into the voice that middle-class boys often feel obliged to adopt with taxi drivers. Geezer-in-a-cab, Kerenza sometimes teases him. Evan looks at Mark for a second, and, although there is nothing directly threatening in his eyes, Mark lapses into silence.

'If I don't make a call those guys could do something really bad to somebody else. And there might not be an extremely talented out-of-work actor who can play an undercover cop hanging about.'

She passes him her mobile.

'Don't call Australia.'

'Don't worry, I'll send a text.'

She watches as he selects Messages and then Write Message. He types quickly, obviously used to predictive text.

'How do you know how to do that so fast if you don't have a mobile?'

At that point she hears a familiar bleep bleep from his jacket pocket. He takes a mobile from it and inspects it.

'I do have a mobile.' He grins at her. 'And I also have your number now.'

'And what do you want that for?'

'In case I ever need an actor again.'

He smiles and half-bows to her. Again she feels the curious mixture of irritation and affection towards the considered gesture. Something about the whole package: the Welsh accent, the book, the little scar, the eyebrows, the stockiness, his seeming indifference to everything including danger just seems to *work* like a daring combination of clothes on the right person.

'What's your name?' he asks.

'Kerenza.'

'Kerenza.' He smiles as if it pleases him. 'Cornish.'

'Fellow Celts,' Mark says.

Evan turns to him.

'There's no such thing as a Celt,' he says. 'It's a stupid myth made up to satisfy a bunch of whinging losers – principally Glaswegian Irish – who like to delude themselves that they have rebellion and poetry in their souls when most of them are a bunch of backward, superstitious, lazy drunks who'd marry a pool table given half the chance. It's on about the same level as astrology.'

He turns and leaves.

'Arrogant prick,' Mark says when he has left.

'Yeah.'

'Do you think I can get Emily Holt Superagent to change her mind?'

She sighs. 'I don't know, Mark.'

'Fuck it, then. I'm gonna write a cop show. There'll be a great part in it for you.'

Kerenza nods, watching the door from which Evan has just made his exit.

He Who Rules Our Destinies

And there's the slider, and absolutely no doubt about it. Up goes Billy Bowden's finger, Hawkeye confirming the decision . . .

'My husband used to take me to watch cricket.' Grace Holding watches Kerenza at the kitchen sink as she does the washing up while on TV a batsman trudges back to the pavilion, glancing at the replay on the screens as he goes. 'In Bushy Park. And we used to go to Brentford together to watch the football.'

'I don't understand cricket,' Kerenza says, her hands warm in the water. 'It looks very boring.'

'Not really.' The old woman sips at the tea Kerenza has just made. 'It's like most things. You just need to understand the rules.'

'That's the problem,' Kerenza says. 'There are too many.'

'You find them out by watching,' Grace says absent-mindedly. Kerenza glances at the woman who cannot watch anything any longer because she is almost totally blind. She started cleaning for the old lady a few months ago. Today is her last day because she has asked the agency for jobs nearer to her home, and they have found her something in Hackney. In spite of the greater proximity, Kerenza feels a sense of regret; there is something soothing about day-dreaming on the Piccadilly line through Acton and Ealing and Hounslow. And she enjoys listening to Grace Holding's stories about her husband, who joined up at sixteen and was injured in the First World War.

Kerenza lets the water out of the sink and comes to sit beside Grace as the late-afternoon sun spreads into the small suburban living room – a gentle torture for the nostalgic or lonely. A brass lizard crouches on the mantelpiece beside a clump of amethyst like a small purple mountain range. Beside the fireplace is a brass bell with a thick black handle. The clock ticks slowly and definitely, as it has done for the last half a century. There are also some photographs on the mantelpiece – in one of them a grinning young man in army uniform rests his hand on the shoulder of a sailor. They are very young, little more than boys.

'Is one of these your husband?' Kerenza asks.

'Arthur's the soldier and the other one is Sam – his favourite brother. He was blown up on HMS *Bulwark* – it was sabotaged in Sheerness harbour, although that lying sod Churchill said in parliament that it was an accident. Sam was never found, but his pocket-book was washed up. And he wrote a last letter the night before he died.'

'Did it ever arrive?' Kerenza asks.

'It's in that drawer over there. Go and get it and read it to me.'

The drawer is heavy, lacquered, with a thin gold handle, and smells of lavender furniture polish. Kerenza finds the old letter with its forward-sloping handwriting and then pauses. There is also money in the drawer – twenty- and fifty-pound notes casually strewn about. Lots and lots of banknotes. Kerenza stands for a moment and stares at the money.

'Have you found it? It's at the top of the drawer.'

Kerenza shuts the drawer and sits down again with the letter.

'Read it to me.'

'*Dear Kruger and Bill* . . . who's Kruger?'

'It was a nickname for my husband. They used to tease him that he looked like Kruger. You know, from the Boer War?'

Kerenza shakes her head but Grace cannot see her.

'*Dear Kruger and Bill, thanks for the letter and card which arrived today* . . .'

'They must have written to tell him that they had joined up . . .' Grace interrupts. 'My husband was only sixteen. The bloody doctor knew that he was underage as well. Bill was his other brother. He was gassed at Ypres. Go on.'

'*Dear Kruger and Bill, thanks for the letter and card which arrived today. As we are working like nigs for the mobilising, coaling and ammunish etc. I hope you won't mind shortness of note . . .'*

Kerenza breaks off.

'Nigs?'

'They talked like that then. It was the coal, you see, they were covered in it as well.'

The writer of the letter has puts nigs in quotation marks.

Grace glances at Kerenza, who shrugs to show that she understands. She is not going to take against him, reject the pathos of the letter, because he used the language of the time. Then she realises that Grace will not have seen the shrug, so she says it's OK and continues to read.

'Should the worst arrive and it is not impossible, I hope He who rules our destinies will protect you in any danger that you may be in. It's a chronic biz all round but then, Kruger and Bill, our work is rather a gruesome job on any occasion. I wish you luck, boys. God bless you is the wish of devotedly your brother Tosh.'

The heavy ticking of the clock. *Should the worst arrive.* A pocket-book lapping to and fro on the beach at Sheerness. She stares at the careful handwriting, written with a fountain pen. The author could never have guessed that nearly a hundred years later a young woman would be sitting with it in her hand.

'He wrote that the night before he died,' Grace says.

He who rules our destinies.

'Why did they call him Tosh?'

'It was just a nickname. Like Kruger, I suppose. They heard the explosion in Whitstable and Southend. Do you believe that there is somebody who rules our destinies, Kerenza?'

'I never think about it. Not really, no. Do you?'

'If there is, he didn't do much for those boys.'

'If there is, then I must have upset him in some peculiar and terrible way.' Kerenza laughs.

Grace Holding suddenly grips Kerenza's hand tightly. 'You have a beautiful voice. The way you read that. Don't ever let me hear you say that you're giving up. Do you hear me?'

Kerenza goes to put the letter back. The money lies in the

drawer – one note. Fifty pounds. Grace Holding will not miss it, what could she do with it anyway? Kerenza shuts the drawer angrily. It is all very well people telling her not to give up, but here she is sick with temptation at the sight of the savings of an old woman whose mother was a washerwoman and whose relatives have been scattered on the sea or buried in the mud. Kerenza opens the drawer again, slips one of the fifty-pound notes into her pocket. She clears the tea things away, puts the biscuits back into the cupboard and says goodbye.

The afternoon is muggy as Kerenza walks towards the bus stop which is right by Grace Holding's home. As she puts her hand in her pocket for her Oyster card she can feel the fifty-pound note that she has stolen from the old woman. Planes are dropping regularly into Heathrow – too many of them, too many people, too many places, too much pollution.

Stealing from an old woman. An old woman of whom she is fond and whose relatives gave their lives for a cause other than themselves. Who would do that now? Who would offer their life at sixteen for the entirely abstract notion of God, King and Country? For any abstract notion. She could go back and return the money. She could go to the supermarket and buy food and a bottle of wine. *What about the times I've gone round to do stuff and not charged?* Then you should have charged rather than stealing. *What was the money doing just lying about in a drawer?* What business is it of yours where she decides to keep her money, doesn't mean you can just steal it. *It's just fifty quid, it's not like Brinks-Mat or anything.* No, it's worse. The money belongs to an old woman who pressed her hand urgently and told her not to give up, who sits with her bell, a brass lizard, the photographs of young men long gone.

She turns on her heel and heads back towards Grace's house.

Wait! I can put it back later when I have money. I'm not stealing it, I'm just borrowing it, she won't even notice, nothing to stop me going back to see her.

She stops and turns again. That's it. She's not stealing, it's just a loan.

Doesn't the person making the loan normally get some say in the matter?

I'm a street girl, a smart girl, not Netta Longdon but Becky Sharp, cheerfully amoral but not bad at heart.

Excuses, excuses.

The morality of a fish.

On the other side of the bus shelter a man is touching himself as he watches Kerenza. There is nobody else about. Then the man takes his cock out and begins to masturbate. The cock is large but only semi-erect. Kerenza walks back towards the newsagent's and stands in the doorway – near enough to catch the bus if it comes, but a little way from the man. The shop smells of stale sweets – the top shelf is bulging with pornography, meaningless, provocative garbage, invitations and entreaties. An elderly Asian woman is doing a puzzle behind the counter. Really, it is such rubbish, such cheap and sordid rubbish. She has never felt offended by it, she just finds it miserable and demeaning with its stupid puns and graceless euphemisms so far from the idea of real pleasure or deviant abandon. It is a promise as false as that contained in the time-table promising a 293 bus every fifteen minutes over which the man is now spurting his own semen. He turns and waves his semi-erect, dripping cock at Kerenza without really looking at her.

A bag of shopping in each hand. One contains olive oil, salad, ground coffee, peanut butter, tins of tuna, a copy of *Heat* magazine. The other contains two bottles of wine, baby onions marinated in balsamic vinegar, a bag of chicken-flavoured IAMS cat food and a baguette impatiently folded in half at the checkout as she handed over a fifty-pound note which the checkout girl had held up to the light. For an instant Kerenza had felt a shameful flush, as if there were a watermark running through it which said *this person steals from old ladies to buy baby onions marinated in balsamic vinegar*.

Borrows.

This is what one does on a spring evening, this is the way things should be, walking jauntily along with two bags of shopping, a baguette poking out of one. Other people have this, take this for granted. Perhaps there will be a phone call from her agent when she gets home, perhaps letters and invitations, perhaps details of a new post from the cleaning agency, perhaps nothing.

On her street, trees are putting out their white blossom.

Meat Is Magnificent

'Let's go to Mangals and eat meat,' Anna says as she and Kerenza come out of the Rio. 'I need comfort after that pretentious bollocks.'

'It wasn't so bad,' Kerenza says, knowing it was worse. But she wants to enjoy Anna's rage, as her friend always loses her customary tolerance and good nature when it comes to films and books she dislikes.

'It was too long. I hate things that are pointlessly long. Learn to edit, for Christ's sake.'

'*Anna Karenina*? *Gone with the Wind*?'

'Had. A. Story. That was just . . .'

She shakes her curly hair vigorously like a dog trying to get a tick out of its ear. A couple who have also been to the film walk past them. The man has little glasses and is bossily lecturing his girlfriend on the director's genius.

'That's what was wrong with the film,' Anna says, scowling at Mr Know-it-all-film-buff in front of them. 'It was all about the director. Look at me, look at me.'

'I thought it was clever the way he used the film as a vehicle to explore the whole process of film-making,' Kerenza says provocatively, knowing that these were the parts during which Anna had sighed and fidgeted most ostentatiously.

'No! No! I came to see a film, not some smartarse and his playful post-modern exploration of the art of film-making.'

'I wonder if they'll do me that chicken with aubergine and yoghurt thing,' Kerenza says, and Anna laughs.

'Always keep your eye on the big picture.'

In the restaurant, they sit at formica tables and order beers and plates of meat from the big flame grill in the middle. A small Turkish family are sitting at a neighbouring table. Both the little girl and boy swinging their feet and drinking Cokes have great big eyes and curly hair. Kerenza and Anna admire the children, and Anna says that one day she would maybe think about having a kid.

'But it's so difficult,' she sighs.

'Finding a sperm donor?'

'I suppose. But Ivo could fill the turkey baster in return for his passport.'

Anna's husband-of-convenience is a good-natured slacker who likes mainly to eat chocolate and watch football, calls himself an anarchist. He works in a bar, is handsome but – as far as Kerenza knows – has never consummated his marriage to her friend. Last year they all went on holiday together to the Dalmatian coast; Kerenza remembers the smooth surface of the main street in Dubrovnik as they strolled at night, eating ice creams, the smell of pine and sea. Ivo taught them how to ask for beers – *pivo molim* – they laughed at Anna as she stumbled on the pebble beach. They took a ferry to the islands of Hvar and Korcula and joked about preening Italian tourists as they sat out on the upper deck in the sunshine drinking espressos.

'It's just I don't know when I could do it,' Anna says. 'I really like my job.'

'You could still do your job.' Kerenza tries to conceal her dismay at the changes this might produce in their relationship. Perhaps Anna would want Kerenza's room for a nursery.

'No I couldn't,' Anna says simply. 'Not without a real husband, and there's no sign of one of those appearing. How would I leave the nipper to go to conferences? What if I needed to write a paper? And how would I find time to do all the reading? I like a holiday where I swim and eat and visit interesting places – not change nappies and sit by the pool gurgling and cooing like an idiot. I might start hating it.'

'It's tricky,' Kerenza agrees, feeling immensely relieved.

'But then, we're getting older, and soon I won't have the choice any more and maybe I'll be all bitter and frustrated later on and wish that I'd had one 'cos I do like them, they're quite funny.'

She looks wistfully at the brother and sister giggling as they blow bubbles into their Coke. The girl has white ribbons in her hair, the boy is wearing a little suit. Perhaps it is a birthday celebration. Kerenza thinks of her sister Lamorna, to whom she rarely speaks any longer. Lamorna is married to a plastic surgeon and has an SUV with satnav and a house in France and various dogs and two annoyingly precocious children – Matthew and Polly. Kerenza always forgets their birthdays, which angers Lamorna intensely. She thinks of how they have grown so apart, the two sisters, but of how they used to sit giggling – thick as thieves – on family holidays in the back seat of the car. Now Lamorna just seems to have resentment as her default mode. She resents everything about Kerenza, even the fact that she perceives her own life as infinitely more successful and worthwhile – an opinion which Kerenza's own mother seems to fully share – only serves to fuel her simmering irritation.

'What about you?' Anna asks. 'Would you one day?'

The possibility seems so absurd that Kerenza laughs out loud.

'I can't look after myself,' she says. 'How on earth would I manage with a child?'

And what would you teach a child, Kerenza, she asks herself bitterly. Right from wrong? You took fifty pounds from an old lady and you spent it on stuff you didn't really need. You didn't even have the moral fibre to admit it was theft, justifying it in your head as a loan. She longs to tell Anna but somehow she can't, she knows that her friend would not condemn her vocally, but that isn't the point. Somehow by confessing it to Anna she would be affirming their difference, the level to which she has sunk, and here in the restaurant, laughing at the pretentious and boring film, eating magnificent meat in Mangals, chatting about babies, she can forget that, she can feel as if her life is normal, that she has balance and poise.

'The Rio . . .' says Anna as they walk down Kingsland Road. 'It's further than you think.'

Just as Kerenza is about to laugh at the old joke, a boy on a bike wearing a baseball cap shoots past them on the pavement, clipping Anna's elbow.

'Ouch,' she says. 'Watch where you're going.'

The boy on the bike stops and pedals back towards them. He has one hand in the pocket of his tracksuit top. His face – beneath a baseball cap – is white, but he is older than Kerenza had first suspected. A scar runs from ear to jaw, and he has a front tooth missing.

'What did you say?'

'You hit my arm,' Anna says.

'You shouldn't be walking together like that,' he says. 'Blocking the way.'

'You're not supposed to be riding on the pavement,' Kerenza says.

He looks at her and cycles along beside them, wobbling a little, moving into the gutter to steady himself.

'Not supposed to . . .' He shrugs. 'I'll ride where I fucking like.'

'All right,' Anna says. 'It doesn't matter.'

But the man doesn't go away, he continues riding beside them.

'Where do you live?'

'Up there.' Kerenza flaps vaguely northwards, watching the hand that he is keeping in his pocket, looking around to see who is nearby.

The man nods. His tone becomes confiding, almost friendly as he gestures across the road. 'That pub over there? That's a lesbian pub that is.'

Later, Kerenza thinks, we will laugh about this. *That's a lesbian pub that is.* But not now.

'You just been in the pub?' he asks.

'No,' Anna says. 'We've just been to see a film.'

'We've just been to see a film,' he repeats, half-mocking her. Kerenza feels anger mingling with her fear.

'What was the film about?' he asks. 'What *kind* of film was it?'

'Not such a good one,' Anna says.

'Not such a good one,' he repeats again and then falls silent but continues to ride alongside them. What should they do now? Kerenza wonders. Stop somebody? Ask for help? But what can she accuse him of doing to them? His knees are very bony, they seem to be moving in an exaggerated style, the bike is too small for him. There are stains on his blue tracksuit bottoms.

'Listen,' Anna says. 'I'm not being rude but I kind of want to talk to my friend.'

He looks at her with pale eyes.

'What about?' he asks. 'What do you wanna talk to your friend about?'

His bike swerves out into the road, almost – but unfortunately not quite – into the path of a speeding car full of Turkish teenagers.

'Cunts,' he spits after them and then brings the bike in close to them.

'You were blocking my way,' he says.

Anna shrugs helplessly.

'You should say sorry.'

His hand is twitching in its jacket pocket. Kerenza can see submission in her friend's face; she knows that Anna knows that this is the only thing that will make him go away. He will have bullied an apology out of them and this will make him feel better. Kerenza almost wants to look away, biting her lip.

'You ain't good-looking enough,' he says to Anna, 'to have that much attitude.'

And Anna flushes because he has hit the Achilles heel that she always had at school: she thought and still thinks that she isn't pretty enough. Kerenza feels rage pounding in her head, she is almost trembling with it. *How dare you, how dare you*, she is thinking. If the man had been picking on her she might also

32

have said sorry, she might have backed down, but anger is now dissolving her fear.

She laughs out loud.

'Well, you're no picnic, mate,' she says.

'What?'

'You really think *you* are entitled to make comments about anybody's appearance?'

'Kerenza . . .' Anna turns to her, but Kerenza's fists are balled now, she no longer cares.

'Leave us alone,' Kerenza says. 'Take your manky tracksuit and the bike you probably stole from your kid and fuck off out of my face.'

The man hikes the bike onto the kerb and blocks her path so she can no longer walk any further.

'Say that again,' he demands. 'Say that again, you ginger slag.'

But Kerenza is full of the exhilaration of losing her fear, of not caring about the outcome any more.

'Get out of our way, you idiot,' she says. 'Go and have a wash. We're not frightened of you.'

And he can see in her eyes that she isn't. He can also see a police van stopping at the lights ahead and he has seen that she is aware of it. She cocks her head and smiles contemptuously, daring him.

'Slags,' he says. 'Fucking lesbian slags.' And he cycles off down the road, pulling a can of lager from the pocket of his jacket and lifting it as he goes, almost pouring it down his throat.

Anna and Kerenza walk on in silence for a moment, watching his departing figure, totally unthreatening now.

'I read a story,' Anna says after a minute. 'About a man and his girlfriend on a bus. There was some guy throwing chips and some of them hit the girl. So the man asked him to stop and the guy, the one throwing chips, he stabbed him. Then he just walked off the bus.'

'I read that story,' Kerenza said.

'This guy might have had a knife as well,' Anna says.

'But he had a can of lager.'

'Still, he might have had a knife.'

'Yes, he might.'

They continue walking, and Anna hooks her arm into Kerenza's, and they don't say anything more about the incident.

Later that night Kerenza lies in bed unable to sleep again, thinking about the money she stole from Grace Holding, about the man calling Anna ugly, his hand balled in his pocket. She stares up at the suitcase on top of the wardrobe where Smut has made her nest. The black tail is hanging over the end of the suitcase, twitching from time to time, and she thinks how brilliant it would be to be a cat with a loving owner; to need for nothing but warmth and food and the occasional caress and to receive them all in abundance. Her mobile bleep bleeps a text message and she frowns as she looks at it because she does not know the sender. The message reads: *Fancy a trip to Wales?*

She texts back: *Who are you?*

She lies with the mobile cradled in her hand for a few seconds and then the reply: *You saved my life.*

She lets the mobile fall onto her belly. Deep down she had known that, hoped for it even.

Rumours

'I thought that I would have a herb-garden. Journalists would come to talk to me about my latest roles. I would travel to France and Italy, sometimes to the States. They would write profiles about me in the *Guardian*, I would sign letters protesting about human rights violations. It wasn't about fame or even money really, it was about being able to live gracefully.'

'Well, it *is* about money, then.' Evan moves the silver BMW convertible around a slow-moving vehicle by overtaking on the inside. 'Nobody lives gracefully without money.'

'I'm not sure,' Kerenza says.

'OK, maybe people who have some kind of divine mission – Jesus, Gandhi or Che Guevara. But you don't strike me as somebody with a divine mission; in fact, you care more about your career than you do about human rights. Don't get me wrong, I like that approach, I couldn't give a flying fuck about anybody's rights except mine. Talk of rights is nonsense, talk of human rights is nonsense on stilts. Bentham said that and he was fucking right. I just can't understand why you're so surprised and indignant about it.'

'Because I was good.'

'And you know what they say about the cream always rising to the top? It's a lie. Nothing floats quicker than a turd.'

They have just passed Reading on the way out to Wales. Kerenza is happy to be sitting in the car with this relative stranger, happy with the audacity of her decision to go with him, happy with the feeling that she is leaving London behind on this spring afternoon, happy with his opinions firing up like flares from a roman candle. There had been a tricky moment when a young black man driving an SUV had cut him up and then given him the finger and screamed a stream of hostile threats out of the window when Evan sounded the horn in warning. In response, Evan had shouted, 'Oh, fuck off, you black cunt, you don't scare me,' which had precipitated a whole further bout of threats, counter-threats and bumper-to-bumper driving. Evan had remained unapologetic when Kerenza had remonstrated with him. 'I was about eighty per cent certain that he was a black cunt without even looking,' he said. 'What does that tell you?'

'That you're a racist?'

'Racist is a stupid label that doesn't mean anything any more.'

'It means calling somebody a black cunt.'

'No, it means discriminating against the black cunt. Or voting for people who discriminate against him. Which I don't do.'

'But not all black people . . .'

'Oh, please . . .' He laughed. 'I said he was a typical black cunt, not that he was typical of all black people.'

'The distinction must have been too subtle for me.'

'It's easy. You're driving blind. Behind you is an ill-mannered, self-righteously aggressive cunt with no volume control on his stupid in-car stereo. He cuts you up and then threatens you before driving off at one hundred miles an hour, ignoring any pedestrian crossings. What colour is he likely to be?'

'You don't notice the black drivers who aren't like that or the skin-colour of the white ones.'

'Yes I do. And I'm perfectly happy to admit that there are white cunts. But there is something distinctive about a black cunt – often much louder and bullying for a start, relies on you being scared of him, which I'm not. Usually disposed to pick on somebody weaker, like an Asian shopkeeper or a woman. Thinks everybody can be intimidated by teeth-kissing and in-comprehensible shrieking about your mother's anatomy. Fuck him, he was a black cunt. And if you don't recognise that, then you're either in denial or you're a racist yourself, because you think it's all ebony and ivory when the one thing the so-called ethnic minorities have in common is that they hate each other's guts.'

Kerenza told him about the man on the bike demanding that Anna apologise for him hitting her with his bike.

'So here we have two complete cunts, and what do they have in common? Is it their racial origin? No. Hmmm, what could it be . . .'

Evan groaned.

'Oh no, a feminist in the car.'

While Kerenza is looking out of the window, still trying to demonstrate indignation at their conversation, Evan opens the glove compartment and takes out an iPod with an iTrip attached and turns on the radio.

'Now we're out of London,' he says, 'we should be able to find an FM station that doesn't have DJ Derek playing grime from his bedroom.'

He finds an empty FM station for the iPod to tune into and tells her to choose something. She scowls at him but scrolls through his music – it's a mixture of names she doesn't know combined with the surprisingly conventional: Bessie Smith; Bjork; The Cardigans; The Cure; DJ Misjah + DJ Tim; Doctor John; E-Type; Echo and the Bunnymen; The Fall.

'Don't know what's on there,' he says. 'Lots of compilations when I looked.'

She gives him a puzzled sideways glance.

'It's not my iPod,' he says. 'Or rather it is but I haven't put my own music on it yet.'

She puts the iPod onto shuffle and watches the passing traffic. Her agent called her this morning and told her that she had been invited for an audition in a medical drama playing a woman who is stung by a wasp and crashes her car into a JCB, where she is trapped. The part involves a lot of groaning. She could be using this as an excuse to go out and get drunk with Mark but she had felt vaguely sad at the news. In some ways these fragmentary parts are even more soul-destroying. Somehow, the idea of just taking flight had seemed almost like an imperative. And he has offered her flight.

'I've never been to Wales.'

'Wales is great. Dark.'

'People make fun of the Welsh a lot.'

'Like people who make fun of people with red hair. Ignorant.'

He says *ignorant* with a marked increase in his accent, stressing the last syllable as if the word itself has annoyed him.

'Like all forms of racism,' she says primly.

'Except it's acceptable to slag off the Welsh,' he says. 'Especially for the media tarts. Why? 'Cos an extended family from Bangladesh is fascinating and exotic while an extended family from Bridgend is pikey trash.'

She decides not to argue any more, and he turns up the music as an old Congos track comes on.

'I love this song,' he says.

He sings along in a falsetto.

'Lots of hungry belly pickney they a shore . . . *millions* of dem.'

And he continues to sing cheerfully along just as a squad of police bikes passes them by on the other side and Kerenza points to them and squeaks 'millions of dem' and they both laugh.

They stop once at a service station to buy sandwiches and she thinks that they must look like girlfriend and boyfriend. In spite of his views, she silently admires the way that he does things – with purpose and confidence, tossing his jacket casually into the back seat, fishing out change from his pocket to pay the toll after they have crossed the Severn Bridge. Even the artillery of his opinions has something certain and unevasive about it – he doesn't care what she thinks of them or try and tailor them to make them more acceptable. He reminds her of a snooker player thoughtlessly chalking his cue before choosing his angle. And as they head westward with the sun, his choice of targets increases to encompass more or less every race, sexual orientation and social class.

38

'Is there anybody you like?' she asks.

'I quite like actors.' He grins at her. 'I like self-educated working-class people rather than scum. I love shop assistants, especially Welsh girls who flirt and laugh and don't give a fuck and spend hours on their make-up. I *hate* self-righteous local government lefties who leave their bicycles in the hallway, eat in gastropubs, call Tony Blair a Tory and go to plays about George Bush being bad and stupid. Can't stand people who say the suicide bombers have nothing to do with Islam – course they fucking do. No time for people who don't read 'cos they say they haven't got time, people with bad manners, especially those who are rude to shop assistants, idiots who keep loads of animals in the house and don't feed them properly so they make a noise, mothers who think you should have to walk in the road if they have a pram, human rights and anti-war activists who live in Hackney, fat people who don't exercise, people who smell, anybody with body-piercings or tattoos, backpackers . . .'

'All right, all right, I can see the pattern emerging. Most actors are spoiled little prima donnas though.'

'They're like cats,' he says. 'It's a toss-up whether they should be stroked or strangled. But sometimes they help us to forget what a pile of shit this world is.'

Dusk is falling as they drive past Cardiff, and she thinks that he is right about Wales at least, that there is something darkly bewitching about the landscape, the low hills, and the proximity of the black sea. Sometimes, she goes home to see her mum in Cornwall, but this is different – more primal, less self-conscious, less bothered.

They head across the common, where Evan silently points out some new-born lambs and then winds down the window to roar at a tattooed man on a quad bike. 'You're not allowed up here, motherfucker.' The man gives him the finger and shouts, 'Piss off, thick'ead,' which makes Kerenza laugh.

'Thick'ead?'

'What do you expect from somebody from Maesteg. I hate quad bikes, they scare the lambs.'

'Ah, so you're a big softy underneath it all.'

'Fear affects the flavour of the meat, thick'ead.'

Mining villages run along each side of the valley as they come off the moors: wood smoke rising from the chimneys; pubs in the dips of the road; old chapels; murals with images from union struggles. He points out a basketball court which stands where a pit used to be. It all – to Kerenza at least – seems suffused with rainy melancholy, the shadows of industrial change seared at every turn, way beyond the 1984 strike (which she barely remembers), right back into the last two centuries – a place so deeply seamed in the nation's history that it cannot hide its loss with anything too brash or too new.

She wonders where they are going to stop but does not want to break the silence, he seems to be concentrating quite fiercely. Finally, they stop because they have to stop, the road simply ends.

'This is the end of the valley,' he says, indicating a dense cluster of pines which stop the road from going any further.

'There's no way through?'

He shakes his head.

'I wanted to bring you here.'

'Why?'

'Thought you'd appreciate seeing the end of the road.'

She glances at him to see whether this mockery is cruel, decides that it isn't. He looks at her and she wonders for a moment if he is going to kiss her, knows that she would let him. But he doesn't try any such thing, simply points to a rabbit which is hopping about beneath a tree. She remembers her cat and feels a pang of guilt as she imagines Smut alone on her suitcase perch, looking down at her empty bed, the ringing silence of the flat.

'My dad used to bring me up here,' he says. 'Hunting rabbits.'

'Does he still live here?'

Evan shakes his head. 'He's dead.'

'Oh. I'm sorry.'

Evan shrugs. 'People die,' he replies. He puts the car into gear as a watching rabbit freezes and then scarpers.

'What about your mum?' she asks as they drive back down the valley.

'Works in Bridgend now. In a pub.'

'Do you see much of her?'

'No.'

They enter his village, which has a long Welsh name that she can't even think about trying to pronounce, so she makes a joke about its name, calling it Pant-y-brastrap, and he laughs. She will always refer to it as Pant-y-brastrap from now on to make him laugh.

'Here we are.' Evan pulls up and parks beside a small stream. The hill behind it is slag-black. They take their bags out of the car and trudge up towards an old two-up two-down miner's cottage. Kerenza almost smiles to herself at the absurdity of this voyage with somebody she barely knows, a man of bushy eyebrows, racist views and a car whose provenance she hardly dares ask about.

'Tommy?' Evan calls out as they enter the house. 'Get the chainsaw ready 'cos I've brought the slut for the snuff movie.'

He turns and winks at Kerenza, who puts her bag down. A middle-aged man comes out of the living room, where a wood fire is crackling. He is tall, bushy-eyebrowed like Evan, wearing tracksuit bottoms and a Harley Davidson t-shirt. He does not offer his hand, although she feels him appraise her body quickly.

'Lost one of the birds,' he says mournfully.

'Tommy keeps hawks,' Evan explains to Kerenza.

'Had two,' Tommy says. 'Secret and Promise. But Promise took off.'

'Maybe she'll come back?' Kerenza says.

'Oh yeah? Your optimism is based on . . .' Evan asks spitefully.

'On optimism,' Kerenza retorts tartly. 'Give it a whirl some time, you miserable twat.'

Tommy laughs at this.

'She's got your number, mate,' he says. 'No, Promise won't

41

come back, sweet'eart, 'cos she still had the equipment attached, so she'll get caught in a tree or a post and she'll be trapped. We'll find her swinging from somewhere starved to death.'

'Oh,' Kerenza says, frowning at this image of a trapped bird hanging upside down in a great mass of useless plumage.

'So much for optimism,' Evan remarks.

'There's a red kite in the valley again,' Tommy observes and glares at him as if this trumps any further arguments on the subject. 'Anyway, going down the club.' He puts the can down and departs.

'Man of few words, my uncle Tommy,' Evan says, guiding her into the living room. 'Must have liked you.'

'Does he live here?'

Evan shakes his head.

'Came to light the fire for us. It's just you, me and the chainsaw.'

Kerenza is relieved, certain now that they will sleep together. She can feel her body beginning to anticipate his touch, a slow spinning in her stomach.

She wonders vaguely about contraception.

'You hungry?'

'Not really.' She gives him a look which she hopes will convey what she really wants him to do. It has been a few months now, and that barely counted as she was so drunk and the results were so forgettable.

'I'm starving, think we've got some eggs and stuff. You sure?'

She follows him to the kitchen.

'I'd like a drink.'

He takes a can of beer from the fridge and pours some into two glasses. It's bitter rather than lager, but she doesn't really mind. Evan starts to beat eggs together for an omelette, melts butter, grates cheese, slices tomatoes, cooks them for a few minutes until the middle goes golden, pours the eggs into the pan, slides the omelette away from the sides, lets the liquid flow back into the space he is creating with the spatula, drops the cheese into the middle of the hardening eggs, flips it into an

42

envelope, slides it onto a plate. She watches semi-hypnotised by his purpose, almost crazed with a sudden hunger as he starts to eat, mopping up the egg and melted cheese with a piece of white crusty bread that he tears greedily from the loaf.

'Sure you don't want one?' he asks when he's finished, but she shakes her head, silently longing for an omelette.

'Who lives here now?' she asks as they go into the living room, where the telly is on and the fire is burning, the deep smell of wood-smoke reminding her that they are not in London, that they are somewhere strange and different. Outside, the top of the valley and most of the pines have vanished into grey cloud and rain is being blown hard against the windows. She glances at her bag for reassurance. It contains her clothes, a soap-bag, the book she is reading, a notebook, a hairdryer.

'My mum. But her boyfriend owns the pub in Bridgend, so she's hardly ever here.'

Kerenza looks at the pictures on the wall – old images of the town at the turn of the century. There is a china slipper on the fireplace with a plastic purple flower inside it and the word 'MUM' on the side.

'What had you done to those guys?' she asks.

'Which guys?'

'The ones who tried to set you on fire.'

He smiles at her.

'I stole their money.'

'You stole . . .'

'I cut them in on a deal to bring back some coke from the Caribbean. But there was never any deal. Or trip to the Caribbean.'

'So you were hardly the victim?'

'Did I say I was?'

She shakes her head.

'How much?'

'Ten grand.'

'Which you used to take a girl on holiday.'

'No, that bit wasn't true.'

'Why did you say it, then?'

'To annoy them.'

'Pretty dangerous strategy at that moment in time.'

'Maybe I've got the suicide gene.'

He grins at her.

'Really, they're not worthy of your sympathy. Just low-level gangsters. They used to boast about using drugs to get girls back to their flat and then . . .'

He makes a vague, half-disgusted, renunciatory gesture, and Kerenza shivers. She thinks of late-night situations she has been in when the atmosphere has become laced with a vague sexual threat, when the faces of the men have started to change, the talk become pornographic. She remembers the producer who touched her hair and promised her a part in his sex film about asylum seekers; she flinches as she thinks about the Shoreditch predators, crocodiles waiting for antelopes at the river crossing. There was a time during the 1990s during which it became acceptable to say anything as long as it was done in a certain flip and playful tone. Now she thinks it has become acceptable to *do* certain things, and even the tone is not so important any longer.

On the television an argument has started about the parachuting of an outside candidate into a safe Welsh constituency. A government spokesperson is arguing tactlessly that the local constituency party should accept this imposition because the government stooge happens to be a black woman. It is a weak and insulting argument to all concerned, and there is talk of a challenge from a disgruntled local. Kerenza glances anxiously at Evan, but he makes no comment about this.

'I stole fifty pounds from an old woman,' she suddenly says.

'Why?'

'I was skint. But then I bought wine and baby onions and a copy of *Heat* magazine.'

He laughs. 'Oh well. Reason not the need.'

'She was blind.'

Evan nods but does not say anything, as if this additional information makes it more interesting but adds no gravity to the crime.

'I mean, that's bad, right?'

'Bad?' He says the word in an almost puzzled tone. 'I wouldn't worry about it any more than I worry about the guys in the bar. It's a bit *tacky*, I suppose.'

'She's an old, blind woman who has always been nice to me. Her relatives died in the First World War.'

'That's what I mean. You can be as good as you like, but life lasts as long as it takes a sniper to aim at your head. Nothing matters now.'

'Nothing matters?'

'Capitalism has won and humans are heading towards extinction. Nothing you or I do matters for a minute. So I wouldn't lose too much sleep about stealing fifty quid. The only decision that you need to make is whether you live a comfortable or an uncomfortable life for the short time that you have left.'

She considers this. Evan is not earnest, or impassioned, just matter-of-fact. Once again he appears not to fear the kind of mockery that she – or anybody – might toss at him for this piece of self-conscious gloom-mongering. *Humans are heading for extinction.* She could imagine Mark's raised eyebrow. *Is this guy for real?* But he does not appear to care whether she mocks him or not, and neither is there anything playful or ironic about the way that he imparts his opinions. He appears to say exactly what he is thinking without any kind of prior meditation or consideration of its acceptability. She has to admit that she quite likes this about him.

'You want to earn money acting?' he asks. 'Or is it for the critical acclaim?'

'Both,' she says. 'Either would be nice.'

'But which is more important? Fame or fortune?'

He grins at her.

'Which would make your life more *graceful*?'

She considers this. Money would have meant that she didn't

45

have to steal from an old blind lady. But it isn't really money, or not just money, it's her feeling that she really did have something to offer, and it has simply been examined and tossed aside, rendering her absolutely inconsequential. This is a debate, of course, that she has had with friends, drunken nights with Mark where she has scoffed at his claim that he would certainly accept an offer of a million pounds not to speak another part or write another word.

Evan is looking at her quite earnestly now. She shrugs her shoulders, but he looks cross, as if he won't accept this.

'Why do you care?' She laughs. 'I don't know. Won't that answer do for once?'

'For your own state of mind maybe,' he says. 'But not for my purposes, I need an answer.'

'You need an answer?'

'That's why I asked you down here.'

'I did wonder.'

'You can make a lot of money if you want.'

She feels something stir inside her. A lot of money.

'Doing what?'

'Acting.'

She stares at him. Is he another pornographer? Is Uncle Tommy part of the audition? Is she actually in danger? No, dangerous people don't talk about the definitive victory of capitalism. But please please please, she silently begs him not to start lecturing her about how pornography can be liberating or alternative and is liked by as many women as men.

'I saw you in the bar. You were good and I could use that kind of . . . performance.'

'And who are you?' She flashes a mocking glance at him. 'Harvey Weinstein or Ben Dover?'

'Who's Ben Dover?' he asks, genuinely puzzled.

'Makes porn.'

'Oh.' Evan makes a dismissive gesture. 'I'm not interested in porn or drugs.'

'Didn't you make a lot of money out of a fake coke deal?'

'Yeah, precisely. There was no coke. Do you do drugs, by the way?'

'Not any more.'

'Didn't think so. I hate drugs. I especially hate older people who do them.'

'You saying I'm old?'

'You're on the borderline when it comes to drug-taking. Forty-year-olds shuffling around discos and still doing coke, though – that's humiliating.'

She smiles as he pronounces it yumiliating.

'Well, chill out, 'cos I don't any more.'

'Good, 'cos they're no good in my line of work.'

'Your line of work?'

He picks up a small piece of glowing wood, examines it and puts it back onto the fire.

'I steal from people or I rip them off. The car we came up in, the iPod, pretty much everything I own is stolen or conned out of people.'

She watches him for a second but knows that he is not joking. Then she takes refuge in banter.

'But you only steal from the bad guys, right?'

'I wouldn't bother taking fifty quid from an old lady – more on aesthetic than moral grounds, though.'

She smiles at the teasing thrust.

'And we'll be Bonnie and Clyde?'

'No, you'll be my employee. I have various projects at the moment and I use a variety of different people for all of them. But I need somebody more versatile, somebody I can trust, so I'd like you to stay across some of them.'

Stay across them? He talks as if this is a real job he is offering her. As if reading her thoughts he says,

'Or you could go back to London and scrabble around for parts in medical dramas.'

Her heart sinks as she remembers wasp-sting woman and the JCB crash. The only coherent line she can remember is *Somebody must fetch the kids from school.* That's another thing, she keeps getting cast in older and older parts, even though she is only in her early thirties. By the time she's forty she'll be playing grandmothers.

'What kind of projects?'

He shrugs.

'I'll explain the details if you agree to do it. It involves a bunch of people who . . . let's say they're clever idiots, which is a worrying combination. You'd deal well with them.'

Kerenza decides not to ask why she should be well equipped for this particular task.

'And how are you ripping them off?'

'We can discuss the details later. This is something I can't do on my own, though. I've needed an assistant for some time and I think you'd be perfect.'

'Why?'

'Because you're hungry and disillusioned and angry. Because you know that talentless fucks prosper in almost every field. Because you're smart. But most importantly for my purposes you're a good actor.'

She stares into the fire, watches the shifting patterns in the flames. It is all nonsense, of course, the kind of thing you talk about when you're drunk, crazy plans of revenge, fantasies of retribution. And yet, as she stares at the pattern of the flames, the crackling, smouldering wood, she also sees young men felled by bullets or smashed to pieces by shells, pocket-books with last letters bobbing on water, news footage of civilians blown apart by car bombs, all of them victims of decisions over which they had no control, decisions taken usually to favour the interests of powerful elites or fanatic hearts. And outside in the dark valley, the unmined coal beneath the surface and the basketball pitch where the mine once stood, and all the powerless despair that still clings and whispers long after the rhetoric of workers united never being defeated has vanished. And Mark in London writing his script, still banging furiously on a door she knows has been closed to him for a long time, and Anna lecturing on international law at a time when it is being most

48

contemptuously flouted. And she's tired of it all, tired of the auditions and the condescension of stupid people and – most of all – tired of waking in the night heart racing with worry, sick and fucking tired of being poor. She here she sits, little Ms Faust facing Mr Mephistopheles, towards whom she has felt an intense desire that she has not felt for some time, and if he had been a bigshot movie producer, would he be any less of a conman, his worldly goods any less tainted?

Evan yawns and stretches.

'I'll give you some time to sleep on it,' he says.

She turns in her bed and stares at the crack in the door, which is held shut by a large stone. Somehow the expected transition just did not happen. *Story of my bloody life*, she thinks bitterly. At every moment, as she brushed her teeth, watched him wash up the omelette plate and beer glasses, she expected something to change, but it did not. He remained fairly calm and then – to her astonishment – he had announced that he was going out for half an hour to see a friend, and she should go to bed if she felt like it. And she had neither dared to remonstrate with him or to ask if she could go with him or even where he was going, and so she had blithely nodded as if that were perfectly normal. The friend was not from the village because she heard the car ignition outside. Now she is a little nervous at being on her own and cross with herself *for not having dared*; even at this early stage it seems that he is calling all the shots.

About five minutes ago she heard the slam of a car door and then the front door open as he came into the house – away for half an hour just as he had promised – shuffle about downstairs for a while and then clump up the stairs to the second bedroom, which is right next to hers. She lies silent for a moment, listens to him getting into bed, sees the crack of light disappear.

She can't stand this.

Maybe he is timid, although she has to concede that she has had absolutely no evidence on the journey so far to favour such an explanation. But she also knows that she can't go to sleep like this and so she gets up and pads to the door, opens it slightly. Then, wearing only t-shirt and knickers, she crosses the landing and pushes open the door to his room. It is very dark and she can just see the shape of him, still and silent in the blackness.

'Evan?' she says.

He makes a noise, she's not quite sure whether he has pronounced a coherent word.

'Shall I get in with you?'

Silence. She can feel the agony of humiliation, but it is too late to turn back now, perhaps he is still sleeping, perhaps this is silent assent. The choice is simple and retreat is too painful to contemplate.

Still he says nothing as she slides into bed next to him. And she lies on her back for a moment with her heart pounding and a sense of her own terrible absurdity ringing in her ears. She reaches out in the darkness and takes his hand and for an instant – or is she just imagining it – she seems to feel the tiniest of squeezes in response. And so, emboldened, she takes her hand out of his and lets it slide down. Still he hasn't said a word, offered any reaction to show he is awake. She can feel the opening to his boxer shorts and moves her hand inside, feels his average-sized, limp penis.

Which remains totally limp.

She starts to caress it slightly.

Nothing.

'Evan?' she whispers.

No reply. No reaction. Nothing. Not even 'Go away.'

She takes her hand away and lies for a moment in the awful, roaring blackness. Then she gets up and pads back to her room, slides back into bed.

Council Flats, Bowler Hats.

Perhaps she can rhyme herself to sleep.

Squinting Bats, Rubber Mats.

Lonely Cats.

A bird of prey snagged in a tree, hanging helplessly, the

50

ground swinging below it, exhausting itself, field mice and voles strolling unconcerned beneath it, defeated majesty.

She is lying in a strange bed miles from home; she can hear the sound of water from the dark outside, a rain-swollen channel, oddly sinister. Lying in the next-door bed is a man she seems to have fallen for. An impotent Welsh racist conman. And suddenly in the darkness, something of her good spirit saves her and she smiles at the description, she is already reinventing the tale for humour. It will be a story for Mark, he will howl with laughter and say *what on earth possessed you?* And she will have to go out and fuck somebody as soon as she gets back to London to prove to herself that his lack of interest was caused by his own failings and nothing to do with her. In fact, she half-wishes Uncle Tommy was about because the way he had casually appraised her body did not suggest a man with any particular problems in that department.

She rolls herself up in the old-fashioned waffled bedspread and curls into the wall. Sleep will come, it will come in the end.

Pulled Pork

INT. POLICE STATION – DAY

Detective Inspector Matt Hambleton is young, good-looking, stylishly dressed, albeit with an apparent disregard for the normal restrictions of fashion. Alongside him is his younger colleague, Detective Constable Kathleen McGuire. She's attractive, flame-haired, although there is a sense that life has disappointed her. In front of them is a very beautiful girl with long dark hair. We will know her as Milena Reyes – she's Colombian.

> MILENA

I used to live on the side of the volcano raising chickens. Then one day the soldiers came . . .

(She pauses and studies her hands.)

> HAMBLETON

They killed your whole family?

> MILENA

Yes.

> MCGUIRE

But they spared you?

Milena turns her large dark eyes on McGuire.

> MILENA

No. They did not spare me.

(beat)

                          MCGUIRE
So you became a drugs courier.

(Hambleton glances at her. His colleague can be harsh in inter-
rogations.)

                          MILENA
(bitterly)
You understand nothing.

                          MCGUIRE
(impatient)
I understand . . .

(Hambleton restrains her with a look.)

                          HAMBLETON
Milena. We need your help.

                          MILENA
How can I help you?

                          HAMBLETON
You have to help us catch Jamie Miller.

                          MILENA
If they find out they will kill me.

                          HAMBLETON
We'll protect you.

'What do you think?' Mark looks at Kerenza across the plates of
pulled pork and back ribs they are eating at Bodeans in Poland
Street – one of their favourite meeting places, where she has
offered to buy him dinner.
    'Yeah, it's good.'
    She catches his slight look of disappointment.
    '*Really* good.'
    Mark gestures to the waiter for his fifth mojito of the evening.
Kerenza signals for another cosmopolitan, although she is not

really sure why she started drinking them and she is getting a bit bored with sweet cocktails.

'So. Reservations?'

'Well . . .' Kerenza knows that she has just stepped into a potential minefield, buys a little time by moving the sample pages of his script out of the way of the empty mojito glasses with their sodden clumps of mint. If she doesn't offer some kind of criticism, Mark will accuse her of only wanting to please him. Which of course she does, as he is down in the dumps after his ex-lover discovered that he was hacking into his Hotmail account and threatened him with an injunction.

'This character Milena . . .'

'What about her?'

'Just her type is a bit . . . familiar. You know, very beautiful with long dark hair, used to raise chickens until she was tortured and gang-raped by the soldiers . . .'

'You think a flashback would be considered in poor taste?'

'Let me guess what happens next. She shows Hambleton her scars, he caresses them sensitively, she stares at him through traumatised yet lovely black eyes, then it's a hot bath and a tasteful shag for lucky old Milena.'

'All true except for one minor detail. Hambleton won't shag Milena.'

His eyes gleam triumphantly.

' 'Cos he's gay.'

'Hambleton's gay?'

He hands her another page of script, which smash-cuts from the scene in the police station to Hambleton dancing without a shirt in a gay club.

'If I can't do *Sad Fucking Losers* then I will subvert gender and social expectations by putting the first left-footed cop on TV.'

'What about *The Bill*?'

'Typically marginalised as small-time PCs. But not like the big cheese. Not like, say, Morse or Columbo or Cracker.'

'His name wasn't Cracker.'

Mark shrugs.

'It should have been. I never liked him anyway.'

'No,' Kerenza agrees. 'He was smug.'

'Smug fat cunt wasn't even a copper anyway.'

A woman eating chicken wings on the neighbouring table glances at her partner, who scowls at Mark. Kerenza would normally sympathise, as she also has a dislike of loud swearing in public. But like late-night music it's always OK when you are the perpetrator. The couple seem locked into miserable murmurings. A couple of times, Kerenza has caught fragments of their conversation and deduced that their relationship is in its terminal stage, and they have made this mistake of coming to a restaurant, probably because home has become so unbearable. Big mistake. They are on display, and there are no channels down which their anger can flow. Now it is as if everything has become the enemy of their happiness: the menus, the chairs and especially the drunken friends talking about gay cops, it is all conspiring to increase their suffering. They should have stayed at home.

Just because you've changed the way you look at things it doesn't mean I have to.

I can't go on like this. It's killing me. I think I'm going crazy.

You're a control freak.

This last accusation had made Mark scowl as it had occasionally – and most unjustly according to him – been levelled at him.

'Not that old chestnut,' he had grumbled into his mojito.

And Kerenza can't help feeling irritated with their neighbours for dragging their relationship failures to the neighbouring table, for their tiresome, everyday suffering.

'OK, then, what about Morse and his sidekick? *The* other *light switch, Lewis.*'

Mark laughs at her passable impression of Morse's world-weary exasperation.

'You don't get anything for sub-text. Not in this game, 'cos then every copper with a male partner would be one of the chosen ones.'

'Columbo doesn't have a work partner, and we only have his word for Mrs Columbo. And what about Hamish MacBeth?'

Mark scrunches up his face.

'That's a tricky one. Was Hamish gay?'

'He had that little dog.'

'It's just the name Hamish that's gay.'

The woman stares with dumb hatred at them again. Mark shrugs.

'OK, he's borderline, but this guy Hambleton is the opposite of Hamish MacBeth, his trousers cling to his muscular buttocks, he's like a gay Bergerac.'

'It's what the world of television drama has been crying out for.'

They order a bottle of wine to mop up the cocktails, and Mark asks her about Wales, and she tells him a slightly edited version, although generously leaves in her nocturnal humiliation, and he roars with laughter and says *what on earth possessed you?*

Sleep had come at last and she had got four or five hours' dream-fragmented rest. When she had woken up, she had gone downstairs, where Evan was sitting reading the *Sun*, eating breakfast. He had offered her fresh toast and coffee and made no mention of the events of the previous night. In the end she had introduced it in an allusive half-joking way, but he had frowned as if puzzled and not followed it up. So she had let it drop.

They had driven back across the moor to Bridgend to give the key back to Uncle Tommy, who lived on an estate on the outskirts of town. Kerenza waited in the car and looked at the tangled streets of council houses that had once been white but were now mostly a kind of singed ochre, some boarded-up shops, a couple of burned-out cars, dealers skulking under their hoods. And in the middle of it all, a few brightly painted properties defying the tone of the rest of the estate – salmon-pink, lime-green – with UPVC windows and gardens filled with roses and hydrangeas. She had commented on it to Evan when he had returned with a bag of chips for her from Munchies fish and chip parlour, and he had smiled as if pleased with her for noticing and told her about the people who had bought their properties under right to buy and who had then been shafted by negative equity as the estate fell apart in the 1980s and the junkie scum took over. He told her about how his Uncle Tommy had caught one of them burgling his house and discovered that the guy had shat on the bed. So he had broken both his arms and pushed his face in the shit before kicking him out into the street.

'Maybe the person whose car and iPod these are would like to do the same to you,' Kerenza had said.

'I'm not a burglar,' he said. 'I don't shit in people's beds. Anyway, you can shut up, you steal from old ladies.'

'I'm giving that back.'

'That doesn't buy you absolution.'

They had driven back listening to a Buddy Holly compilation and voted for their favourite song. His was 'Raining in My Heart', hers was 'Love Is Strange'. And when he had dropped her back at her house, he had handed her an envelope.

'What's this?'

'Call it expenses,' he said, 'for attending the interview.'

'Is that all it was?' And this time she had stared him full in the face, not evading what had happened, allowing him to comment.

'That's all it was,' he said quietly.

She had gone inside calling for her cat, and Smut had finally swallowed her rage at being left overnight and come and stared into her eyes and pounded furiously on her breasts which – Kerenza thought – was about as close as she had come to sexual activity all weekend. And when she had opened the envelope she had discovered that it contained 500 pounds in fifty-pound notes, so she had decided to take Mark out for a meal and tell him all about it, although Mark is disturbingly untroubled by the account of Evan's racism and says that he thinks that he had a point.

'Not you as well,' Kerenza says. 'The whole world's turning BNP.'

'Remember when I lived on the Nightingale estate in Hackney,' Mark says. 'I used to be terrified coming home sometimes because of the gangs of yout' dem shouting that they were gonna burn the batty man. And one guy they did pour battery acid over. Fuck 'em, always whinging about racism when it suits them and sitting on the bus as if sharing the seat is like the reintroduction of slavery.'

Unfortunately this mojito-fuelled diatribe is proclaimed loudly enough to be heard by several tables, and somebody taps Mark on the back. It is a startlingly handsome young black man with a male companion who grins good-naturedly and makes a gesture to him with finger and thumb as if turning down a volume dial.

'Although I don't really disagree with you about those kids on the bus,' he says. 'Which should really tell you something.'

His white partner leans across the table.

'Juliet Bravo,' he says. 'Wasn't she a lezzer?'

'Smut, Smutty . . .' Kerenza makes kissing noises as she comes through the front door that night. She grins as she hears a wail of recognition and then a thud thud on the stairs. She puts the bag down, lifts the cat up and nuzzles her, the almost metallic smell of fur, the delicate symmetry of whiskers, eyes narrowing with pleasure. She walks into the kitchen, where Anna is sitting with her husband-of-convenience Ivo. Anna is solemn; it looks as if she may have been crying. For a moment, Kerenza thinks that maybe Anna has suggested that he impregnate her, and that he has said no.

'What's up?' She tosses Smut to the kitchen floor and the cat stalks away with her tail raised and kinked at the end.

Ivo and Anna glance at each other.

Anna says, 'I had a hospital appointment this morning.'

Kerenza winces as she does when she realises that she has forgotten the birthday of her niece or nephew.

'Oh, I'm sorry, I forgot all about that. How did it go?'

Ivo glances at Anna and in that moment Kerenza knows.

'I've got breast cancer.'

Anna turns her face away and Kerenza feels a weight on her chest, dizzy and nauseous. She sits down at the kitchen table and runs her finger around the rim of a coffee cup as if trying to make it sing.

'What are the doctors saying?'

'Ah, doctors . . .' But Anna cannot speak any more because her eyes are full of tears. Kerenza has rarely seen her friend weep – Anna the sensible, Anna the organised, Anna the clever, Anna the indulgent. She laughs at Kerenza, teases her, but in a way that always makes her feel secure and loved. Now Anna picks up the old copy of *Heat* magazine – bought with the money stolen from Grace Holding – and looks closely at the familiar cover story about the matrimonial problems of a couple whose life nobody could ever really imagine, a gaggle of actresses who lose weight but never diet. Ivo and Kerenza watch her looking at the magazine. Then Anna wipes her eye and pushes it over to Kerenza.

'Isn't that your nemesis?'

Olivia Scott simpers out at her. She's at an award ceremony and has been given a big tick for 'frilling' an award ceremony in her Emmanuel Ungaro frock.

'I wish *she* had cancer,' Kerenza says, and Anna laughs.

'Take that back.'

Kerenza shakes her head.

'I do. I wish it was her instead of you. She's horrible and talentless and rude and stupid.'

'Still. Take it back. Unsay it.'

'You want me to?'

Anna nods.

'I take it back. Only because you want me to.'

Ivo says, 'But there are some people from my country who I wish had cancer.'

'That's different,' Anna says.

Kerenza feels a pain so sharp that she blinks several times.

'What happens now?' Kerenza asks.

Are you going to die?

The question hangs in the air between them. Anna shrugs, blocks it.

'More tests, more doctors, they won't know for a while.'

Kerenza nods slowly, and Anna says she fancies watching some TV, so they go into the living room and watch a programme about very fat kids, and somehow this seems to work as the conversation moves onto actresses who don't need to diet and whether it's the parents' fault that fourteen-year-old kids weigh twenty stone. For an instant, all the sly shifting changes that are going on under the skin, the multiplying malignancies, the betrayals of the body, are temporarily forgotten.

Coal

The air is muggy and oppressive as Kerenza sits on a hot Piccadilly line train out into the West London suburbs. The woman sitting opposite her is smack-skinny, has two kids that she cannot control. They are called Sophie and Rhys. Kerenza knows this – the whole carriage knows it – because every time one of the kids punches the legs of another passenger or lets out ear-piercing shrieks or tries to smash something, the woman raises her head and yells their names – *Sophie! Rhys!* – and then takes no further action. Sophie has a moon face and the half-healed spots of recent chicken-pox, and people withdraw slightly as she tries to climb onto their laps in a way that is more aggressive than affectionate. Rhys has a head as wide as it is long, he is cross-eyed and his nose seems to be growing back into his face. Kerenza doubts whether their mum heeded much ante-natal advice when it came to fags, booze or drugs, and Rhys appears to be paying the consequences. And for an instant she puts on hold her natural sympathy for the woman, whose own childhood probably wasn't too great, and sends silent waves of contempt towards her. *You despicable freak*, she thinks and takes some pleasure from thinking it. *Look after your fucking kids properly.*

Sophie and Rhys don't seem to have a great deal going for them – how will they end up, these two little children, what chance of happiness can they possibly have? They'll bump into people and pavements and demand apologies from them. When Sophie kicks her brother, the mum hits her hard in the face, and everybody on the tube train winces but nobody says anything –

probably out of a mixture of cowardice and an understandable reluctance to get entangled with this family of such genetic and social misfortune. They finally get off the train and people start clucking and shaking their heads and talking to each other as if they have just come through some traumatic ordeal, which, in a sense, they have, because they are all scared by what they have seen.

A big Polish girl called Magda opens the door to Grace Holding's house and stares sullenly at Kerenza. She doesn't speak much English, and Grace appears relieved at the arrival of her predecessor.

'She was an industrial engineer in Poland,' Grace tells Kerenza when Magda has gone and she is making a cup of tea. 'And she has a baby over there but can't get work. That's sad, isn't it?'

'Yes,' says Kerenza vaguely as she pours a little boiling water into the bottom of the teapot, something Grace always liked her to do. Fussiness over tea protocol is one of the idiosyncrasies of the old, she thinks, like worrying about the length of phone calls in the belief that they still carry some punitive expense. She doesn't really care too much about Magda's plight, although she wants to suggest that Grace is more careful with her money, but refrains from doing so on the grounds that it seems both hypocritical and an admission of guilt.

She carries the tea back into the living room and sets it down carefully. The brass lizard, the black-handled bell, the photographs on the mantelpiece – all still there. Grace Holding is wearing the same crocheted shawl that she was the last time; Kerenza can smell lavender furniture polish.

'So how are you?' Grace asks her. 'Nice of you to remember me.'

'I was doing some acting work at Ealing studios,' Kerenza says. 'Thought I'd drop in and say hello.'

The old lady turns her sightless eyes towards her. Her gnarled fingers touch the tassels on her shawl. Outside the window in the little garden, Kerenza can see a jay on the windowsill; the streak of blue in its wing is almost the same colour as the shawl.

Another jay joins it, they begin a noisy game of courtship jockeying and Kerenza thinks that Grace Holding was young once, that she has known what it is like to have a man touch that body that is now gnarled and wrinkled.

I stole some money from you. Fifty pounds. I came to give it back.

Over the small garden a jet drops in low to Heathrow, light glinting from its powerful silver belly. Kerenza thinks of all the passengers on board unaware of her below looking up at their vehicle. One of the jays takes flight. Kerenza feels for the fifty pounds in her pocket, looks across to the drawer with its slender gold handle. She'll just return it to the drawer.

'I was thinking about that letter you showed me,' she says. 'The one from Tosh. I wondered if I could take another look at it.'

'Why?'

'I might be playing a part of a woman from around that time. I was interested in the handwriting and the tone.'

It is lame but not entirely implausible.

Grace gestures. 'It's in the drawer.'

Kerenza walks over to the drawer and opens it. There is now no money inside. She looks back to the old woman, who is staring straight ahead. Confused, Kerenza does not know what to do, so she scrunches the note back into her pocket.

'Used to keep some money in there but I had to put it away.'

'Why?' Kerenza croaks.

'Well, I always knew that I could trust you, but I wasn't sure about this Polish girl. She seems decent enough, but you can't tell.'

Kerenza feels a pang for poor, heavy Magda who probably wouldn't dream of stealing from Grace. She shuts the drawer.

'You got it?'

'Got what . . . oh, yes, the letter.'

Kerenza opens the drawer again.

'It's in a folder. There's a long blue box in there as well. Bring it to me with the folder.'

Kerenza puts the fifty-pound note back into her pocket,

fetches the box and the folder over to Grace Holding and puts them down in front of her on the small coffee table. Grace feels carefully for the box.

'These are my husband's medals,' she says.

Kerenza peers into the box as Grace opens it. The jeweller's name is embossed in gold letters on the inside of the lid, the medals lie on navy velour. A label attached says '3076 Pte Arthur Holding. Middx Regiment'. Kerenza lifts out the medals with their rainbow ribbons. One, shaped like a star, with two crossed swords, says 1914–15. She passes it to Grace, who feels the tips of the little swords.

'Not many people got those medals,' she says.

'Is it for bravery?'

'It's for surviving until 1915.'

The second medal says 'THE GREAT WAR FOR CIVILISA-TION 1914–19'.

Kerenza turns both medals around in her palm. Arthur Holding's name and regiment are on the back of both of them.

'What happened to him?' she asks.

The old woman settles back in her chair and looks at the ceiling as if the story is somehow written up there.

'Arthur was seventeen when the battle started. The Germans sent poison gas over. During the fighting, he killed a man with a bayonet – a boy really, not much older than himself. He used to wake up screaming about it in the night, never recovered from the nightmares of meeting him again.'

'Like in that Wilfred Owen poem,' Kerenza says. '*I am the enemy you killed, my friend.*'

Grace nods.

'He used to dream like that, that he was somewhere meeting him again, or his family, or his girl. When you stuck the bayonet in you had to twist it to kill them and he always remembered the man's face when he twisted the bayonet. Sometimes it was once or twice a week he would wake up like that. I've never seen anybody so scared, crying, white with fear. So many of his friends died during those weeks. Middlesex boys he'd grown up with were shot or gassed or blown up. Some of them just vanished; it was as if they'd never even existed. That happened to Wilf, who used to breed springer spaniels and worked at Syon Lodge. He just disappeared, nothing of him left. Some of them went mad, some were shot for cowardice. That's how it was. One afternoon, Arthur was repairing some duckboards and a shell landed behind him and that was that. He was lucky because he was injured so severely that he'd never get sent back to the front-line.'

'What happened to him?'

'He was taken first to a field hospital and then shipped back home to dear old Blighty. He was in a hospital in Kent somewhere, I forget quite where, but his back and legs had been really damaged in the shell blast. Well, conditions in the hospital were no good, and Arthur was always a bit of a rebel, so he got into trouble. It was very cold, but the authorities wouldn't give them any extra heat, so Arthur and his friends went to steal coal to warm them up a bit. I mean, there were men in there with their legs and arms blown off, blinded by gas, and they were freezing. That was the great war for civilisation. And it was discovered they'd stolen the coal and lit a fire and there was a terrible row and the authorities tried to punish Arthur and his mate. The commanding officer was a man known as the Prince by the men because of his manner; he hated Arthur, and Arthur hated him. Arthur said afterwards that there would always be men like the Prince, men who enjoyed beating and humiliating others, and that humans would never be free until we had put them up against the wall and shot the lot of them. He became quite a Bolshevik as he got older. He was a reader as well: always took the *Daily Herald* every day and he loved Dickens because he had a social conscience but he could be so funny as well, especially the names. Arthur was good at nicknames as well. So where was I . . .'

'The Prince and the stolen coal.'

'Oh yes. Well, they were going to court-martial Arthur for stealing the coal, and the men protested about that and barricaded themselves on their ward, so the Prince ordered that hoses be brought and they turned water on injured men. That was how they were treated for having run away at sixteen to serve their country. They turned hoses on them, and Arthur was court-martialled and punished for stealing coal to keep them warm. If it had been in the trenches they would probably have shot him. But he was a man who knew right from wrong. When he got back, he worked as a clerk in a bedding factory for people who couldn't sing his praises highly enough. Read me this, would you?'

Grace takes out a letter and passes it to Kerenza to read.

Waring and Munro Ltd.
White City Factory W.12
11th April, 1919

Dear Holding,
In reply to your request for a reference I should be very pleased indeed to do so if I were allowed; but it is the rule of the firm that all such matters should be dealt with through the Superintendent as representing the firm, and in that case it is only done on application from the new employer.

However, I don't think you need fear because your persistence and the all-round efficiency of your work during the two years you have been under my control as clerk at the bedding department, coupled with the progress you have made in your general equipment (and in this I have been proud of you taking into account your youth and the disabilities you suffered from the war), these I think may make you quite confident in referring to the firm officially for recommendation to any position you may apply for.

Hoping your good health may continue.
Yours sincerely

Joseph Watts.

'Mr Watts was a good man, always looked after Arthur. You think, he was only eighteen or so and he's seen things that no young man should have to witness. Joseph Watts knew that and always kept an eye out for him.'

'Did they stay in touch?'

'Yes, but Mr Watts was killed later in the blitz. He was a firewatcher for the factory when it took a direct hit, and that was that. Arthur was very upset about it.'

Kerenza looks at the letter, written in a scrupulous hand, the hand of the senior clerk, section-head for the bedding department of Waring and Munro. She thinks that it was a nice thing to say: he was proud of the young Arthur Holding, noting his war injuries, his desire to reassure him in spite of his ingrained bureaucratic insistence that the reference should come from the right department.

'They were the two men he always talked about,' Grace says. 'The officer called the Prince, who turned the hoses on wounded men, and Joseph Watts, who tried to look after him when he came out of the army.'

'You said Arthur also became a firewatcher in the war,' Kerenza says.

'Yes,' Grace says thoughtfully. 'But that's another story.'

Kerenza feels the banknote scrunched in her hand in her pocket that she has forgotten about while Grace has been telling the story of her husband. She swallows and says, 'When I said that I came back because I had an acting job. That wasn't true.'

'Wasn't true?'

'No. I came back because last time I was here I stole some money from you.'

There is silence for a moment. Then Grace smiles.

'I know.'

'How did you know?'

But Grace shakes her head as if this is unimportant.

'Why didn't you say something?'

'I thought you must need it if you took it. You're not a bad girl.'

And Kerenza suddenly feels as if she is going to start weeping at the kindness but also the vague humiliation of it all. Pardoned like this – it seems pitiful almost.

'I came to give it back.'

'I thought you might be wanting more,' Grace says. 'When you went to the drawer.'

Kerenza shakes her head and looks at her hands.

'I came to give it back,' she repeats miserably. Grace reaches out and takes her hand.

'You'll be all right,' she says.

'Will I?' Kerenza says. 'I think that I've got problems and then you tell me that story about your husband and the bayonet, and my best friend's got cancer and the hawk in the tree . . .'

'The hawk in the tree?' Grace looks puzzled, so Kerenza tells her the story of Promise, who thought she could fly away but got hauled back to an ignominious and undoubtedly painful death, hanging from a pine, the slow and diminishing beating of wings.

'Yes, and I'm so stupid and full of self-pity I thought that I was like the bird in the tree, all snared up and unable to fly, and that's just so self-obsessed and silly, but I don't know what to do with my life any more.'

Grace Holding squeezes her hand.

'Oh dear,' she says. 'You're in a bit of a pickle, aren't you.'

And Kerenza half-laughs at the expression.

'And I think I like this man but he doesn't like me,' she says.

'How do you know he doesn't like you?' Grace asks.

Kerenza thinks that failing to stimulate an erection does not portray anybody in the best possible light right now, so she says, 'I just know.'

'But you're such a beautiful girl.'

'How do you know that?'

'I just know.'

For a moment, there is silence. Outside the window the two jays are hopping around each other again, the jets landing relentlessly at Heathrow. Grace says, 'You can keep the fifty pounds.'

'I can't, no I can't . . .'

'Yes, you can. I don't need it and you did. But I want you to do something for me in return. I want you to come and talk to me sometimes. That poor Magda is OK, but she's terribly *big . . .*'

Kerenza laughs. There is something huge about Magda.

'She's big and she doesn't speak much English and I love the way you read those letters. I get so . . . it's not lonely exactly, because I don't mind being on my own . . . but I'm just sitting here waiting to die and sometimes I get scared with all these ghosts around me and I don't understand what it's all about, what it all means. So I just want you to come and talk to me sometimes, read me the letters.'

'I'll do that anyway, I should still pay you back, I've got the money now . . .'

'No, you keep your money, you work hard enough for it. Just come and see me each week if you have the time. And talk to me.'

'All right,' Kerenza says. 'Actually, I'd quite like that as well.'

'That's why I didn't mind about the money.' Grace squeezes her hand. 'You're a good girl underneath it all. And don't worry about this man. My Arthur didn't pay me any attention for months no matter what I did. He was a lot older than me, of course. Then he started making love to me all of a sudden.'

Kerenza smiles at the old-fashioned use of the term.

'We used to go out and about. Bushy Park, Kew Gardens was our first date – the bluebell woods. It was May . . .' Grace looks past Kerenza. '. . . there were bluebells everywhere. I haven't been back there since.'

'I'll take you one day,' Kerenza promises.

Grace smiles at her and takes her hand.

'Everything will be all right, you'll see, everything will work out perfectly for you.'

Anna is sitting at the window reading *The Kite Runner* when Kerenza stumbles into the flat later on. She thinks that Evan would have wanted to pick on Anna for being a middle-class lefty academic who goes to plays about George Bush being bad and stupid, and how unfair that would be because Anna is good and clever and kind.

'I've got to have chemotherapy,' she tells Kerenza.

Kerenza nods.

'But that will sort it out, right?'

'They're not saying.'

Kerenza sits down beside her and takes her hand.

'I'll come with you to the hospital any time you want,' she says. 'Put the appointments on the calendar so I know.'

Anna nods absent-mindedly.

'Come and watch some TV with me?'

They sit on the sofa together and turn on the TV to watch the *Late Review* and pour scorn and derision on the panel except for Mark Lawson, whom they both like. Anna says that she has always found Mark Lawson's powerful bald head, fish-lips and general weightiness to be oddly arousing, and then they discuss whether he might be gay and unattractive (in the conventional sense) and men they have had great sex with.

'So what happened with this guy in Wales?' Anna turns away from the TV.

Kerenza thinks about telling her about the things she had done recently to get money. Stolen from Grace Holding and taken dodgy money from a conman. But she can't tell Anna *that*, even though she knows that Anna would try hard not to be judgmental. She could tell Evan, she feels she could tell him almost anything, but there has been no contact between them since their return from Wales.

'Did he make a pass at you?' Anna asks.

Kerenza shakes her head. 'He just offered me some work.'

'Work?'

'Yeah, just training videos, boring stuff like that.'

'You went to Wales to talk about training videos with a man you'd never met before?'

Kerenza bites her lip and looks at the TV.

'I hate Germaine Greer,' she says.

Anna half-nods, aware that Kerenza is changing the subject but half-reluctant to let her get away with it.

'She can be tiresome,' she agrees absently. 'Too many bossy opinions.'

But for a moment they are both distracted by a discussion about their favourite American TV series – the penultimate series is about to debut on British TV, the last is currently in production and will show some time next autumn. Kerenza suddenly shivers as she watches Anna; her habitual expression when she is listening of tilting her head and twisting a curl of hair, her familiar position on the sofa – feet tucked up beneath her. And in that moment, Anna turns and catches Kerenza staring at her. Just for a second, neither drops their gaze and Anna stares hard, almost fiercely, back at her. Kerenza blinks – the harshest gaze she normally receives from her friend is one of tender dismay – but Anna still does not drop her stare, it becomes more intense, as if she is not seeing her friend at all. Then as if unaware of the moment that is passing, has just passed, it softens into a smile.

'Are you going to see him again?' she asks. 'The guy from Wales?'

Remembering the night when she crept across to Evan's room still sends the sudden adrenaline of humiliation coursing around Kerenza's body, a low involuntary moan of discomfort and embarrassment. But she can recall other things: the casually expert way he chased the egg around the pan as he made an omelette, singing happily about hungry belly pickneys as they drove, the half-smile with which he delivered his own bossy opinions, the weight of the money-stuffed envelope and his expression as he handed it to her.

As if he knew what her answer was going to be.

PART TWO

Burberry Beret

Burberry caps, pink polo shirts, sovereign rings and white Reebok Classics – the party in a Clerkenwell bar is in full swing. Almost everybody on the dance-floor is also wearing a lime-green wristband with the words *Dancing with Life – TBF*. Giggling girls go in pairs to the toilets, although some of them haven't quite been able to sacrifice their Marc Jacobs handbags for the fancy-dress code the charity evening has demanded. The blond DJ in a Nickelson shirt is scratching his six-pack stomach while playing Gwen Stefani, which the faux-chavs from advertising are greatly enjoying; boys are doing mock wind and grind with pretty girls in sun visors and pony-tails. Good-natured booing breaks out as he interrupts his set to allow the event organiser – Ella McCarthy – to get up on the stage and just say a few important words about the evening and the reason we're really here tonight.

'It's great to see everybody having such a good time,' Ella says, her voice reassuringly home counties, 'but let's not forget the reason we're really here tonight and make sure that we all spend a lot more at the bar, which shouldn't be too much of a hardship for you.'

She smiles at the cheers.

'Although those of you doing the marathon in a couple of weeks should perhaps watch those trips to the toilets.'

'The chavathon!' somebody shouts from the dance-floor, and everybody laughs, and the girls fan themselves with beer-mats and lean good-naturedly on the shoulders of their partners and friends while they light cigarettes and sip their drinks.

'I'd like to thank Tom and Roo, who own the bar, for generously allowing us to keep the proceeds from tonight and remind you all to keep looking for sponsors. So far, we have thirty people committed to running for the Taylor Bright Foundation and – for those who don't know – Taylor was a very brave little boy who suffered from a rare genetic heart disorder. You can find out all about that on the TBF website, from which you can also order the *Dancing with Life* wristbands that I'm glad to see most of you are wearing.'

Those on the dance-floor wave their wristbanded hands in the air.

'OK, well, carry on, Wild Things,' Ella says and abandons the stage to whoops and cheers.

She descends from the stage and kisses the cheek of a tall, blond man who is waiting for her with a vodka-tonic clasped in each hand, his eyes wide with love and admiration.

'Brilliant evening, Ella,' he says.

She brushes a curl behind her shoulder and smiles at him.

'Thanks, Rory.'

'Chunk's just called. He's coming down with a *sack* of beans if you want one. I've ordered a couple for later. Might be some chang along in a while as well.'

'Maybe I'll wait for a changy nose-up.' She smiles as he steers her towards a little table. A girl and boy in sun visor and Burberry cap respectively are already sitting there. The boy is wearing white Reeboks and pink Ralph Lauren shirt. His face is a taut geometry of cheek-bones, although he also seems to carry a trail of distant discontent. The girl with him is called Hetty: very pretty, a sweet face underneath her sun visor framed by soft curls, one long leg casually crossed, her cigarette hanging from two long fingers. She is sporting giant gold hooped earrings as her concession to the dress code, but one of her long, elegant fingers also sports a large lapis lazuli ring. Ella admires the ring and Hetty tells her that she bought it in Chile after a skiing holiday and never takes it off – not even to be her chav persona of Jasmine-Chelsea.

'Is Chunk bringing some beans?' she asks anxiously.

'He's on his way. Just been to talk to a few corporate sponsors,' Rory replies. 'Looks like SMP might want to join the fun.'

'Great party, Ella,' Hetty says. 'Don't you think Jamie looks pretty in pink? Also, he's got some fantastic news for the fund-raising.'

Ella McCarthy arches an eyebrow expectantly.

'My dad's rowing club are going to have a barbecue and raise money for the Foundation. It's quite an *exclusive* club.'

'They're fucking *minted*,' the girl says. 'Almost every one of them's a company director. You can expect at least a grand each from some of them.'

'I dunno if it's that much, Hets, but you can definitely expect quite a lot in the end. I'm guessing twenty K, but that might be conservative.'

'Brilliant,' Ella says.

'I've given him your mobile so he can get the account details,' Jamie says. 'That's OK, isn't it?'

'Of course.'

'He's really into this 'cos he thinks running the marathon will stop me from taking drugs. It wasn't very jolly at home for a while when he found all those rocks in my bedroom,' Jamie says.

'I had a message from Charlotte and Frog – they're coming back from Singapore,' Rory tells them.

'They were really lucky with the tsunami,' Jamie says, and Rory nods.

'Not as lucky as Pearl and Justin. She was unconscious for three days after getting hit by that mini-bar. Juzzer was literally *fishing* bodies out of the water.'

'Is Frog going to go back to Young and Fletcher?' Jamie asks.

Rory shakes his head.

'Charlotte's got this idea of setting up a bonsai nursery in Devon.'

'I love Froggy,' Hetty says. 'He's so *funny*.'

'He's such a *Westminster* boy,' Rory says. 'Westminster boys have got a dark sense of humour.'

'Where did you go to school?' Ella asks Hetty.

'Bryanston,' she says.

'Figures,' says Rory.

'How's that?'

'Rich liberal dad works in the film industry . . .'

She sticks her tongue out at him.

'What does your dad do?' Ella asks.

'Oh,' Hetty flaps a hand vaguely, 'he's a director. Out in Hollywood now.'

'Is he making a film now?'

'He's always making something. Think the next project's a rom-com called *Love You Tomorrow* with one of the guys from *Friends*. Liv's just got a part in it, actually.'

'Liv?'

'Olivia Scott,' Hetty says. 'British actress, but this will be her big movie break. Lovely Livvy, she's such a sweetheart, came to my birthday last year. Brilliant in that thing on TV recently – the Henry Miller adaptation.'

'James,' says Jamie delicately picking some fluff from his pink shirt. '*Portrait of a Lady* was written by Henry James. Henry Miller wrote soft porn.'

'Oh, right.' Hetty shrugs good-naturedly. 'What about you, sweet-pea?' She turns back to Ella. 'Where did you go to school? You've got a Saint Paul's look about you.'

'It's true,' Rory says. 'Saint Paul's girls are different.'

'Oh . . .' Ella glances across the dance-floor. 'I did a bacca-laureate. With Dad being in the army, we were all over the place really.'

'My best friend Hugo's in the army,' Rory says.

'The Mad Lieutenant,' Jamie explains to Ella. 'Mentalist.'

'*Fucking* radio,' Hetty agrees. 'Proper mental. He stuck his hand up my skirt at Freddy H's party. Then he was like virtually *raping* me.'

'He can be a sex-pest.' Rory nods.

'*Did* he rape you?' Jamie asks.

'No, he gave me lots of chang, so I let him. That's not rape, is it – if you give in.'

'If it's down to the promise of drugs rather than the threat of violence, I think you'd have a hard time convincing a judge. If I give you lots of chang tonight will you fuck me?'

'No, Jamie, we had baths together when we were kids, you're virtually my *brother*. I thought I might try Chunky tonight, actually.'

Ella glances at her sharply.

'Hugo's still gonna run the chavathon,' Rory says. 'He'll drink a few pints, stop for some smokes and still do it in under five hours. Then he'll stay up for four nights and be back in charge of his tank on Monday morning.'

'It's true,' Jamie says. 'Blew up a house full of rebels in Iraq.'

'Are they called rebels?' Ella asks. 'Thought the appropriate term was insurgents.'

'They're fucking scum is what they are,' Rory says. 'What I hate is that they're always going on about this or that convention and ill-treatment and whatever but they don't mind flying planes into buildings full of civilians and cutting the heads off defenceless prisoners. So they got their photo taken on the end of a dogleash – like they wouldn't do far worse to an American they captured.'

Jamie turns to Hetty.

'Iraq's a Middle-East country we helped to invade a while back.'

'I *know* what Iraq is,' Hetty says. 'Samira's half-Iraqi, remember. She's still got relatives there and she says it's pretty awful – no electricity, car bombs going off all the time, kidnappings.'

'We didn't have any choice, though,' Rory says. 'Saddam was a madman. Bonkers in the nut.'

'And those underpants . . .' Hetty giggles.

'Samira can't want Saddam back,' Rory insists. 'What Blair did was quite right, and it took balls with all the commies marching against it and slagging him off.'

'No, well, she doesn't live there any more, though. Her dad used to be an ambassador or something like that. Can't remember but I think he fell out with Saddam, and then they moved to Paris when Samira was small.'

Ella stands up suddenly.

'Won't be a sec,' she says.

She walks across the dance-floor where a game of piggy-in-the-middle is being played with a Burberry cap, and the crowd are roaring 'Burberry beret' to the Prince song. A man comes into the bar and looks around, catches her eye and gestures with his head towards the street outside. She follows him back out into the Clerkenwell street and away from some of the fancy-dress chavs making calls on their mobiles in the doorway.

'How's the posh druggies?' Evan asks.

Kerenza sighs.

'Millions of dem.'

'They're certainly no hungry belly pickneys.'

'No. And that fucking girl is doing my head in.'

'Which girl?'

'Henrietta. They're talking about how Saddam's mad and has dodgy underpants.'

'Both of which are true.'

'Rory is doing his pro-war rant.'

'Don't disagree with all of it, actually. Only thing worse than those psychotic goatfuckers who want to stone people for laughing are the British lefty trash kissing their arses and making excuses for them.'

'And Hetty's saying she might try and fuck you tonight.'

'Excellent.'

She stares at him.

'Sure you're . . . *up* for it?'

He doesn't bat an eyelid.

'Don't see why not. Always liked a girl who's very pretty but acts very stupid. How's it all going with Rory?'

'I'm fighting him off.'

'OK, but remember he's the one we absolutely must keep on

board, the one I've worked on from the start. If he likes you . . . that's in our favour. Right, I've brought some more wristbands and a bag of pills for them.'

'Real pills?'

'Course they're real pills. One thing these people know is their drugs – they were doing them on the dorm from the age of eleven. I didn't pay for them, though.'

'Course not,' she says half-bitterly, although she doesn't care at all about the pills. The idea of him going home with Hetty at the end of the party makes her feel sick and miserable.

He regards her steadily.

'We stand to make a good amount of money out of this. More than you'd make standing in for somebody at a script read-through.'

This is cruel, as Kerenza's last offer of work had been to read-in for an actress at the readthrough of a new show about a specialist group of detectives working on unsolved murder cases.

'If you're not up for it . . .'

'Course I'm up for it. I just can't stand that girl.'

He grins at her.

'Let me deal with her.'

They make their way back into the party and across the dance-floor, where a white Reebok Classic is now being tossed about to Destiny's Child. Hetty's face lights up as she sees Evan.

'Chunky,' she squeals as she kisses his cheek and lets her hand trail artfully down his chest as she releases him. There aren't enough chairs, and so she insists that he take hers and then sits down on his lap, one long arm draped around his neck, holding a cigarette.

'So,' Evan says, 'how are the posh druggies?'

'There's nothing wrong with a posh druggy,' Hetty says. 'We look nice and we don't hurt anybody.'

'Somebody got hurt somewhere for you to have your little trust fund, Henrietta,' he says.

She clenches her fist in mock-acceptance. 'Respect,' she says.

He grins at her and Kerenza feels the terrible accordion-squeeze of jealousy on her stomach.

Kerenza turns to Rory.

'Fancy a dance?' she says.

Kerenza paces curiously around Rory's Primrose Hill flat as he opens a bottle of wine in the kitchen. The flat is not tasteless but it lacks much originality – Philippe Starck bathroom, a large chrome fan in the living room, galaxies of carefully positioned spotlights, expensive kitchen implements, an electric guitar that looks as if it is rarely – if ever – played, framed pictures of movie stars and Mapplethorpe portraits. She scans his books quickly – books about Tiger Woods and Jonny Wilkinson, books about the history of advertising, Hollywood in pictures and a couple of Tony Parsons novels. A Basement Jaxx Greatest Hits CD is playing through tiny wall-mounted Bose speakers, although his collection – also mainly of greatest hits – contains Elton John, Queen and a Billy Joel box set. Kerenza has a secret soft spot for Billy Joel and suddenly wishes they were listening to the song about Eddie and Brenda and their wine choices in the Italian restaurant.

She picks up a family photograph of Rory as a young boy playing alongside a little girl on some swings in a back garden. They are both on the up, mouths wide open with hilarity. Behind them, their parents are pushing them. It's a nice photo of movement and laughter.

'This your sister?' she asks as he comes back in with the wine.

'Charlotte,' he says.

'What does she do?'

'She drowned.' He puts the wine down carefully. 'When I was thirteen and she was ten. My little sister.'

Kerenza stares at him.

'That's horrible.'

'We were in Cornwall, playing on some rocks. One of those big waves came in and swept her out to sea.'

'Did they find her?'

'All I remember is my mother's face. I remember her shouting at my dad. Shouting and shouting. At the time, I didn't know what she was shouting but obviously she was screaming at him to do something. Her face was all red, and it was windy, and I remember she was trying to get her hair out of her mouth. The wind was just whipping her hair back into her face and carrying her screams away. My dad jumped in the sea but he got swept out as well and nearly drowned. They saved him and reached Charlotte not long after, but it was too late, she couldn't really swim. After that I was sent away to boarding school and my parents split up, partly because they blamed each other, even though it had been a really calm day and the wave just came from nowhere. The last thing I remember about us as a proper family was eating sandwiches on the beach before it happened. Pâté in baguettes my mum had wrapped in tin foil. She got up that morning and made us sandwiches, wrapped them in foil and then . . .'

He shrugs and sips his wine. Kerenza looks at the little girl in the photo and once again feels a dizzying bewilderment. A van marked McGeery's Motors, a scarf over a head made hairless by chemotherapy, a wave foaming over rocks where children are playing, a hawk hanging from a tree and blinking at the fading ground. Cordelia's limp body carried on stage.

But there are also survivors.

A shell fired from a German gun exploding just far enough behind the trench to save a young soldier's life, shipped out of a war in which he would otherwise certainly have died. A conman saved from burning alive because an out-of-work actress happened to be in the bar. And still the greenfinches, still the onlookers with their arms folded, still one day melting into another.

'There's so many bad things.' Rory has returned to his take on the world situation, which clearly causes him a few sleepless nights. 'All that shit about Iraq, people blowing up tube trains, it could really do your head in.'

'It could,' Kerenza agrees.

'That's why Chunk's such a breath of fresh air. He doesn't take life so seriously but he's really passionate about the Taylor Bright Foundation.'

'Lucky you bumped into each other,' Kerenza says.

'Literally,' Rory laughs. 'I was training in the park and he just ran straight into me.'

His name's Rory St John. Public school boy who works in advertising. He's training for the marathon and runs on Primrose Hill near to his flat. Likes his drugs but he'll also like the idea of a good cause, 'cos sometimes he worries that his life's a bit pointless and empty, thinks he might be missing the big picture.

And a nasty thought twists inside Kerenza. Evan has never explained to her the source of his original information about Rory, but if he knew all of this, did he also know about the drowned sister and think that it might make Rory even more susceptible to the tragic story of little Taylor Bright? Is that why Evan also invented the story of a brother who had died of the same condition?

He's got a ton of mates who we can rope in if Rory's on board. All trustafarians of one type or another with corporate and landed relatives.

Kerenza takes a mouthful of wine. Good wine, an expensive white burgundy. She swills it around her mouth; the glasses have long snappy stems and are uncomfortable to hold. Eddie and Brenda sitting in their Italian restaurant, Rory choosing his wash basins, deciding he likes the idea of the stand-alone ones, maybe feeling excited by his chosen bathroom aesthetic, his mum wrapping pâté sandwiches in foil the day of a family picnic on the Cornish coast. She remembers Evan telling her that she would have to confront the fact that the people they were scamming were human beings, that there was no such thing as a con that didn't leave victims. The problem is that it is not just the little sister helplessly flailing in a far more powerful sea, the family broken by grief, that is stirring her sympathy, but odd things like the Moulinex 500 that Rory had carefully explained was considered the Rolls-Royce of food processors and half-jokingly told her was his favourite possession; even the sports biographies and the surfeit of shiny chrome seem slightly lonely rather than creepy.

She gives herself a mental pinch.

'Whose idea was it for you all to run the marathon dressed as chavs?' she asks.

'Oh, well, Chunky likes to say it was his idea, but it was me and Jamie. You seen that brilliant website chavscum.com?'

She shakes her head.

'Heard about it though.'

'They've got this thing. You put your name into it and it generates a chav-name for your baby. Mine was Brandon Kyle.'

Kerenza laughs.

'That's brilliant.'

He moves over to her on the sofa, and she knows what's going to happen next. He fingers a curl of her hair.

'Such an amazing colour,' he says.

'Thanks.' She smiles. She finds nothing particularly attractive or unattractive about Rory but she knows that this is probably in his favour, that it is what will allow her to let him because she has always found something sexy about 'Oh, fuck it, why not?' It is partly why she will let him lead her to the huge bed next door with a large picture of Bogart above it that reminds her of pizza parlours and menus with names like The Maltese Falcon, The African Queen or The Casablanca, and she thinks about Billy Joel singing about Brenda and Eddie in the Italian restaurant, red, white, or maybe rosé wine, and this almost makes her laugh, but it would be inappropriate when Rory is murmuring about how sexy she is and how he has fancied her from day one. His hand is lingering on her cheek.

The other part of sleeping with him is, of course, to do with Hetty and Evan, where they disappeared to; she tries to imagine them together, can't. She remembers plotting with Evan as they chose her name to sound almost identical to the yachtswoman, which would be reassuring for people who probably spent a lot of time just messing about on their boats. She remembers Evan laughing at the yachtswoman's tears from the video-diary: 'Well, what did you fucking expect on your own in the middle of the ocean, thick'ead?'

Now she can feel Rory's lips opening hers and she pushes him away with the delicate theatrics of rejection-but-try-again and he persists and this time she lets him, lets his hand cup her breast, lets him slide his hand up her skirt, fingers fluttering over her belly. He slides off the sofa and stands above her, unfastening his Seven jeans, kicking off his trainers, slipping off his Calvin Kleins, and he has got quite a nice body, she likes the shape it makes as he bends to step out of his boxer shorts and she knows – in a kind of relieved flash as she looks at him – that she is going to enjoy this because she doesn't care too much and that he is at least hard and desiring her and that he is going to make her come probably more than once, here on the sofa and later in the huge bed under Humphrey Bogart. And he kneels down again, lifts her skirt carefully around her waist, says, 'God, you're beautiful,' pushes her thighs apart, moves her knickers aside with one finger and teases her skilfully with little movements of his cock until she arches and pulls him inside her.

Much later in the night she wakes and leaves him sleeping while she goes to the kitchen. She fills a glass with water from the tap and looks out at the quiet, tree-lined street. A taxi pulls up at one of the houses opposite and she cranes to see the people getting out of it. She starts as she realises that they are all famous – a little group of actors and pop stars. It's not so surprising, she thinks, given that they are in Primrose Hill, and she cranes to identify the make-up of the little gang. As she does so, a man who she recognises as Jude Law looks up and waves cheerfully at her, catching her spying and making a quick joke about it to the rest of the group. She half-raises her hand in response but then feels awkward and embarrassed, a Peeping Tom, and she turns away from the window, drinks her glass of water and looks instead at the chrome kitchen, the gleaming Moulinex 500 – Rolls-Royce of food processors.

Expositional Thematic Dialogue

INT. CAR – DAY

Hambleton and McGuire are sitting on stake-out, drinking
coffees. They are watching the entrance to a snooker hall.

> MCGUIRE
>
> I'm not sure about Milena.

> HAMBLETON
>
> She's our only chance of nailing Jamie Miller. He's the number
> one link with the Colombian cartels.

> MCGUIRE
>
> Why don't we just pull him in now?

> HAMBLETON
>
> Because this will allow us to get not just Miller but his entire
> gang. We've got to collect the evidence.

> MCGUIRE
>
> If he doesn't show up then we'll have to call this off.

> HAMBLETON
>
> Sometimes you have to take risks, Kath. I'm prepared to live with
> the consequences of my decisions.

> MCGUIRE
>
> Oh, look, here's Milena.

(They watch as Milena comes into view with a man we will know as Jamie Miller. He's a swarthy man in a leather jacket but no suggestion of the violent psychopath he really is.)

MCGUIRE (CONT'D)

I've got a bad feeling about this.

HAMBLETON

Success is about a mixture of hard work, good luck and risk. We have to take a gamble here.

(McGuire nods. She knows he's right.)

MCGUIRE

I just don't want to see her get hurt.

They watch as Milena and Miller enter the snooker hall and adjust their listening devices.

MILLER (V.O.)

You say you know Carlos Baeza?

MILENA (V.O.)

Yes.

MILLER (V.O.)

I have some people checking that out. In the meantime why don't . . .

(He glances at her lithe body in its light summer dress.)

MILLER (V.O) (CONT'D)

. . . we go in and have a drink.

(They enter the snooker hall together. McGuire glances at Hambleton, whose expression is determined.)

HAMBLETON

This is our only option for getting Miller. We're doing the right thing here.

(She looks him full in the face, and behind her anxiety we also see her tremendous love and respect for her senior officer.)

I know, Guv.

'What do you think?'

Kerenza and Mark are drinking cappuccinos and eating baguette and jam in Borough market. Kerenza is wondering whether the staff are starting to keep tabs on how much jam they are eating, as they only ordered one portion but are eating enough for four.

'Yeah, it's really tense.' Kerenza watches one of the waiters watching them closely.

'I think so too. Milena's under threat. Lots of *sexual* tension obviously.'

'With Miller appraising her lithe body through its light summer dress? I picked up on that.'

'Gotta throw something in for the boys. Soon McGuire will also be in great danger – enabling Hambleton to do what he does best.'

'Trousers clinging tightly to his buttocks as he cuts a swath through the villains?'

'Exactly. Any reservations? Don't hold back. I can take absolutely any criticism.'

'It's shit.'

'Funny girl.'

'OK, well . . .' Kerenza picks up the script again and pretends to scrutinise it carefully. '. . . This piece of dialogue here where Hambleton tells McGuire about the villain being number one link with the Colombian cartels.'

'Miller?'

'Yeah. I mean, I know why you need the audience to know who he is and everything, but it's a bit strange that he tells her something she must surely already know if they're already sitting on a stake-out.'

'Copy that. My life is a daily struggle with exposition! But a bit always sneaks through like a crafty suicide bomber.'

The couple sitting on the bench next to them raise their

eyebrows slightly at the questionable taste of this piece of hyperbole. Mark continues oblivious.

'The only thing that's worse is expositional *thematic* dialogue.'

'What's that?'

'Erm . . . well . . . see, if I wanted the theme of this scene to be . . . let's say . . . fear of failure. It's always a bad sign if characters start lecturing each other on the nature and pitfalls of fear of failure. Then it's not the characters talking, it's me.'

'But it *isn't* the characters talking really. It *is* you.'

'And the artifice of drama should still allow me to conceal that fact from the audience. It must sound like the kind of thing a character might say. You can't have Hambleton wittering on about ethical choices even if we know that he's a deeply troubled but essentially moral man. He must *reveal* that to us.'

Kerenza helps herself to more jam, watched – she is sure – by another of the waiters. Any moment she expects them to swoop on the table.

'Have you been on some kind of writing course?' she asks.

Mark flushes.

'No.'

'OK.' Kerenza lets her head loll back, watches the media types buying their organic meat. Hopefully, this will be the end of her script interrogation.

'What else?' Mark asks slightly crossly, not allowing her to escape quite so easily.

'*Oh, look, here's Milena* isn't a very strong line.'

Mark purses his lips crossly.

'OK? Anything else.'

'I thought you were subverting social and gender expectations. But it's all a bit conventional. Hambleton's not very gay any more.'

'He is a *cop*, he's hard as nails. You want to see him shopping for antiques or going to *Billy Elliott*?'

'Fair enough, but all the ladies – including McGuire – seem to fancy him. In fact, on several occasions you seem to be suggesting that McGuire is in love with him.'

'That's all part of her serial arc. How does she come to terms with the fact that she can never have the man that she loves and admires the most?'

'I suspect she'll cope with the disappointment,' Kerenza remarks drily. 'And that feels a little bit familiar as a contradiction.'

Mark holds up a finger.

'Don't say *Will and Grace* to me.'

'I wasn't going to.'

'It's *not* fucking *Will and Grace*.'

'I know. It's not funny for a start . . .'

She catches his glance and corrects herself hurriedly.

'Intentionally, obviously. It's not a comedy.'

'Although it's supposed to be leavened with a little humour.'

'And that really comes through.'

Mark looks hurt, so Kerenza fights for something that will show how hard she's concentrated on reading the script.

'Do you think there might be too many Ms?'

'What?'

'The names. Miller, McGuire, Milenka. Too many Ms.'

'Oh yes.' Mark brightens – this is the kind of easy script note he really likes and he makes a careful note of it.

'We'll change Miller to Curtis.'

'And his middle name can be Lee?'

Mark looks puzzled and then catches on.

'Oh yeah, well, Saunders maybe . . .' But he does not complete his sentence because he is staring down the street over Kerenza's shoulder. His eyes gleam excitedly.

'I don't believe it!'

'What is it?'

'Don't turn around, but Emily Holt is on her way over for a coffee.'

'Emily Holt?'

'Superagent . . . Emily!'

Mark leaps up and sends the remains of their breakfast flying. Kerenza tries to retrieve – in a none too dignified manner – a jammy knife which has fallen under the table and prevent coffee from dripping onto her lap. The woman whom Mark has detained is pushing a small child in a bugaboo frog pram and looks at him with polite lack of recognition.

'Mark Hambleton,' Mark says.

'Mark . . .' Emily still seems bemused.

'Pendleton. You read my script *Sad Fucking Losers*.'

'Oh God, of course. Very funny script, just not quite . . .'

She flaps her hand vaguely.

'And you were in *Shiver*, weren't you? I loved that show.'

Kerenza studies her carefully, as this puts Emily in either a) a club with very few members – fans of *Shiver*, or b) a club with an infinite number of members – blatant liars. But she seems totally genuine. Disturbingly, Emily Holt has a pleasant face and rather a nice demeanour; a bunch of peonies lies across the top of the pram.

'I mean, I know it got a kicking from the critics, but they so totally missed the point, I thought it was great fun. Christ . . .' she glances around Monmouth's, which is now packed with people waiting for their lattes and cappuccinos, '. . . it's very busy in here.'

Mark whisks an empty chair from the table behind them.

'Here, I'm just going to get us some more coffees. What are you having?'

For a moment, Kerenza thinks that Emily might pass on the opportunity of breakfast with a pushy writer, but she looks tired and overladen and doesn't need another invitation to grab the chair.

'Latte decaf, please, Mark.'

'Kerenza?'

'Erm . . . normal latte please.'

Mark skips towards the queue, pausing to examine the sleeping baby.

'Oh. My. God. Aren't you gorgeous.' He turns to Kerenza. 'Isn't she just divine?'

'He,' Emily says a little wearily, as if this is a very frequent mistake.

'No! A boy and so pretty. You're gonna be breaking hearts in Old Compton Street, baby.' Mark camps it up even more in an admirable recovery, and Emily Holt laughs good-naturedly.

They watch Mark queue-jumping, smiling charmingly when he receives dirty looks, and Emily raises an eyebrow at Kerenza.

'Kerenza. That's an unusual name.'

'It's Cornish.'

'Beautiful.'

Kerenza nods, wondering if anybody will ever say that her name is unusual but grotesquely ugly for a change.

'Do you live locally?' she asks.

'Clapham. But I come here every weekend after baby yoga.'

'Baby yoga!' Kerenza can't quite prevent a flash of mockery in her eyes.

Emily grins.

'I know, I know, don't say anything, my partner gives me a hard enough time about it. But actually I really enjoy it, I'm always so busy and it just takes my mind off the clients – needy little fucks. Plus, there's an absolutely gorgeous single dad that I love flirting with. Baby yoga, flowers and a coffee in Monmouth's. I feel like at least I have some connection with the real world again.'

'Just your luck, then, to bump into a writer.'

'Oh well, compared to some of the freaks whose fragile egos I have to soothe it might have been a lot worse. If ever they need a collective noun for writers I think "a whinge" should do the trick nicely. You know what one of them said to me yesterday? "Phone the BBC and tell them I won't do the rewrite. I'm not a slave." And he's getting eighteen grand an episode and then the same again in principal photography fee, so he's a long fucking way from Kunta Kinte. You're not . . .'

'I'm an actor.'

'Kerenza . . . ?'

'Penhaligon.'

'Right.' Emily nods earnestly – the name clearly meaning nothing to her – as Mark returns with the coffees. He and Emily sit and chatter and gossip good-naturedly about the world of television and shows they have seen both under- and over-rated and ratings battles and whether a clever drama subverting gender and social stereotypes in modern policing could ever stand a chance against *Help, I'm a Celebrity*, while Kerenza nods and throws in the odd comment. And she realises that Mark is never going to give up, that this world is right under his skin, and that he will not stop or swerve until he is a part of it, until it has embraced him fully. And she can understand his desire to belong, the way he would enjoy it – all the script meetings and gossip and shiny product. She watches him laughing, exaggerating his campness, teasing Emily gently, judiciously deferring to her opinion from time to time, and she suddenly things, *he's going to do it, he's going to pull it off*, and, just for an instant, she knows that she would be glad if he did, if he was able to mark out his little corner of territory and live there happily. Eventually, Emily Holt departs with baby in tow, having urged Mark to send her the script of 'Gay Bergerac', which she playfully agrees is a *fantastic* working title.

'She was nice,' Kerenza says a little disconsolately.

'Yeah,' Mark replies. 'Glad I came across that *Guardian* media piece on her.'

'What *Guardian* media piece?'

'The one where she said she loved a coffee in Monmouth's on a Saturday morning, of course.' He grins at her.

'*That's* why you were so insistent on coming here . . .' Kerenza laughs and shakes her head. 'You scheming little bastard.'

Mark nods proudly, as if fielding a compliment.

'Detective work that might make Hambleton envious. You said you wanted to buy some food anyway.'

'I wondered why you kept looking over my shoulder.'

'Do you think she was really interested in the new script or was she just saying it?'

'I think she was just saying it.'

'Really? I think she seemed genuinely keen.'

'So then,' Kerenza shrugs, 'why are you asking? Yes, she seemed to like both you *and* "Gay Bergerac".'

Mark tilts his cup and plays with the dregs of his coffee.

'But when she said "fantastic working title", what do you think she meant by that?'

'She hates marzipan?'

'You think?'

'Or I'm guessing she meant it's a funny working title, albeit one nobody could use – a bit like *Sad Fucking Losers*.'

'I'm scared,' Mark says. 'My love-life's shit, I've got no money, and a proper agent is my only hope.'

'Excellent.' Kerenza squeezes his hand. 'For a moment I was worried you might be getting your act together.'

'And leave my fellow sad-fucking-loser behind? No way.'

They leave Monmouth's and wander around the market, watching people munching on pork and apple sauce in baps, queueing for organic burgers, inspecting the manchego cheese, cathedrals of olive oil, debating the relative merits of grilled over-roasted peppers as people walk past clutching little bunches of flowers for their flats or moaning about their hangovers. Kerenza buys some pork-belly and peaches for the dinner she is making for Anna and Ivo that night. Mark glances at her.

'You seem to be doing well for money these days. But you're not doing any work.'

For a moment, Kerenza remembers the advertising chavs, Chrome Rory – as Evan has mockingly nicknamed him – standing undressing in front of her, the picture of Bogart above his bed. She had told him instantly that she had slept with Rory and how enjoyable it had been, something for which Evan had coolly congratulated her, as it would help dispel any doubts about their project. *I didn't do it for that,* she had protested, and he had shrugged and smiled infuriatingly and told her not to get too close to him as she would not be seeing him again once the last of the money had come in for the chavathon. She had fished for information about where he had disappeared to with Hetty, but he had refused to rise to the bait, as if daring her to ask him directly – something which was a desperate temptation but which she had resisted.

'I am working, actually,' Kerenza says. 'I'm working with Evan.'

'The handsome Welsh fascist? Has he managed to rise to the occasion yet?'

She shakes her head sorrowfully. 'Haven't given it another try.'

'A crazy salad and no meat,' Mark observes. 'Why do you bother with him?'

'I like him.'

'Why? At our admittedly brief meeting I thought he was an arrogant, self-conscious prick.'

'He is.'

'So . . .'

Kerenza picks up a bunch of basil, breathes in its strong aroma. For a moment she thinks she might, absurdly, be about to cry. Mark spots her looming distress and steers the subject away from her feelings for Evan.

'What kind of work are you doing with him?'

Kerenza is tempted to spill her heart to Mark. He's a conman and we're working to rip off a bunch of advertising executives and trustafarians. I hosted a fundraising party, urged people to access sponsorship pages from a fake give-us-your-donation website designed by Geraint Roberts – an unemployed computer maverick in Bridgend whom Evan knew from school. Oh, and I provided coloured wristbands for a non-existent foundation to a group of people who – however absurd or foolish they might be – are having fundamentally decent charitable impulses cruelly deceived. Soon I'll be watching them run the marathon dressed up as a social category they fear and despise in equal measure before handing over all their sponsorship money to two individuals who will then disappear without trace.

Then on top of this there is Evan, a man who is consistently and casually cruel with her and yet whose presence she has come to long for as the accident victim yearns for morphine. And he knows this, must know it, because he is so adept at the heartless manoeuvres that keep the besotted so bewildered – now you see him, now you don't. There are just some people who can do that, who can light up a room and make everything seem empty when they are not there. She has fallen in love with the most unsuitable man, for no reason that she can properly work out but in one of the most old-fashioned of ways. What does she want from him? she sometimes asks herself, and the truth is she doesn't know. She just has Evan-images stuck in her head like bits of glass – the bushy eyebrows over his book in the bar, the text message inviting her to Wales to which she had so rashly responded, the shape of him in the little miner's cottage with its smell of wood-smoke, the sound of his voice: mocking, intolerant, clever.

'Training videos.'

Mark furrows his brow.

'*That* guy makes training videos?'

'He's got a contact who does and he . . . put us together. It's quite lucrative.'

'It's not porn, is it? I know you had that offer before and thought about it . . .'

'It's not porn.'

'Good,' Mark says determinedly. 'You really wouldn't suit that.'

'Some women are supposed to enjoy it, find it liberating.'

'Maybe.' Mark inspects a bunch of rhubarb. 'But it's more likely you'd be anally raped and strangled by some fat cunt from Texas. And while I'd never want to second-guess your sexuality, I don't think you'd find that very liberating.'

'I wouldn't.'

'Well then. Stick to training videos.'

He signals to the man that he is going to buy the rhubarb, turns and smiles at Kerenza.

'Think I'll make a crumble tonight.'

'I hate hospitals,' Ivo says gloomily as they sit waiting for Anna to come out of the appointment with the consultant in the oncology unit. Kerenza nods, although she actually thinks they're great, their sense of quiet purpose, their absolutely collectivist nature, one of the very few challenges to the dismal segregations of the British class system. She loves the geography of the corridors with all the coded signs to wards and suites and units, the little shop with the flowers and magazines and boxes of Celebrations chocolates, the blue- and white-gown hierarchies of radiographers and therapists and nurses and doctors, the pregnant women cradling their bumps and groaning at the first contractions, elderly patients slipper-shuffling with their drips, the porters joking as they push a trolley with some stricken patient on their way to theatre.

'How do you think she is?' Ivo asks Kerenza, and she tells him that she thinks that Anna has definitely been better recently now that she has stopped throwing up everything she eats after the chemotherapy.

'But she's frightened and angry,' she adds.

Ivo nods.

'You know, back home there were guys from some of the villages in Bosnia. One of their tortures was to force people to eat live birds. But they are still walking about drinking their plum brandy, going to weddings, playing with the kids like they never did anything wrong.'

He tells her how his family were from Istria, staunch communists and supporters of Tito. At the time war broke out he was doing his military service in the Yugoslav National Army stationed in a strongly nationalist part of Serbia where care had to be taken in bars if you spoke with a Croatian accent. He knew his unit was being despatched to lay siege to Vukovar, so he deserted, fleeing first to Germany and then Britain, where he lived in a squat in Camden and worked for a while serving crêpes on a stall near to Waterloo.

'I knew nobody apart from the guys from home I was squatting with,' he says. 'Man, I was fucking depressed.'

One day he sold a crêpe to a young British woman who was carrying some books about Yugoslavia, and they got chatting. She invited him for a drink, cooked him meals, introduced him to friends and colleagues, inquired about college courses for him. And when he was having problems with his national insurance number, she took him off to Marylebone register office and married him.

'Now she's got fucking cancer. Where's the justice in that?'

Kerenza shrugs.

'Anna's a good woman. She didn't even ask for money to marry me.'

After the wedding, Ivo and Anna rented a car and took a honeymoon around Croatia and Bosnia, driving to Mostar, where drunken Croat forces had blown up the historic bridge that once used to stage diving competitions, roars of boozy laughter at the puffs of smoke as shells landed in the spots where young men had once arced their lean, muscular bodies into the summer sky for the sheer pleasure of the spectators, the brief illusion of flight. Then they went to Rijeka in Istria – a stylish port that the war had hardly touched because the Istrians, according to Ivo, 'couldn't be bothered with all the tribal backward shit that was convulsing the rest of the country'.

'They're all pigs,' Ivo says. 'Ustashe and Chetniks and Taliban. Nationalist, religious pigs.'

Ivo had got into a fight at a wedding back home in Croatia when some of his friends started to berate the British. And he had lost his temper and pointed out that, whatever faults the British might have, they weren't at least sitting around in the ruins of cities ripped apart by the most vicious of wars, they had not entered villages and forced members of the same family to rape each other. On the whole, their society worked, people rarely killed each other for reasons of race, and when they did it caused a scandal and there were inquiries. Some of their politicians were fools and charlatans, but there was no systematic corruption, and British cops didn't even carry guns. They had a health service you didn't have to pay for.

'The one thing I still hate, though, is the way that asylum seekers are treated . . .'

'Yeah, it's bad . . .'

'. . . on TV. Why do they always show us like we're cowering under floorboards? Terrified of the immigration service or recounting stories about our traumas?'

'I dunno . . .' Kerenza says. 'What do you want instead? Asylum seeking: another top night out?'

'No, but most of the people I know are still going to parties and getting drunk and trying to get qualifications or despatch riding while studying at night and watching the football. It's not all drowned cockle pickers and the widows of Srebrenica, you know.'

'Maybe they think people getting on OK in life doesn't make for riveting drama.'

'There are just some people in this country who like to wallow in it all, tell themselves how shit everything is. If it's so shit, then why are there so many people trying to come here?'

'Yeah, well, you can say that 'cos you're an immigrant.'

'That's exactly what I mean. Why can't you say it if it's what you think? If you don't value the things that are good about your country,' Ivo says, 'then how will you know how to defend them? There were loads of good things about Yugoslavia once. We all fucking moaned about it and look what happened.'

The wait is now getting rather long, and Ivo buys them both coffees and chocolate muffins that they pick at disconsolately, because muffins always promise far more than they deliver, and Kerenza worries slightly about the meat which might be going off in its bag. But finally Anna emerges with her headscarf tied over her head, and Kerenza can tell immediately that she has been crying.

'How did it go?' Kerenza asks.

'They're worried about metastasis.'

'What's that?'

'The cancer spreading through the lymph nodes to other parts of the body.'

'Oh.'

'I've got to go on with the chemo.'

Nobody can think of anything much to say as they walk down the winding corridors to the exit, because what is there to say? Kerenza calls a cab, and they sit in almost silence until it arrives to take them back through a city which suddenly seems dirty, shabby and poor.

Back in the house, Kerenza starts to make the food, drawing sharp scores in the skin of the pork even though her heart isn't really in it any longer. Anna has barely said a word since they returned home except to snap at Ivo when he mentioned that there was a big football match on TV that night involving Dynamo Zagreb, and then at Kerenza for not having cleared Smut's litter tray for a couple of days. Kerenza can feel an increased sense of desperation as she empties the small, dried cat turds into a plastic bag, twists a knot in it and throws it into the bin. Then she washes her hands and starts to shove peaches viciously under the skin of the pork. In the end, she can't bear the terrible atmosphere in the house any longer and opens a bottle of wine, downing two large glasses and almost sighing with relief as she feels its sweet anaesthesia coursing through her blood stream. She fills a glass and takes it to Ivo, who smiles gratefully at her and then glances at Anna, who is sitting biting her nails, half-reading a book.

Kerenza is just contemplating her third glass of wine before eating when the doorbell rings.

'Can somebody get that?' she calls, as her hands are covered in peach juice.

She hears Anna go down the hallway and open the door and the low murmur of a man's voice. Something stirs in her belly, and she looks expectantly as Anna returns.

Behind her is Evan.

'Hi, thick'ead,' he says.

'Hi.'

She can't ask him what he's doing here, especially when she has never even given him her address. She hopes Anna will leave them alone for a while, but she goes to the sink to get a glass of water.

'You must be the friend Kerenza told me about.' Evan smiles pleasantly at Anna. 'The one with cancer.'

Kerenza rolls her eyes skywards. Anna stares at him crossly.

'What gave you that idea?'

'Well, I'll give you a tenner if you take that scarf off and there's any hair under there.'

Anna lets out a sudden bark of laughter.

'Cheeky sod. I can't take that bet.'

'Thought so. I had an aunt had breast cancer.'

'Really. Did she stay positive and beat it like I'm always being told to do?'

'Nope, she died pretty quickly. It was one of those really aggressive ones. Inflammatory breast cancer or something, made her tit go like orange peel, she said. Any chance of a glass of wine, by the way?'

Kerenza signals apologetically to Anna that she'll get it, but Anna moves across to the fridge and takes out the bottle. Something about the presence of this complete stranger, his don't-really-give-a-shit-about-you-or-your-feelings attitude, seems almost to have perked her up. Very gradually, the atmosphere seems to improve with his presence. Anna hands him a glass of wine, while Kerenza switches on the radio to a digital channel which is playing a Martha Wainwright track that everybody agrees is great, and then Ivo wanders in and gets a glass of wine as well.

'You're cooking?' Evan says as he watches Kerenza finish preparing the pork and peaches.

'Very observant. So?'

'So nothing.'

'You sound surprised.'

'I like watching people cook,' he says. 'Tells you a lot about them.'

'What does it tell you about me?'

'You're good at it. You want it to be nice for the people you're cooking for.'

'I'd never cook just for myself. Apart from fried courgettes. I lived a whole winter on fried courgettes and cheese.'

'Courgettes are good.'

'Courgettes are the stuff of life.' She smiles at him and gestures to the food. 'You want to stay and have some?'

He glances at his watch. 'Sure, why not?'

Smut wanders in and stares indignantly at him.

'That your cat?'

She nods as Smut curls around his leg, crackles out a purr and leaps onto his lap.

'What's he called?'

'She. Smutty.'

Evan laughs.

'Good name for a cat.' He strokes her from head to tail and Smut crackles and pounds his leg with her little black paws. 'Stupid thing,' he says. 'You stupid, idiotic cat.'

Strange, Kerenza thinks, as they sit eating the pork and peaches with asparagus and mashed potato while she prays that Evan will not start a rant about black cunts, goatfucker fundamentalists or lefties in gastropubs moaning about George Bush being evil and stupid. But, of course, once the pleasantries over the superb crackling on the pork have been dispensed with, the mmmming at the added flavour brought by the peaches, there is virtually no topic of conversation on which she can trust him not to be offensively opinionated. Least of all international law and human rights, which he quickly discovers are Anna's academic speciality.

'What is that?' he asks her aggressively as Kerenza tries desperately to think of a way of changing the subject.

'What is what?' Anna answers coolly.

'International law. There's no such thing.'

'Isn't there?'

'No. Apart from that charade at The Hague for poor scape-goats like Milosevic.'

'Any more for any more?' Kerenza asks brightly, using – to her horror – a phrase that her mother always did when a domestic squabble seemed likely to turn into a major con-flagration.

'You feel sorry for Milosevic?' Ivo asks.

'Yeah, I do. 'Cos those Albanians are a bunch of CIA-sponsored terrorists who'd pimp out their own sisters given half a chance. As I understand it, Kosovo was a province of Serbia, which means that when they started shooting Serb cops, Milosevic was well within his rights to send in the army to kick their backward peasant arses. More within his rights than that freaky-looking little Russian who gets invited to the G8 summit rather than the international war crime tribunal.'

He helps himself to more mashed potato.

'Milosevic was a scapegoat,' Ivo agrees. 'But he played the nationalist card, so he's not innocent.'

'Oh, innocent, guilty.' Evan shrugs. 'What does that mean?'

'What does *that* mean?' Anna says, imitating his shrug. 'Innocent, guilty, like it doesn't actually matter? People who carry out mass murder or give orders to do it are guilty.'

'How can you even be bothered to talk about international law after Iraq? There isn't any. The Americans wanted a second UN resolution but they didn't get one, so they went in anyway.'

'You have to have a law to know it's been broken,' Kerenza says, but Evan ignores her.

'That thing with Pinochet was a joke as well. Just because he had a bad name all the liberals were applauding, although if it had been somebody like Castro the hypocritical motherfuckers would have been screaming blue murder. All this stuff about international law is just a façade, a gravy-train for lawyers and lefty academics.'

'That's rather rude,' Anna says calmly. '*I'm* a lefty academic.'

'I'm not knocking it, I bet it's a great gig, travelling the world, going to conferences, writing papers about human rights and talking to loads of interesting people who think the same as you and listen to world music compilations.'

Anna laughs.

'I certainly miss it,' she agrees. 'But here's the thing. I quite like you, Evan, whoever you are. You've cheered me up being here, and I was really fucking depressed when I got home. Oddly, I often get on better with arrogant right-wing people and I even agree a little with some of what you say, although, let's face it, they're not exactly the most original of arguments. But as part of the gravy-train on which I've been lucky enough to hitch a ride, I've sat through a ton of conferences and conscientiously read almost every book and journal article about the topic. One of the interesting things about contemplating my mortality and our general insignificance as a species is that I don't believe I was wasting my time and I still believe that international law and human rights are important, which is kind of reassuring and makes me feel I haven't completely wasted my life.'

Evan starts to speak but she holds up a hand.

'And I'm certain that if we were to continue the discussion any further than the current superficial level I would be more than capable of kicking your arse. But I'm tired now, so I'd rather not have to waste time making you look stupid.'

She smiles and chases a bit of mashed potato around her plate with her fork. Kerenza holds her breath, but Evan just looks puzzled.

'I'm not right-wing,' he says.

'How would you describe yourself, then?' Ivo asks.

'Anti-establishment,' Evan replies immediately. 'And that includes the British liberal establishment trying to find excuses for suicide bombers living off our taxes.'

Ivo nods in agreement at this. He hates religious fundamentalists and taxes in almost equal measure.

'Yes,' Kerenza observes to Evan. 'Your own tax return must have made sombre reading last year.'

Once again Evan ignores her.

'If they hate decadent Western society so much why don't they leave it and fuck off back to their religious schools and herd their goats under Sharia law?'

Anna rolls her eyes.

'Well,' she says. 'Tomorrow you can write a letter to the *Angry Times* about it all.'

Evan laughs.

'If I wrote about all the things that made me Mr Angry from Angry Town I'd never do any work.'

'What do you work at, Evan?'

Without blinking he says, 'I make training videos. That's what Kerenza and I are working on right now.'

'Training for what?'

'At the moment, how to fill in a CV, how to do well at an interview, basic job-seeking stuff. It's boring but lucrative.'

Anna gazes sadly at Kerenza, and Kerenza knows that she is feeling sorry for her at having been reduced to this.

Kerenza says, 'It pays the rent.'

'You never have to do anything you don't want to to pay the rent,' Anna says. 'You're an actor – being skint is part of the territory.'

'It's OK, I don't mind it,' Kerenza says. 'I get a lot more lines.'

'So what are you doing here?' Kerenza asks Evan when Anna has gone to bed and Ivo gone home.

'Came to see you.'

'All right.'

She regards him steadily. The cat stalks into the room, looks at both of them and chooses Kerenza, which is a big relief to her, as the treachery of cats knows no bounds. In spite of everything, she likes Evan sitting in her living room making cheeky remarks about the Guatemalan cushions and mock-inspecting their CD collection for the Buena Vista Social Club.

'She's all right, your flatmate,' he says.

'Thought she was a lefty academic.'

'Not a *real* lefty,' Evan says. 'Real lefties would have used the word offensive several times and probably asked me to leave. She was wrong about being able to kick my arse, though. But speaking of lefties, I've had an idea and I want to know what you think of it.'

'Go on, then.'

'It's one of several possible projects. I thought we could go to Wales again.'

'To Pant-y-brastrap?'

'Yeah. Kind of a barnstorming session.'

'Brainstorming?'

'That's what I said, isn't it?'

She looks at him, teetering so close to absurdity and still crackling with personality and charisma. She shakes her head slowly.

'I dunno.'

'Go on, we can play the Manics as we go over the Severn Bridge.'

'Not Sooper Furry Animals?' Kerenza rolls each vowel up in the strongest Welsh accent, and Evan laughs and says that, while that's a funnier name, it wouldn't be as poignant since none of the Super Furry Animals have jumped off the bridge, and they toss about the names of other Welsh bands – *it's the Stereophonics, see. No, it's Gorkis Zygotic Mynki, thick'ead.* Their conversation is like this, Kerenza thinks, sliding into the kind of cheerfully aimless banter that a normal girlfriend and boyfriend might have. But they are a long way from that, and she knows that she could never have turned up at his flat in this casual, proprietorial way, knows that he would never have offered her some of the meal he was cooking with his flatmates. Maybe if she were more like him he would demonstrate more feeling for her, but she knows that that is one role she would never be able to play – it has never been in her nature to be aloof or issue the ultimatum and have the *sang-froid* to carry it through. In arguments, she is not the one to storm out and stay away, she has never been very good at sulking, unless it's sulking at more successful peers from drama school, which is a different thing altogether.

'So you'll come. You want to stay involved?' Evan asks her.

She hesitates, remembering Chrome Rory and his little sister who drowned. Then she shakes her head.

'I don't think I can do this any more. I'll see the chavathon through, but then I'm done.'

He takes an envelope out of his pocket and hands it across to her. She feels it thick with banknotes.

'That's an advance. You can buy your mate a new headscarf with it.'

She looks at him.

'You're a real bastard.'

'Maybe. But I'm the only bastard who's offering you proper paid work.'

'I'll think about it.'

'All right. Let me see your room before I go.'

'What?'

'I'm curious. I wanna see what your room looks like.'

She shrugs and leads him to her bedroom, watches him as he inspects stuff – some photos of her family, the books on the shelf. He snorts derisively at a *Chomsky Reader* that Kerenza borrowed from Anna but couldn't be bothered to finish. 'What about East Timor?' he asks sarcastically, before pulling out a copy of *Cloud Atlas* that Mark gave her for her birthday.

'Now this is a great fucking book,' he says. 'Should have won the Booker Prize, but no surprises when they gave it to the posh gayboy instead.'

Kerenza rolls her eyes.

'I still haven't read it. A gayboy gave it to me, though.'

'That guy you were with in the bar?'

'Him.'

Evan nods dismissively, but Kerenza's not having this.

'He has the same look on his face whenever your name comes up.'

'You talk to him about me?'

Evan looks genuinely alarmed.

'God, yeah. He's got a brilliant plan to break into the Bank of England.'

Evan half-smiles and continues his odd snooping around her room, as if her possessions define who she is, give him some special access to both her personality and motivations that he has not previously had. He fingers her perfumes and make-ups, inspects a bottle of Marc Jacobs scent that she bought with her last 'advance' on a joyful trip to Selfridges which also included an iPod Nano, some Earl jeans, Myla underwear and Bliss vanilla and bergamot body scrub. She has also paid £1,000 from her credit cards and felt confident enough to set up a standing order to Anna for the rent.

'These are what I love about girls,' Evan says as he sprays a little perfume on his wrist. 'All this kind of *stuff*.'

'What do you want, Evan?'

He turns to face her.

'You weren't made to be poor.'

'Nobody was.'

'I'm not bothered about the swinish multitude. You wanted to live gracefully . . .'

'On tainted money?'

'All money's tainted in some way. That's the first lesson in life. Don't go back to stupid auditions for parts that are beneath you. You should see the sponsorship pages for the chavathon – we're going to make a lot of money out of this. I'm thinking at least fifty grand of which fifteen is yours.'

'We're not a profit-sharing cooperative, then?'

'Course we are. Just not equally.'

Kerenza contemplates him miserably. Why don't you just stay, she thinks, stay and be kind. You've got this brilliantly deviant imagination, why don't you turn it to something real and interesting. We can work on it together, I can help you, we'll be a team, a little gang. She almost shudders as she imagines his ridicule were she to say anything so naive.

'I find this difficult,' she says.

'Why?' he asks. 'It's like taking candy from babies.'

'Not that.'

'Then what?'

'This is hurting me,' she says, and he furrows his brow in incomprehension, even though she's sure that he knows what she means.

But at this moment his mobile rings.

'Hetty,' he says and clicks it to silent. Then he adds, 'She's got an eating disorder. Bulimia or something.'

'Snackhead Hetty.'

Evan laughs appreciatively. 'Snackhead,' he repeats. 'That's very good.'

'Answer it if you want.'

'I'll talk to her later.'

She stares angrily at him.

'You go and take candy from your baby,' she says, 'before she gorges and regurgitates it. I'm done with all of this.'

He smiles at her. There is both sympathy and mockery in his smile.

'Sleep on it, thick'ead,' he says, turns and leaves.

That night, as Kerenza lies in bed unable to sleep, the door softly opens, and Anna comes in. She tells Kerenza that she's scared and can't sleep, so Kerenza pats the bed, and Anna comes and lies down beside her. They talk and laugh softly in the low light, and Anna asks Kerenza if she likes Evan, and Kerenza says yes, and Anna says he's sexy but trouble, and Kerenza says she knows that already.

'He's awfully silly,' Anna says.

'I quite like his silliness,' Kerenza answers. 'I prefer silly to boring.'

'What's really going on with him?' Anna asks. 'You're not making training videos together.'

'I don't know what you mean,' Kerenza says.

'You can talk to me about it,' Anna says. 'You don't need to do anything that you don't want to.'

But this only confuses Kerenza even more, because she

doesn't know what she wants, except of course that she wants Evan's presence, nothing else seems to quite measure up any longer.

Anna is looking at her expectantly, but Kerenza says nothing, and Anna's eyes suddenly flutter and close, exhausted by the day and the news of metastasis and all the anxious speculations chasing around her head.

Smut creeps into the room and lies in the warm space between them, and gradually Kerenza sinks into sleep, dreaming that she is on a plane which is taxiing down a never-ending runway in a faraway land, but the runway is winding and hemmed in by hedges as if their 747 is traversing country lanes. Kerenza thinks that soon they will come to a normal, straight tarmac runway and the engines will roar into life, but they don't. Eventually, she jerks awake and looks around confused for Anna, but her friend has gone.

A man she wants to sleep with who thinks that ethical choices come down to what makes your life more comfortable.

A woman, her best friend, who still has faith in international law and human rights, even though half the world is in flames and she is dying.

Swept from a rock, entering the wrong carriage, jerked out of flight by the tug of the leash.

Bluebells

'Stop here,' Grace Holding says. 'It must be quite a struggle.'

Kerenza brings the wheelchair to a halt on the barky path and looks out at the constellations of bluebells all over the woods in Kew Gardens. She is a little out of breath from trying to navigate the wheelchair over the uneven path.

'Can you see them?' Grace asks.

'Bluebells everywhere,' Kerenza replies.

And it is amazing, like the glitter glimpsed from a plane landing at night in a foreign city – every tiny light a home.

The old woman fingers her shawl with her gnarled fingers. 'I think I can smell them,' she says. 'Or maybe I'm just imagining it.'

Kerenza sniffs the cool spring air, imagines the small roots of each flower clasping the earth like a baby's fingers.

'I think you can probably smell them,' she says.

She had picked Grace Holding up that morning and taken her in a taxi to the bluebell wood in Kew Gardens, where she used to walk with Arthur Holding. Now Kerenza checks nobody is looking and plucks one of the little blue flowers and hands it to Grace, who holds it in her hand on the tartan cover as Kerenza wheels her out of the wood to the tea-shop, where she parks Grace at a table and brings them a pot of tea and some cake. They talk a little about a warning of imminent terror attacks on London, and Grace says that while the tube bombings were terrible, the casualties were still the equivalent of maybe one bomb during the war. She tells Kerenza about the different bombs: the screamers, the breadbaskets of incendiaries that dropped fizzing and glowing magnesium-white, later versions booby-trapped to take the arms or legs from the firewatchers trying to extinguish them; the high-explosive bombs that could suck the air out of a man's lungs half a mile away; the landmines and torpedo bombs and the delayed-action bombs that might explode many hours later; the phut-phut of the doodlebugs; the silence of the V2s, which gave no warning until they turned buildings inside out. Grace tells her indignantly that the government fed fake information to the Germans so that some of the rockets would fall on civilian streets in South-east London rather than on the centre of government.

'Except you can kind of see their point,' Kerenza says mildly. 'You can't fight a war if the nerve-centre has been blown up. And at least that war was worth fighting.'

'It was terrible in the public shelters, though,' Grace says. 'Not all sing-songs and cockney spirit. Women got raped, people had their money stolen, fights over sleeping spaces, gangs and card-sharps trying to muscle in. And a terrible smell because there were no real sanitary facilities and they were so overcrowded. People were sleeping on the tracks, fighting to get spaces by the wall, but outside the shelters people were having nervous breakdowns because of the terrible noise, and there's only so long you can go without sleep, and it was kind of a torture the sound of those planes droning endlessly overhead. The Germans always had one engine out of kilter.'

'Why?'

'Something to do with not being picked up by our ground defences.'

She fumbles in her bag and takes out her purse. Kerenza watches her fingers as she opens it and takes out a ring with a blue stone. She tells Kerenza that it is the first gift she ever received, that Arthur had laughed, made her close her eyes and said he had a real bluebell for her.

'Is it your engagement ring?' Kerenza asks.

'No,' Grace says. 'I hardly ever wore it because it's so valuable. Preferred the simple wedding band he bought me.'

'Why don't you wear it now?' Kerenza asks.

'Because of my joints,' Grace says. 'I take it out and look at it sometimes.'

Kerenza admires the ring, and Grace says that it is a sapphire surrounded by tiny diamonds. The stone is large and Kerenza wonders how she might politely express surprise that a clerk from a bedding factory who had become a minor civil servant could afford such a magnificent stone. As if reading her thoughts, Grace tells her that the ring is valuable and that there is quite a story attached to it.

'In 1941 the spring raids were very bad. They hit everybody: the East End, the West End, young and old. There were stories of babies being sucked out of buildings by the blast and smashed on the pavements outside. I'd left the bedding company and was working as a receptionist in the hospital. Arthur was working in High Holborn and he was a volunteer firewatcher in the West End at nights, so we didn't get to see too much of each other. I was awfully lonely, our little girl, April, was only young.'

'I didn't know you had a daughter,' Kerenza interrupts, surprised.

'She's married with four children, lives in New Zealand. I get a Christmas card.'

The terse way that Grace pronounces the last sentence makes it clear that the mother–daughter relationship has not always been a harmonious one. Kerenza decides not to pursue the topic or ask why there are no photographs of April in the living room.

'I nearly sold the ring once so that she could go to college, but that never happened,' Grace says.

'Why?'

'She got married. To *Richard*.'

'Oh.'

Richard, clearly, was part of the problem.

'So what's the story of the ring?' Kerenza asks.

'Well, like I said, Arthur was a firewatcher in the West End, and it was a terrible night, one of the worst of the war. It was the day of the cup final, I remember – I think they called it the War Cup back then. Arsenal were playing Preston North End, it was a draw. Anyway, I went off to the hospital for a night-shift, and Arthur stayed in town. He walked from High Holborn to a club in Soho where he liked to have a few drinks with friends. Some of the boys in those clubs were quite wild, actually, but Arthur usually went early because he liked a game of cards as well, and there were plenty of places around at the time where you could do that – have an after-hours drink and play some cards, although they sometimes got raided by the police. But he had his chum Jim there, who was a whole heap of trouble but a good boy underneath it all and treated Arthur like a brother. Well, anyway, the raids started, down came the incendiary bombs in their thousands, and there were fires everywhere, it was as if the whole city was burning. The heavy rescue squads and the fire brigades were all out while the German bombers were still up there pouring bombs down on the city. That night, a high-explosive bomb fell on to the street where Arthur was based, and it brought down several buildings. Arthur was with the Heavy Rescue Squad, and they could hear cries coming from under the rubble of one of the buildings that had been partially destroyed and was about to collapse. The air was still thick with smoke and burning particles from some of the buildings that had been set alight, and there were fractured gas mains burning – oh, it was like hell that night. But they could hear these terrible cries and so they started to dig through the rubble. It was very dangerous because, like I say, the building the cries were coming from was on the point of collapse itself. But they started digging anyway and Arthur always had quite a slight build so he was the obvious choice to take a rope and crawl into the rubbish with one of the men from the Heavy Rescue Squad. It was filling up with water as well because another bomb nearby had burst a water main. In the end, it was likely that everybody in the building, including Arthur, might either be drowned or have the building collapse on top of them. But still they could hear this shouting and they couldn't have it on their consciences

115

that they had just left these people inside trapped in the building that was filling up with water from the burst water main. So Arthur volunteered to go in and they gave him some morphine to take to anybody who was injured down there and he managed to inch his way through the rubble using a stick to make his way. And above them still the German planes dropping their bombs on the city, it was a truly terrible night. But in the end, he managed to get into an air pocket and there was a woman in there, but she had already died of her injuries. Arthur thought that it had all been in vain and he was turning to go back when he heard a kind of whimpering. So he goes back and he discovers that the woman is cradling a baby – no more than a few months old this little mite – and the baby is alive. Very, very gently he takes the baby from under the dead woman and he tries to soothe it as best he can and he crawls back through the rubble. Just as he's about to get out, another bomb explodes quite close and the whole building comes down on him and the child.'

'What happened?' Kerenza has completely forgotten about her tea and cake as she listens to this rescue story.

'Arthur woke up in hospital. For a while he couldn't remember who he was or what had happened to him. Then bit by bit he remembered and he started asking about the child and they told him that the child had survived as well. The dead woman was called Catherine Sheldon, and it turned out that her husband was a very wealthy jewel merchant. The building had once been a jeweller's, you see. Mr Sheldon came to visit Arthur in hospital and, although he was mourning the death of his young wife, he was also grateful to him for saving his only child. So he offered him some money. Quite a lot for those days. Arthur refused, of course, and said that he didn't want the money because he was only doing his duty, but Sheldon gave him a ring instead as a gift. And later on, Arthur gave it to me here in the bluebell wood.'

Grace Holding fingers the bluebell that Kerenza plucked for her in the wood.

'You know what Churchill said afterwards? He said he was

glad it was London that took the blitz because London *could* take it. He said London was like a great animal that lay bleeding, wounded but still alive, still able to move. And although he could be a callous sod, Churchill, and a downright liar sometimes, he understood that, he knew a thing or two about this city even though, like I say, it wasn't all sing-songs, there were people who would wait to loot bombed-out houses, steal from the wounded. The blitz was a terrible, terrible thing, I don't think people really understand that now, it's become . . . falsified, just a word, there's no real meaning to it any longer . . . I'm trying to say . . .'

Grace Holding stops as if frustrated by her inarticulacy.

'They just don't understand the smell of it, how real it was for everybody, we were real people.'

She lifts the bluebell to her nose.

'Anyway, that's the story of the ring,' she says simply.

In the taxi on the way home, Grace tells her that she is going to go into a home.

'Surely you don't have to do that,' Kerenza says, alarmed.

'I don't *have* to,' Grace says. 'But I want to. There's a nice place in Brentford. A friend of mine's there. I think that when you're old you should be among people, not sitting staring into space in your living room. In fact I've always approved of communal living, I remember them talking about the Russian communists breaking up the family and making people go to eat in canteens and do washing together and I always thought it sounded like a really good idea.'

'I'll still be able to come and see you, though?' Kerenza says, anxiously. She has grown very used to her trips out to West London to sit with Grace and listen to her stories, especially as she now has the money to stop at the supermarket on the way home and buy bottles of wine and *Heat* magazine and baby onions marinated in balsamic vinegar without having to steal it from Grace.

'I release you from your debt,' Grace says. 'Think I've had a very good deal for my fifty pounds.'

'But I don't want to be released from my debt.' Kerenza is becoming distressed. 'I like coming to see you.'

'A young girl like you with an old lady like me,' Grace scoffs. 'You shouldn't have to. There'll be plenty of people for me to chat to in there.'

'But I hate that,' Kerenza wails. 'Everybody will be old some time. There are lots of young people who are far less interesting than you. All the people who are on programmes like *Big Brother* are young but they're disgusting and vulgar and horrible, I wouldn't sit next to them on the bus. Anyway, I always assume that people I like are kind of the same age as me – whether they're older or younger.'

Grace reaches out her hand and takes Kerenza's in her own.

'You're a lovely girl,' she says. 'And the best thing about you is you don't even know it.'

Kerenza genuinely does not think that 'lovely' is an adjective which can properly be applied to her given the source of her current income. For a moment, she once again has the impulse to blurt out her secret to Grace but she does not dare to do so.

'You'll make time for me,' she asks now, feeling ridiculously close to tears, 'in your old people's home? You know, when you're not having parties and flirting with elderly gentlemen.'

Grace laughs – a little peppery cackle that turns into a cough.

'I'll always have time for you, Kerenza.'

That night, Kerenza cannot rid her mind of the images from Grace Holding's story. She tries to imagine the London skies all heavy with bombers droning across the moon, wave after wave of them navigating by the curves and bends in the Thames, pale faces in cockpits – boys from Berlin and Dortmund and Hamburg and Munich. Other cities with coffee houses and dance halls and factories. It was only sixty-five years ago: nothing, no time at all. Had the baby sucked out of the house by the blitz had a chance to grow it would have been about the same age now as her own mother and father. It would only have been in its early thirties in the year that Kerenza was born. Or it might have died of TB at ten years old or it might have gone on to write poetry or join a bedding firm as a clerk or enlist to fight in subsequent wars and squeeze the trigger which sent another human being – oceans and continents away – to his death. In a second the bombs are released, the Junkers 88 jerks up, relieved by its lighter load, down below babies stir in their cots, watched by nervous mothers, they gurgle and blink like babies do.

She thinks of Grace Holding, who was young then, imagines her laughing and joking with the other girls at hospital reception, flirting with young servicemen. And London – the wounded beast of Churchill's great rhetoric – still shifting, moving, alive in spite of everything. It has lost something, she thinks, London, since that time, and suddenly she remembers Evan and his anger at those memories and experiences that it is still acceptable to ridicule or ignore. She thinks about the women raped in shelters and houses looted and firemen killed and men from the Heavy Rescue Squads crawling through rubble with sticks to save survivors and the droning and droning of death-filled monsters overhead and people walking to work around craters and people falling in and out of love and drinking in bars just like today and over it all a kind of terrible, moving, defiant spirit to the city. And perhaps in another era even Chrome Rory would not have been a chang-snorting advertising executive, an easy mark for a con, but would have been a young journal-keeping RAF man, would have piloted a night-fighter to defend his city, dying tragically young but having achieved the purpose in his short life that he now longs for.

To the German bombers, every fire they started – in the British Museum, the Houses of Parliament, Waterloo Station, every warehouse, corner house, music hall, blocks of flats, pie-and-mash shop and barber's salon – must have seemed tiny and far removed from the suffering caused, the breadbaskets of incendiaries scattered like bluebells on the forest floor, thousands of them blinking back up at the German pilots as they gripped their controls and their gun handles in tight, fear-strained hands, young men thinking of the return journey across the Channel to a chateau in France and some food and sleep and a game of cards after the dangerous mission. The stars in the sky from the cockpit, the incendiary bombs fizzing, tiny spring bluebells – the only constant being the human eye that views these different lights, the blinking jelly gazing through its uncertain window of time to try and make some sense of it, bring order and meaning to it all.

Chavathon

'Christ, Ella.' Rory looks gratefully at Kerenza, who is dutifully massaging his thigh. 'I need a drink.'

'Chunk says we should go to that bar in the Aldwych and have champagne.' She smiles admiringly at him.

'I didn't wear my Burberry cap all the way round,' he says. 'It was too warm. You think that's cheating?'

'I think the kids who are going to benefit from the Taylor Bright Foundation will forgive you.'

Jamie flops down next to them, rubbing his ankles. 'Bloody brilliant,' he says as high-fives are exchanged, and for a moment they are basking in their accomplishment of running twenty-six miles – albeit dressed up as chavs – and they look young, happy and healthy, and even their outfits are more endearing than irritating.

'Here come Chunk and Hetty,' Jamie says. 'Chunk, you lightweight, you could still have given it a go.'

Evan is walking on a crutch with Hetty the Snackhead carefully supporting the other arm.

'Don't be so horrible,' Hetty defends her wounded knight. 'Poor Chunk was distraught at not being able to do it.'

'I agree with Jamie,' Kerenza says. 'Chunk could have joined the deep-sea diver and finished next month or something. He doesn't look nearly distraught enough to me.'

Evan glares at her.

'To train so hard and then sprain my ankle just before the event . . .'

'Devastating,' Kerenza says but still with a trace of mockery in her voice, because she feels both irritable and reckless. Nevertheless, her tone is noticeably sharp, and they glance at her, slightly puzzled.

'To be fair,' Rory says, 'Chunk was out training with me right from the early days, so he must be quite pissed off.'

'Always next year, eh, Chunk?' Kerenza says and returns to massaging Rory's thighs. And when Rory asks her what she is doing later on that night, she grins at him and says, 'Spending the night with you, of course,' but Evan doesn't even look at her. Jamie and Hetty start bantering with Rory about a trip they have taken on the Silverlink (hilariously renamed 'Tinkerlink') train service from Dalston (drugs) to visit a friend (Richmond). This allows Evan to slide alongside Kerenza.

'Can I just have a quick word about the publicity?'

She slaps Rory's thighs affectionately and moves away from him.

'What the fuck's the matter with you?' he asks.

'Keep your voice down.'

'Never mind that. Watch the sarky tone, people are noticing.'

'Oh, fuck off, you cunt.' Sometimes, Kerenza thinks sourly, this is the most satisfying combination of words in the English language.

'What is it with you?'

'Nothing. Go and buy your girlfriend a family-sized bar of fruit and nut.'

'She's not my girlfriend, she's somebody we need to keep on board. Her dad's just donated £10,000 to the Taylor Bright Foundation, and at least I haven't *fucked* her, unlike you with that weak-chinned idiot.'

Kerenza is still so full of rage towards him that she wants to ask whether the lack of sex was through choice or necessity and whether Hetty felt very let-down afterwards but she doesn't dare because Evan's temper currently seems to be on as short a fuse as hers. Perhaps it is the warm weather, perhaps it is the tension, perhaps it is the sight of people so at ease with their own bodies after exercise while she feels hot and uncomfortable after eating some street-food tortilla ridiculously over-laden with cumin that she can still irritatingly taste, and Evan is hobbling about pretending to have an ankle injury. Although she doesn't feel at all sorry for him about this and thinks if he really wanted to get in part he should have run the marathon with Rory. She suspects that his real reason for not doing so is that he would have had to run the marathon dressed as a chav – something she cannot imagine him ever doing, however large the pot of gold that lay at the end of it.

They stroll up from the river towards the Aldwych, where Jamie says he will stand them all champagne at Number One rather than some pikey pub, Hetty says just one then because she's going to meet her friend Tabitha, who's thinking of starting a chinchilla farm in Cumbria, and Rory asks Kerenza if she fancies eating at J-Sheeky afterwards. As they approach the Aldwych they spot more marathon runners with similar ideas but also men in black tie and women in evening dresses.

'It's the BAFTAs tonight in the theatre next door,' Hetty explains. Kerenza feels a little ache in her stomach. She has never been to the ceremony, although Mark did once when he was still acting in a well-reviewed, gritty legal drama that didn't get any viewers or a recommission but won an award in what was described as a 'calculated snub for ratings-driven drama'.

The bar in the Aldwych is filled with a strange mixture of award nominees waiting for the ceremony and marathon runners drinking cocktails and champagne. Kerenza spots Andrew Marr talking animatedly in a corner with Gillian McKeith and wonders whether they are discussing the benefits of colonic irrigation. Rory orders champagne for them all, and Kerenza heads for the toilets to do her make-up. She is standing at the mirror adjusting her mascara next to a very beautiful girl doing the same thing, wearing an astonishing evening dress which seems to just float around her lithe body. The girl glances a couple of times in Kerenza's mirror and then says, 'Kerenza? Kerenza Pen . . . ?'

'Penhaligon.' Kerenza looks in her neighbour's mirror and

sees through a perfectly styled mane of soft curls the smile of Olivia Scott, a face and body made for the red carpet, the popping of flash bulbs, the graceful acceptance speech.

'Olivia!'

'Oh my God,' Olivia says. 'What are you doing here? Are you up for something?'

'Up to something?'

'An award.'

'Oh.' Kerenza laughs, looks down at her jeans and Converse. *Does it fucking look like it?* 'No, I'm with some people who just ran the marathon.'

'Oh yes, spotted a few of those in here.'

'Are *you* up for something?' Kerenza asks.

'Best actress.' Olivia puts her make-up away in a little Miu Miu bag and smiles at herself. 'For *Portrait of Lady*. Don't stand a chance, though.'

With your wholly undeserved good fortune? Don't count on it.

'I heard fantastic things about that.' Kerenza smiles insincerely.

Wouldn't have caught me watching it, though.

There is nobody in the toilet.

INT. ALDWYCH BAR – DAY

DI HAMBLETON and his attractive colleague DC McGUIRE step through a police cordon. Shocked people in evening dress and marathon runners are milling around, several of them with their hands to their mouths.

HAMBLETON
What do we know about the victim?

MCGUIRE
Olivia Scott?
(shakes her head)
Second-rate actress who appears to have gone a long way on the back of connections, nice tits and lucky breaks.

124

HAMBLETON

Any witnesses?

MCGUIRE

No, they were all swilling champagne and networking at the bar
when it happened. Some guy on crutches claims to have seen a
girl running out.

HAMBLETON

What did the girl look like?

MCGUIRE

Just like me, apparently. But I have a bad feeling about this
witness.

HAMBLETON

Bad feeling?

MCGUIRE

Remember that song – there's a guy works down the chip shop
swears he's Elvis?

(Hambleton laughs appreciatively at his colleague's trademark
wit.)

HAMBLETON

He's a liar and I'm not sure about you?

MCGUIRE

Exactly. An untrustworthy, disloyal, scheming, cheating,
opinionated, bigoted, impotent, Welsh motherfucker who was
too lazy even to run the marathon.
(beat)
Guv.

HAMBLETON

You seem to have strong feelings for this witness. Make sure they
don't interfere with the investigation.

(They push through the bar area and go into –)

125

where they both recoil at the sight that greets them. A girl in a red
Stella McCartney evening dress is hanging from the toilet cubicle
with a copy of a programme for the BAFTAs stuffed in her mouth.
Her face is blue, staring, lifeless.)

HAMBLETON

What kind of sick mind would do this?

MCGUIRE

The clue's in the awards programme, Guv. I'm guessing we're
looking for somebody infinitely more talented than Olivia nursing
a burning sense of injustice.

(Hambleton looks at his colleague admiringly. Once again her
dazzling detective skills almost put his to shame.)

HAMBLETON

Let's find that red-haired beauty seen running from the building.

'Kerenza?'

'What, sorry?'

'I said what are you up to now?'

'Oh, erm, well, you know . . . between work.'

Olivia smiles. Her smile says: of course I *don't* know, but that
gives me the inner calm to sympathise with those less fortunate
than myself.

'Well,' Kerenza cocks her head at her nemesis, 'good luck
tonight.'

'Thank you.'

But suddenly from behind her she hears the cry of 'Lovely
Livvy!' and Hetty glides into the toilets. For an instant Kerenza
can't think of what to do, racks her brain for possible explana-
tions as to her split identity, then realises that Hetty is paying
her no attention and so she takes advantage of the air-kissing
and astonishment at their meeting to retreat into a cubicle and
lock the door before Hetty can see or engage with her.

Hetty and Olivia start to exchange small-talk about fashion labels as Kerenza huddles into a protective ball on the toilet seat, scratching miserably with her fingernail at the tiny track marks of cocaine almost worn into the cistern. Olivia tells Hetty modestly that she does not expect to win anything tonight, and that the award must surely and deservedly go to a previously unknown actress for her harrowing depiction of a pregnant teenager from rural Ireland who has been raped by her cousin.

Yeah, sure, Kerenza thinks, scratching even harder at the cistern and contemplating licking the tiny grain of coke she has extracted. But then she freezes as Olivia starts to tell Hetty about the amazing coincidence of meeting an old acquaintance from drama school.

Olivia says. 'I always envied her her name.'

'Her name?'

'Kerenza Penhaligon. It was the sort of name you expect to become successful.'

'Didn't she?'

'Not really,' Olivia says. 'Bits and pieces here and there. She was a good actress, though, and everybody at college liked her. Always meeting people after classes, always *doing* stuff, fizzing about all over the place. She seemed to have the whole world at her feet. Funny how things work out, it's all such bollocks really. Anyway, lovely, shall we have a quick drink before I have to go to this ceremony?'

'Have to be another time, sweetheart. I'm off to see my friend Tabby. You're on the same mobile, right?'

Kerenza hears the toilet door swing shut behind them. She sits dumb with surprise and sorrow. Her comfort-enemy, the distillation of injustice – she is actually quite inoffensive, insecure, nice even. Is this not the cruellest cut of all? Bits and pieces here and there – no arguing with that one.

Outside the toilet, she finds Evan leaning on his crutch, doing calculations on his Palm organiser. He seems in a far better mood and grins happily at her.

'Ten to fifteen K from online sponsorship, fifty from daddy-donations, couple of grand from the party. We'll clear seventy K at the end of all this.'

'Has Hetty gone?'

'Yeah, her and Tabitha are going to guzzle knickerbocker glories sprinkled with ketamine.'

A joke about eating disorders among posh druggies is clearly his idea of a peace-offering, and Kerenza explains about the conversation in the toilets between Olivia and Hetty.

'But did they say anything that might make Hetty realise that you were Kerenza?'

Kerenza shakes her head.

'Then we're fine,' Evan says and studies Olivia across the room; she is laughing delicately at something a portly producer is saying.

'She's up for an award?'

'Yeah.'

'Isn't she the one you really hated . . .'

'Yes but . . .'

They're interrupted by Rory and Jamie and another large and rudely healthy man, who turns out to be Hugo the Mad Lieutenant – the lecherous, chain-smoking, tank-driving scourge of Iraqi insurgents – whose large and forceful presence prompts Evan to smile politely and glide away to make some calls. After the basic hellos have been exchanged, the Mad Lieutenant leans in confidentially to Kerenza and suggests a quick trip to the cubicles for a line and 'then we'll take it from there and see what happens'.

'Sounds good but . . .' Kerenza glances apologetically at Rory.

'I am the biggest cunt in the world,' Hugo pronounces cheerfully, grabbing Rory and pummelling his head. 'Sharking the delicious floozy of one of my oldest buddies. Although you'll forgive me if I ask the obvious questions about matching collar and cuffs.'

'I probably won't,' Kerenza says.

Hugo grabs more champagne and starts to regale them with

tales about various war-zones, tales which Kerenza finds oddly compelling until she looks across the room and notices that Evan is talking to Olivia Scott and that she is laughing at something he has just said. She tries to concentrate on Hugo's stories of psy-ops, his promise to get inside all their heads and some lovely's knickers by the end of the evening, but all the time she can just see Evan out of the corner of her eye. And he and Olivia Scott are laughing heartily as if they've known each other for years until, finally, Evan departs with a cheery little wave.

'Excuse me a moment.' Kerenza follows Evan out towards the entrance, where he is making a mobile call to Geraint the web-designer in Bridgend.

'What do you think you're doing?' she asks him.

He grins at her.

'Getting you a little retribution.'

'What do you mean?'

'If Olivia wins an award tonight she won't be in much of a position to make her acceptance speech.'

Kerenza feels dread tightening her veins, her chest is heavy.

'Why, what have you done?'

'I spiked her drink.'

Kerenza stares at him in horror. 'That's not . . . you can't do that.'

'Why not? It'll be funny watching on TV if she wins.'

'Because that's . . . it's just a stupid, spiteful thing to do.'

'I hate these people congratulating themselves like this, giving themselves awards.'

Kerenza turns and hurries back into the bar area, where Olivia is still sitting on a settee, trilling away to a producer. Her untouched champagne flute is on the table beside her. Kerenza breathes a sigh of relief and strides through the bar with the intention of knocking it off the table. But as she gets near, Olivia stretches out a long, bare, pale arm and lifts her champagne glass to her lips. Kerenza stops, considers and realises there is only one thing she can do.

'Look out! Oh!'

The person next to Olivia cries out and jumps back as the champagne glass goes flying and spills all over her Stella McCartney awards-ceremony dress.

'What the . . . Kerenza? Jesus, my dress, what the hell do you think you're doing?' Olivia is wiping herself furiously with a napkin proffered by the person next to her and angrily spurning those offered by about five other young males. A large wine stain is spreading from breast to stomach.

'Oh my God!' Kerenza clasps her hand to her mouth. 'I'm so sorry, I just lost my footing.'

'Lost your footing?' The producer who was talking to Olivia stares at her incredulously. 'You just charged into her. That was deliberate.'

'No it wasn't.'

'I saw you. It was deliberate.'

Olivia stares balefully at Kerenza. 'Why did you do that? I've never done anything to you.'

And it is true. Kerenza stares at the pretty, pale-faced actor who was once envious of her but is now regularly on the cover of most celebrity magazines. Olivia Scott is not a very good actor but she has never done anything to her, she is not responsible for any of the problems in Kerenza's life.

'I didn't. I . . .'

A waiter comes over with a cloth, the producer angrily demands that Kerenza is removed from the bar, but unfortunately this only brings Hugo the Mad Lieutenant into the fray, and a general exchange of threats and counter-threats.

'One touch!' Hugo is drunkenly bellowing. 'I only have to touch you once and you'll be paralysed for life, you cunt.'

And while all of this is going on, and people are assuring Olivia that the damage to her dress is not serious and will dry out before the awards ceremony, and several waiters are trying to restrain Hugo from paralysing a film producer or, worse, getting inside his head, Kerenza glances across the bar and sees that Evan is watching the whole debacle, and an infuriating smile is playing across his lips. She strides furiously across.

'Proud of yourself?' she asks.

He takes out a napkin folded in half and shows it to her. It reads 'I have no talent.' Then he unfolds the other half, which has a signature that he has obviously just tricked Olivia into giving him.

'Now I admit that's a childish joke,' he says. 'But I thought it would make you laugh.'

'You didn't . . .'

'Spike her drink? You really think I carry Rohypnol around with me? I don't mind a bit of bodice-ripping in films but I've never wanted to rape anybody.'

'Assuming you were able to,' Kerenza snaps, but he just shakes his head, puzzled at this, and she doesn't know of course what Evan does or does not carry around with him. She has no idea where he draws the line, what he would stop at, whom he might not consider fair game.

'Why did you tell me . . .'

He raises a bushy eyebrow.

'I wanted to see your reaction.'

He was playing with her, testing her, watching to see how she responded to his vicious trick. The whole episode, the humiliation, has been artificially manufactured simply because he wanted to see the impact it would have on her.

'I have to get out of here,' she says dully.

'We're done here anyway,' he says. 'Mission accomplished. If you can get away from that freakshow in there we could go for a drink.'

Kerenza shakes her head.

'I want to go and see Anna,' she says.

'I'll come with you.'

'No.'

'All right.' He shrugs, looking at her curiously because there are angry tears in her eyes.

And Kerenza fights her urge to give in and go for a drink with him as she makes her way out of the bar, pushing past tired marathon runners and award ceremony nominees. Outside it has become a no-weather kind of day, cloud has rolled in and is hanging grey over London, holding the city down. She stands in the street uncertain of what to do now, watches disconsolately as Olivia Scott and her party emerge from the bar to make the short walk to the awards ceremony, Olivia still inspecting the damage to her dress. The pay-as-you-go mobile in her bag bleep-bleeps an incoming text message. Evan gave the mobile to her when she agreed to work with him on this project, and still her heart surges a little as she thinks that it might be him calling her back and maybe she should go, they could go to some pub nobody knows about, with old geezers sitting in the corner and a bored landlord and they could choose Blondie records on the jukebox and call each other thick'ead and drink beer and go home and spend the night together. The message is, however, from Rory, saying that Hugo is insisting on coming with them to the restaurant, would that be so wrong? He's got more chang than Colombia and they can get rid of him later. She can no longer be bothered with these foolish people and their drug incontinence and so she texts back: *Sorry. Feeling ill. Gone home.*

Then she turns her mobile off.

Broadwings

Two mobile phones spin down through the dark air, two faces crane over the side of the bridge, but it's too dark to see or hear them splash into the river below. Kerenza and Evan turn back to the car with its hazard lights flashing and drive from England into Wales as Evan puts 'You Stole the Sun from My Heart' on the iPod in tribute to all thick'eads everywhere. And in spite of the ironic way in which it is done, Kerenza looks out at the estuary, the sinister mud of the flats, and shivers at the idea of the dark currents taking possession of a warm body, sweeping it out beyond the city lights, towards the dark ocean beyond.

Ella and Chunk are no more.

Once again she has driven across London with Evan, out on to the M4 towards Wales. She could tell herself all she liked that she wasn't going to do it, that she was still furious with him for the incident with Olivia Scott, but it was too irresistible. Quite apart from the fact that she has grown very used to not worrying about money. It is some time since she has had to chew her fingernails in the supermarket queue as she hands her card over to the check-out girl.

Anna had been going to stay with her grandmother for a few days in Suffolk but had looked suspiciously at Kerenza when she had said she was also going away.

'With that guy?' she had asked.

'No,' Kerenza had lied unconvincingly, and Anna had shaken her head scornfully.

'What are you doing with him?' she had asked. 'Where are

you getting all this money from all of a sudden? I want you to tell me.'

'It's nothing,' Kerenza had said. 'You don't need to worry about it, please don't worry about me.'

'Of course I worry about you,' Anna replied impatiently. 'You're my best friend. But you don't have to tell me anything you don't want to.'

'I can't,' Kerenza said helplessly. 'But it's nothing to worry about. It's kind of acting . . .'

'Oh Christ, Kerenza . . .'

'It's *not* porn, it's just . . .'

Anna had waited but seen that she was not going to get any more out of her friend so she had turned impatiently away.

'Tell him that if he gets you into trouble I'll kill him,' she promised.

Evan was totally unapologetic about the incident in the bar, professing himself perplexed and disappointed by Kerenza's reaction to his prank with Olivia Scott and claiming that, had he possessed the means to do so, he would certainly have thought hard about spiking her drink. Kerenza had woken the next morning to discover depressingly that Olivia had won the Best Actress award and that there were photos of her clutching it in the bright red (stain-free) dress that earned her another big tick in *Heat* magazine. And Kerenza had tried to reawaken her animosity but only managed a tiny flicker.

They drive through Bridgend, stopping to buy bread, cheese and Sicilian wine in Tesco's, and then on into the valley until she sees the lights of Pant-y-brastrap twinkling on the side of the hill and the pub by the stream with the Welsh red dragon sticking its forked tongue out on the flag above it. She has none of the trepidation from the last time – oddly she thinks that she could just retreat here indefinitely and go for walks in the valley and read books and watch the rain slating down over the pines and be quite content. Evan laughs when she says this and tells her it's rubbish and that she would go mad like all the residents whose permanence is not a matter of choice.

'Why?' she asks, slightly cross that her idyll of retreat has been dismissed so lightly.

'You'd miss your friends,' he says. 'That drama queen you give so much time to and your sick housemate and the old girl you're always going on about.'

'You don't have to make them sound like such losers,' she retorts. 'If you weren't so judgmental all the time maybe you'd have some friends.'

'Why would I want that?' he asks. 'I don't need friends . . .' He glances at her maliciously. 'I don't need anybody.'

She picks up the iPod and scrolls through the artists. Evan hasn't changed any of them from the last time they drove up. She finds 'Fisherman' by The Congos and says, 'Well, I've got friends. Millions of dem.'

'Hello, sweetheart.' Uncle Tommy grins at Kerenza as they drop their bags in the hallway of the little house. 'I was wrong about you, you must be stupid coming back here.'

'She's a thick'ead,' Evan says.

'I like it here,' Kerenza says.

'Why's that, then?'

Why is it? Because of the misty valley and the rain-heavy pines dropping wet needles onto the blackened valley slope that the locals call 'the mountain' even though there isn't anything resembling a mountain in sight, and the way she feels more aware of herself and her surroundings as if a kind of loosening has taken place inside her, as if she can suddenly see herself and her small bag of possessions, and they are all that matters – the change of clothes and her make-up and book to read. And because she drives in a car alone with Evan through the darkening night to get here, through British towns and cities that you can almost lose sight of in London, the crossing of the Severn cutting them off from it all, and past Cardiff and Bridgend to this place that now seems familiar, almost a sanctuary, a retreat almost, where she can just sit and take stock and stare at slatey skies. And if she gave up Evan she wouldn't have this, she would have early-morning awakening, her stomach churning to thoughts of direct debits and phones not ringing and familiar days of nervy emptiness.

'Good just to get away from everything,' she says, and Tommy shrugs and says that if she wants he'll take her out with him to see the hawks tomorrow morning.

'Watch your arse,' Evan says.

'Watch your mouth,' Tommy snaps back at him. He has trained a new bird called Spitfire, and Kerenza might want to watch.

'Sure.' Kerenza smiles. 'I'd like that.'

'I'll pick you up around ten,' he says. 'Going down the club for a pint now.'

Evan watches as he descends from the cottage into the street, where his car is parked.

'You really want to go?' he says.

'Why not?' Kerenza replies. 'I've never seen anybody doing falconry before.'

He stares at her, and there is both curiosity and irritation and something else – almost patronising affection – in his stare.

'Tommy's a weirdo. Most people would have made an excuse.'

'I didn't want to,' Kerenza says.

'Fine. Go and watch his stupid bird display, then.'

And he turns his back on her.

'OK,' Evan says as they sit in the living room eating their baguette, cheese and wine – a meal which Kerenza ranks almost as highly as fried courgettes – 'these are the projects I've been giving some thought to.'

'Fire away.'

She pulls her legs up and tucks them comfortably under her on the seat as she sips the crisp white Sicilian wine and watches the spluttering flames from the fire he's built.

'OK, project one is called "The Baby Charlatans". There's a massive market in people writing books and running courses with their revolutionary ideas on how to train babies. Feeding, sleeping, all that stuff – turning previously accepted wisdom on its head. The good thing is you need virtually no qualifications and you don't have to worry about being contradictory or completely out of touch with reality. Put it on a routine, don't put it on a routine; feed on demand, starve them; take them to bed with you, make them sleep on an ironing board. You can say anything and claim it's a new science. We set up courses, charge the earth, fuck about with people's heads, pocket the money of the gullible.'

'And the desperate. Besides, it would take a long time to get established.'

'Yes, good call and my thought exactly. Long lead times, labour intensive and that market's pretty well saturated with con-artists as it is.'

'Project two?'

'Religion.'

'Didn't Christianity have a pretty long lead time?'

'A pseudo-religion, self-help type thing. You know, the best parts of Kabbalism with some New Age spiritualism and Deepak Chopra thrown in. Healing Stones, Seven Steps to Wisdom, run three times widdershins round a dock leaf, you do the Hokey Cokey and shake it all about. The problem with *that* is we'd have to round up the marks, no self-contained group like the advertising types and their posh druggy mates for the chavathon. That's also time-consuming. I want a quick, hard hit on the next one. Maybe not so lucrative but also not such hard work.'

'So we park religion for the time being.'

'I think so, although it's postponed not cancelled. I'm giving some thought to raising money for World Jihad as well. But that has obvious risks – we don't want MI5 breathing down our necks.'

'Plus, would anybody take a Welsh Muslim seriously?'

'Perhaps a little more than a ginger Muslim.'

'I could wear a veil. We could be the Islamic Caliphate of Pant-y-brastrap.'

She draws the seat covering across her face, and he laughs.

'Project three?'

'Now, project three I'm excited about. Originally, I had this idea called IT for Refugees. Essentially, that involved applying for money for a community centre and computer equipment to train Kosovans how to use the internet.'

'I'm not ripping off refugees.'

'Well, I thought you might say that, although it wouldn't be ripping *them* off as such. And remember, there's no such thing as a victim-free con. But anyway, there were problems with the fact that we'd need to be registered as a charity or cuckoo our way into an existing one. Boring bureaucracy. But that idea fed into another one.'

'Which is?'

He smiles at her and stands up.

'My favourite. You heard of the BFDF?'

She shakes her head.

'The British Film Diversity Fund. Classic New Labourish make-art-accessible bollocks, whose purpose is to foster diversity and encourage film-making from the oppressed margins, which really means act as a trough for all kinds of nepotism, rent-seeking and special favours. It's run by a woman called Maggie Thompson, who I've already met.'

'What's she like?'

'Skinny. Lives in Stoke Newington. Thinks George Bush is stupid and bad. Eats the lefty platter in gastropubs, has yoga arms and doesn't look as if she's ever menstruated.'

Kerenza laughs.

'The lefty platter?'

'Yeah, over a feast of rocket with pine nuts we discussed film-making from the margins.'

Kerenza puts her hand over her mouth, spluttering with laughter.

'*You.*'

'It was tough. That's why I want some back-up. I've already paved the way – you're Lizzie Connolly, which I thought was a really good name for a Trot documentary maker.'

'I hate the name Lizzie.'

'Too late now. I just need a CV for you.'

Kerenza considers, remembering a Mexican film-making friend of Anna called Enrique, who has made a number of unshown documentaries about oppressed indigenous groups in Central America.

'OK, I've travelled largely in Latin America, where I've made a moving film about Bolivian coca farmers and justice systems in indigenous Guatemalan villages.'

'What if she wants to see it?'

'I can get my hands on something.'

'Excellent.'

'But what are we pitching to her?'

Evan's mobile bleep-bleeps a text message. He pauses to read it, smiles a little smugly and then turns back to Kerenza.

'*Asylum Songs*. A moving and elegiac film which involves empowering asylum seekers who have come to this country. It's *their* film, we're just facilitators. Our plan is to arm, let's say, about twenty of the fuckers with digi-cams and send them back to retrace their steps of how they arrived in this country, what their individual odysseys were, the obstacles they overcame. Not a dry eye in the house as they end up back in their hopefully war-scarred but definitely godforsaken villages, and finally we all understand that they're not scroungers but pioneers, blazing a trail and helping the economy more than hurting it, doing the jobs we're not prepared to do and enriching our culture, blah blah blah.'

'Won't we need an asylum seeker or two?'

'You know loads.'

Kerenza considers Ivo. It's a tricky one. He has an anarchic and deviant sense of humour and might do it just because it's a funny idea. Besides, she might also be able to pitch it to him as a clever revenge for all the stereotyped depictions of asylum seekers as helpless victims on film and TV. But deep down she knows that he might also consider it immoral and – even worse – tell Anna.

'I'll sort something out,' Kerenza says.

'Great.' Evan looks pleased with her. 'Then we're in business again.'

He gets up and takes the plates out to the kitchen, leaving his mobile on the table in front of them. She stares at it for a moment and then it bleep-bleeps another text message. She picks it up, almost unable to resist the temptation, and then presses *Show Message.*

Hi handsome. Tue at 1 in venue with Toby. Caro xxx PS Unforgettable night!

She stares at it with such miserable intensity that she doesn't notice Evan coming back into the room. One good thing about Evan is that you don't have to feel guilty about anything, so she simply hands him the phone.

'You've got a text message.'

He raises an eyebrow, reads it and clicks it shut, pours some more wine.

'Who's Caro kiss kiss kiss?'

'You don't want to know about Toby?'

She tuts and looks out of the window, biting her lip.

'It's to do with another project.'

'What other project?'

'A more long-term idea.'

'And Caro works for you?'

'Not in the way that you do. She couldn't act to save her life.'

'Then how?'

He sighs.

'She runs an illegal private drinking club in Shoreditch. So she knows a lot of people and possible investors for a project I have in mind.'

'What kind of project?'

'A multi-media, digital art gallery with DJs and performance poets.'

'Which will never happen, right?'

'Just an empty space in the fashionable heart of East London. There's a pleasing symbolism about that, don't you think?'

Kerenza chews her lip.

'Who's Toby?'

'The name should give you a clue. Made shitloads of money by setting up and then selling some internet company and likes to think of himself as a bit wild. So we took him out the other night.'

'You, Caro and Internet Toby. Must have been a laugh.'

'Yes, it was. Caro knows absolutely everybody worth knowing in Shoreditch and Hoxton.'

'How *does* she fit her address book in her handbag?'

Evan grins at her.

'You may mock, but Internet Toby was pretty enamoured of her.'

'Why, because she's totally gorgeous?'

'You don't lure in somebody like Toby Turner by doing coke off the tits of just any old girl.'

'That's what you were doing on your unforgettable night?'

He smiles cruelly at her, enjoying this passive bullying as he always does, safe in the knowledge that he owes her nothing, that she has no claim on him, that she will never dare admit why she craves the detail that wounds her so much.

'Cocaine is for losers, you know that.'

'So all the pieces were in place for you, then.'

'Very good,' he says in the same placid tone that he must know infuriates her. Kerenza imagines Caro – hard-face-good-figure, fashion, cigarette-drawl, been round the block enough times to have very few sexual hang-ups. She looks at the crescents in her palm made by her nails. Then, as if deciding to give her a gift, Evan says, 'She's never been here, though.'

Kerenza looks up, and Evan laughs.

'Can't really see her even having the appropriate footwear for an afternoon watching the hawks with Tommy.'

And he gets up and leaves Kerenza wondering if she has received a compliment or an insult.

That night, Kerenza lies in bed in the room next to Evan's. The kind of plan they have elaborated is the type you might discuss drunkenly as being a funny idea, a wild plan to be cleaned away with the wine glasses the next day. But Evan has already met Maggie Thompson, and she has no doubt that he will put the scam against the Diversity Fund into action. Just as he will befriend Internet Toby to rip him off with a digital art gallery/drinking club in Shoreditch.

Still, she has been a beneficiary; her own bank account is several thousand pounds in credit as a result of the chavathon and she wonders vaguely about Chrome Rory and Hetty the Snackhead and Hugo the Mad Lieutenant and what they will say about it all when they discover – if they haven't already – the extent to which they have been duped, that there is no little Taylor Bright with his chronic heart condition. She suspects that Rory will be the most angry and upset: perhaps he is lying in his flat unable to sleep, just like her, perhaps sipping water and staring from his window, as inconsequential as a single pine needle dropping onto the side of the mountain. She remembers the touch of him, just as he might be remembering the feel of her hips under his hands. And perhaps he will marvel at her callousness – *how could she, how could she*. Perhaps right now he is phoning and phoning the number of a cheap mobile which lies somewhere in the mud at the bottom of the River Severn.

That night she has depressingly obvious dreams of Evan and Caro on a sofa in a Shoreditch flat while she watches them and Evan smiles at her and reassures her that it is all part of the plan.

A craze of wings, the hawk rears up, beating at the air, and, yelping, Kerenza leaps back in terror. Uncle Tommy laughs.

'She's just bating. It's 'cos she doesn't know you, see.'

The bird settles again on his gloved fist, glaring furiously at Kerenza as if pecking her eyes out is project one.

'What is she?' Kerenza asks nervously. 'She's very handsome. Not a kestrel – they're smaller.'

'Harris hawk.' Tommy settles the bird. 'Kestrels and most falcons are longwings. Beautiful but difficult to train and not so suitable for woodlands. Shortwings like goshawks are good for woodland but they're also very temperamental, and you've got to watch their weight very closely. Spitfire's what we call a broadwing, more fun to watch fly 'cos they like to soar. And the Harris hawk is less aggressive to other birds, so you can team them up. Quarry doesn't stand a chance with two of these lovelies coming after it. Course, if you want to move up a level – say a peregrine falcon, which is what I'll be doing next – you've got to tear up everything you know and start again.'

Kerenza shifts uncomfortably.

'Shouldn't she have some kind of leash attached?'

'We're done with the creance,' Tommy says. 'She's been free-flying for a while now.'

'Why does she come back?'

'Well,' Tommy says. 'It's all about food. I've got it and she wants it. Simple really.'

'What do you feed her?'

'Day-old chicks usually. Sometimes a bit of rabbit.'

And he explains about training the bird to accept the fist as a perch, manning her so that she doesn't bate at everyday sights and sounds, how you start with a leash which is called a creance and practise using a swing lure. How you cast them off and teach them to follow you so that you can flush out quarry for them, how carefully you have to control their weight and how they sometimes fly past and kick you if they think that you are ignoring them. And Kerenza, who loves experts and enthusiasts of almost any type, listens and asks questions and wonders that such a wild and raw creature can be tamed to hunt food for the benefit of its trainer, and Tommy says that it's because they know what's good for them.

'She's not a dog, though,' he says. 'Never wag her tail or roll over. She just knows that right now life is better with me than without me.'

He lets the bird go, and they watch her soar for a while, tiny movements, fragile adjustments, high above the valley, searching for the scuffle of wind in fur, the panic-filled scamper of tiny feet. It seems quite impossible that the hawk will ever return to the fist, surely she must keep soaring, keep climbing, keep searching, surely she must disappear over the top of the valley and never return.

'You seen much of the valley?' Tommy asks her as Spitfire balances on the thermals, looking for rabbits.

Kerenza shakes her head.

'Although it just ends, doesn't it? Evan took me to show me the bit where it all stops.'

Tommy glances at her sharply.

'Did he?'

He shakes his head slowly and then checks his watch and says it's time to bring Spitfire in and takes a lure from his bag.

'You want to do it?' he asks.

Kerenza shakes her head.

'I don't think . . .'

'It's easy,' he says. 'Look.'

He stands behind her and takes her hand in his ungloved one. For an instant he looks at it, small and pale with a silver ring against his own large and calloused hand. He turns it round in his own, touches one of her knuckles lightly, lifts a finger and inspects it.

'Little hands.'

He grins at her.

'You right-handed?'

She nods.

'All right.' He lets the lure bag drop. Kerenza does not want to look too closely at it as she thinks it might have a few day-old chicks attached.

'OK, so you hold the stick in your left hand and swing with

your right. Swing clockwise so that you can cast it off easily when I tell you. I'll be right here, right behind you . . .'

He starts to move her hand, swinging the lure in circular motions, she can feel the press of his body.

'Steady now, just nice strong circles, don't be scared of it, she'll come in soon.'

Tommy gives a blast on a whistle, and Kerenza sees Spitfire swoop towards the lure bag. Tommy holds her slightly closer, she can feel the pressure of his knee against the back of her thigh now. She half-laughs nervously, can smell leather, old cotton and perhaps stale beer from Tommy, whose head is almost resting on her shoulder and whose breath is on her own cheek. Tommy jerks the lure away from the bird a couple of times as it swings in.

'OK,' he says. 'Now, the next time she comes, let the rope just cast out but keep hold of the stick, and the lure bag will fall to the ground . . . now.'

And as Spitfire swoops in again, Kerenza releases the line from her hands and its momentum carries it away so that it lands on the ground about twenty yards away. She laughs and claps her hands in delight as the bird lands on the bag in a flurry of wings and a tinkling of the bells attached to its ankle and starts to feast on the tiny bones and cartilage of day-old chicks. Tommy releases her hand and smiles at her.

'Good girl,' he says.

'So what did Evan tell you about the place he took you to?' Tommy asks casually as they are walking back towards the car.

'Not much. His dad used to take him there or something.'

'My brother Gavin.'

'He was a miner, right?'

'He worked in the mine but he was white-collar staff. Gavin was the brainy one, went to college in Cardiff and everything. Seemed to have everything going for him, married Bethan, who everybody was after at the time. That was before she started drinking.'

'Must have been very sad when he died so young.'

Tommy glances at her as if trying to make a decision.

'Evan's dad killed himself. He was always a crazy commie bastard, seemed to go with being clever. But he had problems during the miners' strike 'cos he went out with the men even though he was NACODS and they weren't on strike. So he got victimised by management and lost his job. He could have coped with that, found another job, but it was the strike itself that made him most angry. 'Cos say what you like about Scargill, he told the truth, didn't he? He said they were going to close all the pits, that they had a list, and people laughed at him and called him mad, but he was telling the truth. That's just what they did, the miserable, lying bastards. They don't care about anybody, not the lives they ruin, not about people trying to just get by, it doesn't matter to them. There are some heartless scum in this world. And now we're dependent on oil and there's valley boys dying over there in Iraq for it . . . well, it can drive you mental if you think about it too much. Better to come up here and just watch the hawk fly over the mountain. Anyway, so Gavin's getting crazier and crazier, and that stupid slut Bethan's drinking and going home at night with every Tom, Dick and Harry, and people are laughing at Gavin, and he's getting into all kinds of bother in pubs and he could never fight much anyway – I was always having to get him out of trouble. Evan was only about ten at the time but clever like his old man, and Gavin loved him, he never meant to hurt him.'

'What happened?'

'I knew something was wrong that day, Gavin had been worse than usual. I went to the house and saw the car was missing, and it was like somebody had tried to set fire to the living room. Evan wasn't in the house either, so I thought maybe they'd gone looking for rabbits and I wanted to talk to Gavin 'cos he'd been acting so strange. I had an old Triumph at the time – lovely bike that was – so I rode up to the end of the valley and that's where I found the car. It had the exhaust running, and when I went up to it I saw the hose and I knew that they were both inside.'

'He tried to kill his own son?'

'He loved the boy. Maybe that's why he did it.'

'How did Evan survive?'

'The car was this very old Ford; it had one of those triangular windows that you can push open. When Evan lost consciousness he fell against it and it was slightly open so he got a little air. They thought he'd be brain-damaged and . . . well . . . you can make your own mind up about that . . . but Gavin was dead, and that was a shame, because he had a few screws loose, and all those gossips saying "How could he do it?" but he wasn't a bad man really, Gavin, and he loved that boy.'

Tommy fastens a tiny leather hood to Spitfire and tethers her to a perch in the back of the car.

'Won't she bate?' Kerenza asks nervously.

'She's used to driving now. Sometimes I can even take the hood off so she can see where she's going. I like to watch the kids in other cars pointing when they see her.'

He looks at Kerenza over the roof of the car.

'You seem like a nice girl. And maybe Evan wasn't brain-damaged by what happened but he's not . . . normal.'

She laughs but her throat is tight.

'Are you trying to warn me off him?'

'If I thought it might all work out I'd be happy, because you're the only person he even talks to, let alone brings up here. And I can manage him OK, he's clever and crazy like my brother and he knows I'd kick the shit out of him if he tried anything with me. But if you want my honest opinion there's something broken inside him, and you should be careful is all I'm saying.'

'Well,' Kerenza says. 'We're just friends. There's nothing . . .' She shakes her head.

'He doesn't have friends,' Tommy says. 'Never has done. After his dad died, he just sat in his room and read books and listened to music. That was it.'

147

'We work together sometimes,' Kerenza says. 'Colleagues, then.'

'Colleagues,' Tommy repeats. But he looks at Kerenza doubtfully as they get into the car and drive back down the valley in silence: Uncle Tommy, Kerenza and a Harris hawk under a hood like a grumpy executioner sitting in the back.

Black Out

From: Emily Holt
To: Mark Hambleton.
Subject: Gay Bergerac!!!

Dear Mark, thanks for sending the treatment for Gay Bergerac and
for the sample scenes. They made great reading, and this is a much
more marketable project. Although my list is very full at the moment
I feel that there are people who might be interested in your work and
have mentioned you to a couple of independents.

So, if you would still like me to represent you, then I enclose the
terms of business form, which I would be grateful if you could sign
and return.

Maybe see you again in Borough market!

Emilyx

'That's brilliant.' Kerenza hands Mark back the e-mail.

'She gives me a little kiss at the end.'

'Yes, I saw that.'

Mark and Kerenza are sitting in the bar of the Zetter hotel in
Clerkenwell because Mark fancies one of the Australian bar
staff. Kerenza wrinkles her nose at the sweetness of the cocktail
that Mark's very unobscure, body-pierced and rather garrulous
object of desire had promised her was the 'dog's fucking
gonads'. But right now, Kerenza wants to talk about Evan and
not about Mark's career development.

'Did you talk to him about it?' Mark asks when she has
finished recounting Uncle Tommy's story.

'Yes, I did, Mark. Over onion rings and Diet Coke at Reading Services I said: I've just found out that your dad killed himself, tried to kill you, and your uncle thinks there's something broken inside you.'

Mark cranes past her to try to see the waiter.

'He is a weirdo. Never understood why you hang out with him.'

'Don't you think that story kind of makes him a bit more understandable?'

'Peter Sutcliffe probably had a terrible story to tell, K, doesn't mean I'd go away with him.'

He sips his drink and smiles maliciously.

'To Wales.'

'I like Wales.'

'Please.'

'I like Wales.'

'And the Welsh?'

'Oh, that's such lazy bollocks. I don't know "the Welsh".'

'You just see *people*, right?'

In spite of her irritation, Kerenza laughs.

'What do you go down there for anyway? You're not fucking him, so it's not even a dirty weekend.'

He glances sideways at her.

'Unless that's where you make your "training videos".'

'Yeah, that's very . . .'

But she can't finish her sentence because two girls have just walked into the entrance to the Zetter. And one of them is Hetty, who has not yet seen Kerenza but will at any second.

'Kerenza . . .' Mark notices she is no longer listening.

'My name's not Kerenza, it's Ella.'

'What?'

Kerenza leans forward, ducking under her hair, knowing that any moment Hetty will see her and that her rapidly forming plan relies on the principle of first-strike.

'Listen quickly. My name's Ella, I'm a freelance fundraiser, I've been devastated by being ripped off by a guy called Chunk.

150

Who's actually Evan. Follow me and back me up, or I'm in big trouble.'

Kerenza gets out of her seat and marches down the stairs to the small lobby, where she taps Hetty on the back.

'You want to tell me what the fuck is going on?'

Hetty turns in astonishment.

'Ella?'

'Oh yes. Surprised to see me again?'

She folds her arms aggressively and turns back to Mark.

'This is one of the people I was telling you about.'

He slips effortlessly into role.

'Not the ones who ripped you off?'

'I haven't ripped anybody off,' Hetty protests, confused by the assault. 'Where've you been, Ella? Everyone's going mad.'

'Trying to find that Welsh bastard who hasn't paid me my agreed fundraising fee, which, I might add, was virtually no more than my costs.'

She can feel Mark's eyes widening.

'But Ella, we can't get in touch with him either . . .' Hetty turns in distress towards her friend, who is staring intensely at Mark. Kerenza feels uncomfortable about this, as if there is something about Mark that reveals that he's lying. But she has chosen the strategy of turning the tables on Hetty, and once this has been done there can be no going back.

'Don't give me that. You two were thick as thieves, always giggling with each other and sneaking off. You think it's funny, do you?'

'Come on, Ella.' Mark lays a restraining hand on her arm. 'I'm sure this girl is nothing to do with it. Why don't we sit down and see if we can find out what's been going on.'

'A fake charity is what's going on.' Kerenza pokes Hetty's arm with her finger. 'I've been conned by a group of people who made up some foundation and used *my* name and *my* fundraising skills to manipulate people's good will.'

'No! Ella, I swear we had nothing to do with it. Nothing happened between me and Chunk. Actually, I found him quite weird about sex in the end, but that's another story. It was Chunk who ripped everybody off and . . . well, we thought you must have been in on it. Anyway, *we* raised a lot of the money, and it's all gone. My father's furious, and it's embarrassing, because lovely Livvy sponsored me a couple of grand when we met after the run.'

Even at such a critical stage, Kerenza finds it hard not to smile at this piece of information.

'That's true, Ella,' Mark says, sliding happily into the role of good cop. 'If they raised money why would they rip themselves off?'

Kerenza, who has never needed assistance from tiger-balm on set, starts to cry.

'I feel such a fool,' she says. 'I really believed in it. I mean, the website, the wristbands, Taylor Bright . . .'

She turns reproachfully to Hetty.

'And you and your boyfriend just made all of that up?'

'No! We didn't . . . I'm just as innocent as you!'

'I don't know what to believe any more.' Kerenza accepts the napkin that Mark has tactfully passed her from one of the adjoining tables and blows her nose.

'Why didn't you call Rory?' Hetty asks reasonably enough. 'He's been calling and calling – it's been a week.'

'Not *Rory*?' Mark arches an eyebrow, cleverly setting up any information Kerenza wants to supply. 'Rory who . . .'

He breaks off.

'*That* Rory.' Kerenza nods solemnly.

Mark shakes his head at Hetty. 'I didn't realise you were a friend of *his*.'

'What did he do to you?' Hetty asks. Her lower lip is almost wobbling. 'I thought you two had a thing going.'

'We were supposed to be going out to dinner, and he blew me out and went off to snort fucking coke with that army monster you're all so fond of.'

'He said he texted you, but it was you who blew *him* out!'

'After that guy had been hassling me all night right in front of

152

him without him saying a word? Suggesting a threesome in the toilet cubicle? Telling me how much he loved anal sex . . .'

She catches a glance from Mark – OK, overdoing it, take a step back.

'I thought Rory had a higher opinion of me than that,' she says plaintively.

'Rory really likes you.'

'Look, let's just forget Rory. I really thought that might go somewhere, but he's not involved in this, and it's a personal matter. You, however, I'm still not sure about. I'm not being funny, but I'd like your mobile number, Hetty, in case I need to follow this up. I'm sorry for the people who lost money, but I'm also a victim here, and my professional integrity has been called into judgment.'

While Hetty is apologetically scrabbling for her mobile, her friend is still staring hard at Mark. He can't help but notice this and asks nervously,

'Do I know you or something?'

'Aren't you . . .'

Mark relaxes and smiles in happy expectation.

'Aren't you an actor?'

'Yes, I am.'

'And you were in . . . Oh. My. God. Hetty, this is the guy who was in . . . oh my God . . . you were Conrad in *Shiver*.'

'That's right,' Mark says. 'Ella here handles my PR.' He turns to Hetty. 'I've known Ella for quite a few years and I've met very few people in this business with her integrity.'

'I'm sorry, Ella.' Hetty looks genuinely contrite. 'We were all just so confused.'

'I'm Tabitha.' The girl holds out her hand to Mark. 'God, we all *loved* that show. Every week, we'd never miss it, we'd get completely shitfaced and try to guess what mental plot-line they'd think up next. What *drugs* were the writers on? It was fucking hysterical.'

'Thanks.'

'No, but, you know, in a *good* way. What are you doing now?'

'I'm writing my own show.'

'An actor and a writer!'

Renaissance man smiles again. It would all be quite nauseating were it not so useful for establishing Kerenza's credibility.

'I can't believe I've met Conrad from *Shiver*.' Tabitha takes a photo of him with her mobile phone. 'I've got to send this to Suze and Olly.'

Hetty gives Kerenza her mobile number, and Kerenza promises to text her her own, and they swear that they will find Chunk and force him to return the money he has stolen, and Hetty promises not to tell Rory how upset Kerenza was, because Kerenza doesn't want to give Rory the satisfaction, and Mark and Tabitha chatter away about the heroin addiction of his co-star in *Shiver*, the sexual shenanigans at the wrap party, and Tabitha tells Mark about the plans she has to make duvet covers out of chinchillas in Cumbria, and Mark squeals with delight at the idea and promises to come to any dinner parties she is attending and to let her know when 'Gay Bergerac' will be transmitting.

Kerenza drags him out before he can agree to Tabitha's plan to pick up a bag of coke and go and sit on her roof overlooking the Portobello Road and watch *Shiver* DVDs all night – a difficult task, as this is the closest to heaven Mark will ever get.

'So, then,' Mark asks as they are walking down the Clerkenwell Road. 'You going to tell me what's going on now?'

So Kerenza tells him, relieved at last to have it all out in the open and not to have to pretend that she is doing training videos any longer. Mark frowns during the telling of the story, and when she has finished he says, 'At least it's not porn.'

But there is something in his tone – not outrage, not condemnation, just a kind of quiet disappointment.

'You don't approve?'

Kerenza suddenly feels very dizzy, the air around her is soupy warm. Mark shrugs.

'You could get in real trouble.'

'I was in real trouble before.'

'You might find Holloway Prison a little more troublesome.'

She has never seen Mark like this – he's both serious and sad.

'But that's not what's really bothering you.'

'No.'

'So, then . . .'

He stops and looks at her.

'I expected better from you.'

Her heart starts to thud inside her rib-cage. He carries on.

'OK, this is gonna sound really old-fashioned, but I some-times think our generation is really rubbish. Everything has to be easy, nothing has to be worked for; if you fail it's always somebody else's fault. You know why I didn't make it after *Shiver*? Because the scripts were pony, and my performance wasn't all that, and the only people who really liked it were off their tits at the time. I bet that Evan justifies what he does on the basis that the whole world is a con, so why should he be any different, that his lies and theft are nothing in the grand scheme of things. And maybe, you know, maybe he's right and he's not Enron but he's still a liar and a thief. And I hope you don't go along with his self-serving bullshit, 'cos if we don't try and be different then we're stuck in this shit and it all just gets worse and worse and nobody cares about anything.'

Buses and taxis and cars and bicycles on the Clerkenwell Road. People in windows doing stuff, she doesn't know what. People she doesn't know, lives she'll never penetrate. The grey angles of the Barbican towers built on a site destroyed by German bombs. Netta Longdon on the eve of war: what might she have said? 'Oh, don't be such a bore and get me a drink, there's a good fellow.' A fragment of the Grandmaster Flash song – principles, morals, scruples, love. Things apparently you ain't never heard of. But she has heard of them – she knows what they are, she thinks Evan might also, even though he thinks them nonsense, because Darwin, because hair falling out, because headscarves, because world fucked anyway, because final victory of capitalism, etc., etc. Not to be so easily dismissed, though, because maybe an answer would be nice. More sinned against than sinning. Who doesn't think that about themselves? I expected better of you, you were made for more than to guard over the sensibilities of a sterile dilettante. What good blaming Olivia Scott in her Stella McCartney dress for this or for that? Labels and images and surfaces and names, so many names, pointless names. The air around her getting warmer and planes dropping into Heathrow, staining the warm clouds, and something's happening to her head, her knees . . .

'Is she OK?'

Kerenza looks up into a face. It's a man in a suit, it's Chrome Rory. No, it isn't Rory, it's a stranger. Is she in bed? She hears another voice which she knows.

'She fainted. Do you have any water?'

The plastic rim of a bottle on her lips, water dribbling out of the side of her mouth, she chokes.

'Steady.'

She turns her head and looks at Mark, who squeezes her hand.

'It's OK, it's OK. You just blacked out.'

'Yes.' She can see people looking at her curiously, a despatch rider has stopped by the side of the kerb. 'It's very hot.'

'You're stressed,' Mark says. 'I didn't mean to pick on you.'

'It's OK.'

'No, really. Who am I to judge?'

'Who are you not to judge?' She sits up and feels her head swimming again. 'You're my friend, you should tell me what you think.'

'I want you to be happy.'

'It's hard to be happy when you can't pay the rent,' Kerenza says. 'It's that simple.'

But even now, groggy as she is, she knows that Mark is being kind in not pointing out that it isn't that simple at all, that he has great difficulty paying his own rent for a tiny room in Archway sometimes. That plenty of people can't do what it is they think they're good at doing and so they do something else instead. Her reasons for doing what she is doing now are partly because she likes doing it and she is happy being with Evan in all his strangeness, cruel humour and amoral imagination, happiest when he raises a bushy eyebrow at her and calls her a thick'ead.

But she also knows that, while Mark's assault on Evan's motives and justifications drew blood, she still thinks that it is far lazier to sit on a roof terrace all night in ironic indifference to the world around you and sticking a truckload of cocaine up your nose.

She gets to her feet as her mobile bleep-bleeps. The message is from Ivo and tells her that Anna has suddenly got quite sick and that he has taken her to the hospital.

Kerenza stops at a hardware store on the way to the hospital to buy a fan because she remembers Anna complaining the last time she was there that it had no air conditioning. She remembers Mark's earlier disapproval of her involvement with Evan, but the fact is that she can buy a fan like this, carry out a thoughtful act, because she has money. There is no getting away from it. Unfortunately, though, the hardware store only has tiny handheld fans, so Kerenza buys one of those and some magazines from the newsagent's, where an argument is raging between the owner and a red-eyed, loose-limbed crackhead who claims to have dropped his pound coin under the counter and is demanding a replacement.

'You'll get it when you clean up,' he keeps repeating, but the owner won't give in, and the customer departs hurling ugly insults and abuse as Kerenza raises her eyebrows in sympathy as she pays for the magazines.

The hospital is stifling as Kerenza walks through the ward of emaciated patients, their bedside tables full of their temporary hospital furniture, some of them with headphones on watching the pay-as-you-go TV, some in the weary sleep of the sick. Anna is in one of the side rooms and asleep when Kerenza enters, so Kerenza sits in the high-backed blue hospital chair reading about Sienna Miller's stunning new Boho look in *Heat* magazine until her friend's eyes flutter and open, close again, then open and rest on Kerenza. She smiles.

'Hey, lovely,' she whispers. 'I had a bad dream. I dreamed they could clone us, not just our bodies but our consciousness. If it was exactly the same consciousness would it be me?'

'You've got me there,' Kerenza says. 'My bad dreams are about being back at school retaking exams or not having any shoes on.'

She sits down beside the bed, fiddles with the hospital sheets.

'Why's that such a bad dream anyway?'

'It would mean you could never get away,' Anna says. 'Although it's hard to imagine – not having consciousness any more ever again.'

'No different from before we were born.' Kerenza thinks of Grace Holding – a receptionist in a hospital, bombs falling on London, the tiny specks of Wembley mud on the legs of the players in the 1941 War Cup final. Neither she nor Anna was around then. She sits and holds Anna's hand with one of hers, with the other she blows air onto her brow with the little handheld fan. Somewhere else in the hospital somebody is calling loudly and impatiently for the nurse. It's persistent and irritating. Somebody shouts, 'Shut up, you selfish cunt,' from another window, and Kerenza laughs, and Anna half-smiles, but it's the kind of smile a baby might make, unsure really why it's smiling. She dozes again, and the nurses come in to do observations and go away again, and when Anna falls properly asleep, Kerenza turns off the little plastic fan and sits studying it, hoping that Anna is not having any more bad dreams.

The Ring Cycle

Feb 1941

Michael Young from the end of the street was killed by a bomb last night. Ten years old. His mother Jane and sisters Emily and Linda too. Father (Bert) was not there because he was visiting his mother in Norwich. Poor Bert, having to come back to that. Michael was such a popular boy. I always saw him playing with a football in the recreation park when I went off in the evenings. Now I won't see him ever again. Makes you shiver to think of it, just a boy like that and such a violent death – smashed to pieces, nothing now, nothing left of him or the big smile he always had, we're taking up a subscription for Bert. Small consolation. Grace very fed up – lack of sleep – and we had an argument because she will leave her handbag and if – God forbid – anything were to happen it makes me crazy to think they could not identify her. Why do I write God forbid? There was no God when I was in the trenches, there was no God when that bomb fell on Michael Young's house, there was no God when a steeple fell on the head of Billy Morgan while he was trying to put out a fire in the church. There is no God. That should come as a comfort to us, because if there were a God then he is a stupid, uncaring, all-powerful Hitler of a God able to make our lives miserable for all eternity.

'He didn't like religion much,' Grace observes.

'Yes, I'm getting a sense of that.'

'He was always worried about me being killed and

unidentified,' Grace Holding says. 'You didn't get much of a send-off – they just slung you in a cardboard box.'

Kerenza looks up from the leather-bound notebook she is reading. She has been taking boxes down from the loft in anticipation of Grace's move to the home. In one she has found a membership card for the Communist Party, which Grace joined because they were active in the hospital where she worked and because the Soviets were fighting Hitler so hard and because she liked Harry Pollit, the General Secretary. 'But they despaired of me really, because I was so lazy.' Grace chuckles. 'I was a very bad militant, and some of them really had no sense of humour at all.' Then they found the diary. Grace said she knew that he had kept a journal during the war, but it had vanished afterwards, and she had never thought to ask about it. Arthur had tucked photographs in the pages of the notebook; there were pictures of Grace and Arthur with their springer spaniel called Spam and Arthur grinning and holding a guitar. Arthur is small and slight with a mischief obvious even in the photograph. Grace is willowy and lithe, laughing at something Arthur has said.

'He couldn't play at all,' Grace says, as Kerenza tells her of the photo with the guitar. 'But some of the people in the public shelter could and we would have sing-songs. Arthur had a good voice – he liked to sing "The Butcher's Boy". Do you know it?'

Kerenza shakes her head.

'It's a sad song.'

She starts to sing.

'*In London Town where I did dwell, a butcher's boy I loved right well . . .*'

Her voice is thin as rice paper, her eyes like opaque marbles.

'*He courted me my life away and now with me he will not stay . . .* you really don't know it?'

Kerenza shakes her head again, and Grace tells her it is the old story of a girl who loves the wrong man, the butcher's boy doesn't want to know, sits other girls on his knee, leaves her holding the baby, etc., etc.

'*I wish, oh how I wish in vain, I wish I was a maid again.*'

Grace laughs.

'These poor, silly girls.'

'What happens to her?'

'She hangs herself. But they find a note . . . *oh, make my grave long, wide and deep, put a marble stone at my head and feet, and in the middle a turtle dove, so the world may know I died for love . . .*'

Grace wipes a mock tear from her eye.

'She doesn't want much,' Kerenza says.

'Arthur was a soppy fool, he loved the bit about the turtle dove and dying for love. Men are very sentimental in spite of everything. And we sang "Juanita" and "The Camptown Races" and "Clementine" . . .' Grace starts to sing again, '*She drove her ducklets to the river, ev'ry morning just at nine; she stubb'd her toe against a silver, and fell into the foaming brine . . .*'

'Another silly girl bites the dust,' Kerenza says.

'Yes, poor old Clementine was lost and gone for ever after that.'

'How do you stub your toe on a silver?'

'I don't know,' Grace says. 'It's more unfortunate than hanging yourself, I suppose. It's the sort of thing that Arthur would have known. Or he would have made up some nonsense just to entertain me. Oh, he spoiled me really but he was always playing about. Do you think it's wrong for me to read his diary now?'

'Even if it were . . .' Kerenza returns to the careful, neat calligraphy of Arthur Holding's war diary '. . . it's not a temptation I could ever resist.'

March 1941

London has been taking it very hard. We look back at Christmas and the quiet nights as if it was centuries ago. Some very bad news. Joseph Watts who looked out for me when I got back from Flanders has been killed. He was firewatching in the factory when it took a direct hit. I write this news with a very heavy heart and I try to fight my desire for our boys to give them hell in return. But it would just be some German family, some Hans with a football, no different from poor little Michael Young.

I have tried to keep my mind busy. Reading Charles Dickens. Last night took G to the cinema in the West End. We went to see Seven Sinners and . . .

Kerenza breaks off, half-trying not to laugh.

'What does he say?' Grace demands.

'There were two far bigger sinners in the seats at the back and I remember less about the film than I do about . . . well, really . . .'

Even Kerenza breaks off here, while Grace cackles with laughter.

'Yes, we never really had any problems in that department. I had to watch out for him as well I can tell you because he had a wandering eye. There was a girl from his office I'm still not sure about. Doreen. Maureen. Something like that. He just liked women a lot.'

'And what about you? Did you have an eye for the boys?'

'I wasn't without admirers,' Grace says. 'The chap who recruited me to the party, Joe McFarlane, he was a nice-looking boy. Awfully serious, though, always got very flustered every time I asked him to explain why Stalin had signed a pact with Hitler.'

'Sounds like his mind might have been on something else.'

'And what about you? Didn't you say there was some young man breaking your heart?'

'Well . . .' Kerenza shrugs. She is in Evan's good books because she has persuaded Ivo to pose as an asylum seeker for the British Film Diversity Fund. Ivo thought the whole idea was quite hilarious, largely because Kerenza pitched it to him as a practical joke rather than a fraud. He promised to bring his friend Branka from Zagreb, who had been a comedian for an alternative radio show back in Croatia. Neither had Evan minded her pinning all the blame for the chavathon fraud on

162

him during the encounter with Hetty – 'Quick thinking,' he had remarked appreciatively.

They had booked into the Dorchester for the weekend (in separate rooms, of course) to draw up budgets, preliminary treatments and prepare CVs for the British Film Diversity Fund before dressing up to drink peach bellinis before a lobster dinner. Evan told her that he had met Maggie Thompson again to go to an alternative puppet show which explored domestic violence, where he had given her their document, *Asylum Songs: Witnessing Our Lives*. He was particularly proud of the title because, according to Evan at least, the colon was an essentially smug, know-it-all piece of punctuation. Evan is keen for Kerenza to take over some of the burden of Maggie, whom he describes as spiteful and argumentative, which, Kerenza thinks, is pretty rich coming from him. He also seems particularly obsessed with her footwear, which he describes as Trotskyist but refuses to elaborate any further.

Now Kerenza tells Grace that she doesn't think that Evan has any interest in her at all, and Grace asks what Evan is interested in. To say money would be too easy, Kerenza thinks. Evan certainly wants a comfortable life-style but it is not just that – he is like a stilt-walker who can neither stop nor dismount; while he is up there he can just keep taking big strides, head moving from side to side, the deprecatory gaze. Apart from the cottage in Pant-y-brastrap, she knows virtually nothing about him – where he goes, what he does, whom he sees when he is not with her remain a complete mystery. Well, she also knows about Caro kiss kiss kiss, the sexy hostess from the private drinking clubs, but has tried as far as possible to rid her mind of the sordid imaginings of the unforgettable night out with Internet Toby.

'Well, men are pigs sometimes,' Grace says. 'I was lying when I pretended not to know her name. She was called Maureen, and something definitely did happen. Very pretty girl, I have to admit. Went on for months.'

'Did you think about leaving him?'

'I thought about it but . . .' Grace shrugs. '. . . Arthur was the only man I ever really wanted, and I couldn't imagine life without him. A boring man who was faithful wouldn't necessarily have made me any happier. When he was dying – oh, he was so thin and helpless, it was terrible to see what that cancer did to him, he had seen so much, been so full of life . . .'

She breaks off.

'When he was dying . . .' Kerenza prompts.

'He said sorry. We'd never really discussed it, just sometimes when I was angry with him I would throw things his way, he knew that I knew. Anyway, he said to me, "Anything I've ever done that's hurt you I'm truly sorry for." And he was telling the truth, because he wasn't a mean-spirited man. Arthur didn't want to hurt me, so it was easier to forgive him. Besides, women liked him as well, and he was only human in the end, I suppose.'

But Kerenza can still sense the pale threads of pain running through her words.

'Do you want me to stop now?' she asks, but Grace shakes her head firmly.

June 17th 1941

So much has happened since I last wrote that it almost makes my head spin to think about it. To try and explain this story I have to go back to May – the day of the cup final, Arsenal were playing Preston North End . . .

Kerenza looks up at Grace.

'You told me about this, didn't you? The worst night of the blitz?'

Grace nods.

. . . Arsenal were playing Preston North End and I was cheering for them because although my team will always be Brentford they are a

London side and they had Denis Compton playing for them – magnificent player. Not a great game though and ended in a draw. Compton scored.

G working nights in the hospital so at about six o'clock I went into town because I had arranged to meet Jim at the 77 Club in Hanway Street, where they were playing a few hands of pontoon. When I got there, Jim and Suzie were working a mark of his money, Suze sitting next to him showing him a bit of leg and placing bets with his chips (the mark's). He was about £50 up and eating sandwiches and drinking rum, his hand on Suzy's leg as merry as a lark. He wouldn't be so merry by the end of the evening. These types amaze me – they think that even if they lose they can write a cheque which won't be enforceable in the courts. Which is why Jim is there of course. Handy with his fists and you have to knock him unconscious to stop him. But Jim's a good chap, not frightened of anything and he saved my life. Back in France, I was dog-tired and I fell asleep on sentry duty and the officer caught me, and he's shouting and spitting in my face and talking about having me court-martialled, which would have been the end for me – firing squad and no doubt about it. Well, Jim has a quiet word with the officer, reminds him that I'm a popular boy and only young and this officer – forget his name – Carling or something – wouldn't want a rat to climb on his face in the night and suffocate him or cop a bullet in the back from accidental discharge and that was the last I heard of the court martial. Then Jim made me stick close to him, said I was his lucky charm, nothing would happen while we were together. We're special, Jim says, and we are because there aren't many who marched out of Brentford at the same time as us that came limping back again. Now Jim's working out of West End clubs enforcing debts for men who don't appear at their own card games.

Anyway, Jim and I have a beer and a smoke and we talk about the match that day, and Jim had been to the game and says there was a young boy playing for Preston, Tom Finney, who wasn't half bad and to watch out for him. Then Jim tells me to watch out for myself as well because it's going to be a bad night – Jerry's going to rain hell down on us and I ask him how he knows and he says he just does and

that's good enough for me because Jim always did have a sixth sense,
knew when we were going over the top, and we talked a bit about
those days and Jim said he also has the dreams but then it's all
getting a bit much and so we have another beer and Jim tells me
there's a bag of lamb chops for me round the back. The rationing is
right and proper but G does love a lamb chop and thinking of her face
when I bring them back makes me smile as well – she is awfully
spoiled but what's to be done when I like spoiling her, and she knows
how to spoil me back no mistake about that. Anyway Jim wants me to
stay with them because no bombs will drop on the card game while
I'm there but I say I have to go and so I pick up my chops and say
goodbye to Jim and give Suzy a wink . . .

'I bet you did,' Grace mutters sourly.

. . . and I go for a walk around town and there's not much to beat a
May evening in London although it's chilly this night so I stroll
about for a bit with my bag of chops from Jim and then I take my book
over to the offices and settle down to read Great Expectations and I'm
just at the part where Joe is giving all the gravy to Pip to cheer him
up when the sirens sound and shortly after that the first waves of
Heinkels are over and they're giving us merry hell, there are baskets
of incendiaries everywhere and one of them gets into our building
fizzing and burning with that vicious white heat, so we have to put it
out and it feels like the whole world is on fire and I wonder about Jim
and Suzy and the mark and whether they'll have the sense to get to a
shelter and I think probably not because the mark will have Dutch
courage and what with him wanting a bit of Suzy and them wanting
his money they're probably still in there playing pontoon or faro or
even chemin-de-fer.
   But Jim was right. We were copping it something terrible.
   After the fireraisers came the high explosives and a big 'un comes
down nearby and the blast like a gale and as if the air sucked out of
me and one of the other boys laughs because we look like negro
minstrels all covered in dust and soot and we start to sing
Shenandoah and we're laughing thinking of Jerry up there throwing

down everything he can at us while we're singing down here even though not one of us thinks we can survive this terrible night.

So a shout goes up for help because there's a building taken a direct hit on the street but several others have been damaged and there's people trapped in the rubble and it's shops and flats so I leave Joey to watch the offices and I go out to help the Heavy Rescue Squad and it's as if the air is on fire and if you'd have had time to think about it it would have broken your heart what they were doing to our city.

One of the Heavy Rescue boys comes out of a building that's hanging like an old tooth where there were some flats on top of a jeweller's and he says there's a woman and her baby trapped inside and the building's filling with water on account of a burst water main but they're in this space at the back but there's a lot of damage and he's too broadshouldered to get through the space to them. They all turn to look at me and I say 'hold on I'm just a firewatcher' but I know I'm going to have to do it because of my build and so they give me the morphine and a stick and I have to go back in with the boy from Heavy Rescue and I'm crawling through the dust and the smoke and I can hear water and feel the tails of rats flicking at my face and I'm scared as hell because we can hear the sound of crashing masonry all around and there's wave after wave of Jerry still showering everything they've got down on our heads.

We're crawling on our bellies through the rubble and the boy from Heavy Rescue he points to a part of the building where there's only a small gap and I inch my way in and I can feel it scraping the skin off my back. There's a gentle moaning coming from just behind me and when I turn my head in the torchlight I see a pale little face and it's a slip of a girl – can't be much more than twenty. Her face is unmarked and I think she must be all right but when I look behind her, oh her poor legs! I ask her how old she is and she says that she is twenty-one years old and her baby is six months. The baby is awfully still and quiet and I wonder if it's dead but it's whimpering very softly. The girl says she's called Catherine and the baby's name is Susanna and she doesn't want to die in there, she's only young, won't I save her

167

life. I tell her that I'll take baby out first and that then we'll come back for her and she says that she knows I'm lying, that I'm leaving her there to die. There's not much to say to that because she's got a ton of brickwork holding down her legs and the rest will come down before I'm back, before I'm even out of there. So she gives this funny bitter little laugh and then she takes a ring from her finger – a big sapphire – and she asks me to give it back to her husband so I tie it into the lining of my pocket so that it won't fall out as I'm crawling through the wreckage.

She says that she wants to tell me something important and I'm thinking it will be some words of love or farewell for him but instead she says that she doesn't love her husband, that she married him because he was a wealthy jewel merchant and her family were poor. 'Give him back the ring,' she says. 'I don't love him.' She seems to be enjoying saying this. 'I don't love him,' she repeats this several times. 'I never did. This ring was a curse.' As if that helps her to take the pain away. Then she starts to pray out loud, the Lord is my Shepherd, and I want to scream out that he is nobody's shepherd, he is a cold-hearted murderous Hitler bastard of a God who punishes his sheep in the cruellest ways imaginable and even if I had to burn for an eternity I would do so hating him and this cruel world he created to torment us. I take baby in my arms and I see a tear in her eye. 'Goodbye, Susanna darling,' she says and she's weeping and I want to cry as well but instead I give her the morphine and plenty of it and that does the trick because she gives just a little shudder and she makes a noise which sounds like 'oh' as the last of the air leaves her lungs and her eyes roll back in her head and she dies.

So I push the child back through the gap in the wreckage and crawl after it and all the time I know that the building's coming down at any moment and the child's starting to cry. I'm singing to myself to give me courage and I'm singing oh Susanna, don't you cry for me and I'm remembering us singing as the bombs are coming down and that's all you can do sometimes just sing for your life. Somewhere out there is Grace in her hospital and I'm praying that she's safe and Jim who survived Flanders and even the mark with his hand on Suzy's leg, he's only human after all, just a fool and his money easily parted, *but you wouldn't want to see him all smashed to pieces and the city burning and burning and the terrible noise of the planes overhead and falling masonry and the baby crying. So there am I – Arthur Holding – thinking this is the end of my life, here with little Susanna in this burning building that's also filling very quickly with water now on account of the burst main and me singing how I come from Alabama and I'm bound for Louisiana even though I'll never see Alabama or Louisiana in the whole of my life. Ahead of me I can hear voices and I think I can see lights and I say oh little Susanna don't you cry now, don't you cry for me and then a noise, a rushing, a terrible crashing noise and my eyes are filling with dust and it feels like heaven itself is falling on top of us, as if that spiteful pig in whose honour the stupid build their churches has crumpled the world in his angry baby's fist.*

When I wake up I'm in a hospital bed again. Very very lucky the doctors tell me, a piece of masonry knocked me out cold but a larger piece fell over me without touching so that it was protecting me from further falling and my body protecting the nipper. She saved my life in a way because they heard her crying and after four hours they were able to get in and haul me out with a rope and not a scratch on little Susanna, just hungry and cold, just a baby.

Well now, here's the part of the story that is the strangest of all. Writing this at home now, I still cannot quite believe it, cannot believe what I have done. But still, even if things were to repeat themselves again, I don't think I would do it any different.

One fine evening in the hospital and the nurses tell me that I have a visitor. It is the father of the child I saved, husband of the girl who died in there under all that rubble. The nurses didn't find the ring right at the bottom of my trouser pocket tied into the lining so I take it from where I have stored it in my drawer ready to give it to him. I imagine he will be like her – I am waiting for somebody young and pale and shy. Instead they show in a man who must be in his late fifties and a man I recognise at once.

The Prince.

The officer from the military hospital who had the hoses turned on injured men when they were freezing cold. He's put on a bit of weight but he still has the same little moustache, the same mouth and tiny teeth like a ferret. He has an expression, his teeth draw over his lower lip, half-laugh, half-snarl, unmistakable. But I can tell from the questions he asks me about my health that he neither remembers who I am nor particularly cares. And I'm holding the ring his wife sent back to him tightly in my hand under the sheet. And I'm thinking of the way she repeated that she did not love him and asked me to tell him that.

'She was alive when you reached her?' he asks me.

'Yes,' I say.

He is twisting his umbrella round in his hands like a truncheon. Some men are born to be policemen or fascists.

'Was she suffering?'

'Yes,' I say. 'But I gave her morphine and that eased the pain somewhat.'

He nods and paces around the room, picks up a photograph I have of Grace.

'This your girl?' he asks.

I nod.

'Pretty girl,' he says. 'Catherine was pretty as well.'

I shrug and tell him there was nothing I could see in that place, although I remember her little white face in the torchlight.

'She played the piano,' he says. 'She had good hands for the piano. She used to play Chopin nocturnes very beautifully. In the evenings.'

And to my astonishment I see him wipe a tear from his eye and I think: he loved her. Whatever he did to her – and he must have done some very bad things to make her hate him like that – he felt love for her, he noticed her hands when she played the piano. I can feel the ring heavy in my hand, pressing against my skin, he would have watched it glinting in the light as she played Chopin in their parlour. I remember men with their teeth chattering as cold filthy water was pumped all over their wounded bodies, I remember that little smile-snarl at my court martial, how he enjoyed dispensing my punish-ment, his pious words, the words of a hypocrite who had never been near to the front-line.

'Did she say anything to you?' he asks. 'Any message?'

And what good would it do to tell him the truth so I say, 'She said you should care for your child.'

A strange expression flickers on his face. Like the shadow of a moving cloud on the ground.

'She spoiled that baby,' he says. 'She was a little fool for her.'

I bet she did, I think. I bet she gave her all the love she wouldn't give to you. And I imagine that even though the Prince must have loved his young wife, he would have been cruel and shallow as well because that is the kind of man he is. And it is at this point that I know that I am not going to give him his ring back, that he will never put it on the finger of another young bride and slowly drain the lifeblood out of her.

'Well,' he says. 'I must be going.'

'Goodbye,' says I.

He fumbles in his pocket and pulls out a couple of guineas.

'Keep your money,' I say a little sharp. He looks at me surprised.

'No,' he says. 'You took a risk for my family and saved my daughter's life.'

'Keep it,' says I. 'I was doing my duty.'

He nods with approval. Duty. A word he likes but does not understand the meaning of.

'Well,' he says. 'That is a most commendable attitude.'

I nod and he stares at me and just for a second I see something like recognition in his face.

'You seem familiar,' he says.' Do I know you from somewhere?'

It was over twenty years ago. He sat in front of me enjoying his power over me. He turned filthy water on the broken bodies of my pals. Now I have something of his he will never see again. In my hand the warm stone of the ring.

'No,' I say. 'You don't know me.'

Later he must have remembered the ring because an embarrassed detective comes to talk to me about it but by that time I had given it to Jim to look after. Jim and Suze had survived that terrible night although Jim tells me that Suze was lucky that night because the knocking shop next door took a direct hit and that several of her mates – Lizzie and Sarah and Shoreditch Kate – were found dead

without a stitch on which is a humiliating way to die and also among
the bodies a High Court judge wearing suspenders and a silk muffler.
Anyway, Jim had whistled with admiration when he saw the stone
and told me that a fence could get rid of it for a thousand pounds. No,
at least I told him, I didn't want to make money out of it.

Well, the detective says it's just a routine inquiry but had I noticed
a ring on Catherine Sheldon's finger and I say that conditions were a
little cramped down there to pay much attention to her jewellery. 'Of
course, of course,' he says and chews his lip. I'm getting a bit worried
because I've known firemen sent to prison for taking a mouthful of
rum from a bottle found on a bombsite to cope with the horror of what
they are dragging from the wreckage. But the detective apologises
and says that Mr Sheldon has admitted that his wife did not always
wear the ring and that Mrs Sheldon might have taken it off that
night and it is lost for ever in the wreckage, that the kind of fellow
who risks his life to crawl through the rubble to save a little child
would not take the ring from the finger of a dead woman. 'I didn't,' I
say, which is true. And he goes away saying that it is a crying shame
that he had to ask me such a question and I tell him not to worry
about it, that Mr Sheldon was within his rights to ask if I had noticed
and he scowls and curses Mr Sheldon with the same word that we all
used about him in that hospital in Kent where he ordered the hoses to
be turned on us just because we wanted a little warmth.

And when I leave the hospital I get the ring back from Jim and I
give it to Grace in the bluebell wood of Kew Gardens.

Kerenza stops reading and looks at Grace Holding, who is
gripping the arm of her chair tightly.

'You didn't know?' Kerenza asks. 'You thought that Sheldon
gave him the ring as a reward, you said.'

'I knew there was something about it he wasn't telling me. I
thought it might have something to do with his mate, Jim. He
was a bag of trouble, that Jim, but loved Arthur like he was his
younger brother . . . pass me my bag.'

Kerenza hands Grace the bag and she feels around in it until
she finds the ring. She takes it out and they both stare at it, the

ring that was on the finger of a woman dying under the rubble of a bombed building, the ring that glinted as she played Chopin. Kerenza shivers.

'I prefer Arthur's version of the story,' she says.

'He should still have returned the ring,' Grace says.

'You can understand, though, why he didn't. That man was clearly a monster.'

'Never mind,' Grace does not seem particularly upset by the story or even to think that it reflects particularly badly on her ex-husband. But her face is quite hard and determined. 'He could have got into awful trouble, and it wasn't his to keep.'

She turns it around in her fingers.

'It isn't mine to keep now,' she says.

She looks up at Kerenza.

'But Sheldon will be dead now,' Kerenza says. 'There's nothing you can do.'

Grace holds out the ring.

'Take it.'

'I don't understand.'

'I want you to do something for me. I want you to find out about the baby that was saved. It's her mother's ring and she must have it back and know the true story. That's very important. Will you do that for me?'

'How will I find her?'

Grace shrugs.

'All of this stuff I hear about the internet – it can't be that difficult. Please, Kerenza. I don't feel angry with Arthur, it was wartime, I tried to explain it to you, how it's not at all like the way it's presented now. Such strange times, we didn't know if we'd live until the next day sometimes. But it's not my ring, and I want it returned. Do this for me.'

And Kerenza knows that there is a command contained in the last sentence, that it is the last repayment for the theft of the fifty pounds from the drawer, that if she does this she will have received some final absolution.

She looks at the blue stone on its golden band, the curse for a songbird, the bluebell for a sweetheart, stolen property.

'You trust me with it?' she asks, and Grace frowns.

'Completely. If you don't find the owner you can keep it. That's how much I trust you to try.'

And Kerenza takes the ring and puts it in her own pocket.

The Lefty Platter

'Why do you need to find this person so badly?' Evan asks Kerenza suspiciously.

He is the only person she could think of who would know how to begin tracking down the surviving relatives of the Prince. Besides, the story of Catherine Sheldon's wedding ring is so intriguing she can hardly resist retelling it. He had listened carefully while she waited for his scorn at her decision to try and execute Grace Holding's instructions, but it didn't come.

'Aren't you going to tell me to keep the ring for myself?' she asks now. 'Wouldn't that fit your moral philosophy perfectly?'

He grins comfortably.

'All this time and you still don't get it,' he says. 'If it makes you feel good to give the ring away then that's what you should do. Just don't pretend it's for any other reason.'

'I'm doing it for Grace.'

'But still because it makes you feel better to do that. Personally, I'd keep the ring and tell her that I couldn't find the relatives. But I'm not you.'

'No, you're not,' Kerenza agrees but she finds it hard to feel ill-disposed towards Evan because they are walking down Stoke Newington Church Street, and it's warm, and people look nice and sunny, and Evan has been making her laugh by refusing to be intimidated into walking in the gutter by pairs of mums occupying the whole pavement. And of course the central boulevard of what he considers to be the middle-class lefty capital of Britain provides him with a rich array of targets: bugaboo frog prams; beggars with their dogs sitting outside delis; IVF mothers; Birkenstocks; Stop the War stalls; baby shops; organic supermarkets; bendy buses; ethnic restaurants; bagel bakeries – he is almost glowing with happy contempt.

'I'll do what I can,' he promises. 'If this guy was a soldier and a prominent jeweller it shouldn't be too difficult to find out what happened to him and his relatives. In the meantime, let's keep our eye on the ball: what are our three golden rules?'

'George Bush is evil and stupid.'

'Good, that's still rule number one. Always remember to accompany it from time to time by hilariously referring to Tony Blair as his poodle. Leading to rule number two . . .'

'New Labour are turning us into a police state.'

'Identity cards are OK in Cuba but not here, where they're a fascist indignity. Number three?'

'Everything bad that happens to us is all our fault.'

'People who blow up cleaners on their way to work are expressing their natural grievances at being oppressed into living in social housing without paying for it and, of course, by . . .'

'. . . the atrocities committed in Iraq by evil, stupid George Bush and his poodle Tony Blair.'

'Excellent.'

'I suppose that, unlike you, I don't disagree with all of it.'

'Like what?' Evan demands. 'I hate the excuse-making for those murderers.'

'Well . . .' Kerenza considers. She understands Evan's dislike of the fractious British left but does not share his contempt for all its values. Ideally she thinks there would be a political group that believed in democracy in its fullest sense, and that very rich people should pay a higher proportion of their income in taxes than poor people, and that something should be done for the environment, and the transport system improved, and affordable housing provided for people who did valuable jobs, and an end to social apartheid in the education system, and international law supported even when powerful nations flouted it so blatantly, and it would be secular and oppose nationalism. (If

– after that bright May morning in 1997 when she and Anna drank a bottle of champagne and danced around the garden – New Labour had done, or even showed any desire to do, but *one* of these things, she might have bothered remembering to vote in the last election.) And the people in that group would not be bullying ultras but decent and progressive with a good sense of humour who understood that you can't always get what you want – people like Anna planning policy under the willow tree – and not would-be commissars, jesuitical freaks tearing themselves to pieces over doctrinal differences or swelling with rage over interpretations of dead theory or forming cliques or vanguards. And they would take power in a peaceful revolution and the banners would flutter pleasingly and Britain would become a small but loveable island, a little beacon of hope that the world would quickly want to emulate, and the arts would flourish, binge-drinking would decrease, and the ice caps would stop melting, and there would be no breast cancer, and a man wouldn't get stabbed on a bus for trying to stop somebody throwing chips at his girlfriend and everybody would live happily ever after. She smiles to herself as she considers her absurd utopia, imagining Evan's mockery were she to share it with him.

'I don't support the invasion of Iraq.'

'Makes no difference to the Islamabaddies – they'd still blow you up. And they shed all these tears for their brothers over there yet *they're* the ones killing most of their fellow Muslims, blowing up kids, murdering some poor guy 'cos he's joined the police to feed his family. They're hypocritical scum.'

'We created the conditions for them to flourish, though. And what we've done in Iraq is really terrible, just saying, "we don't give a shit what anybody says, we couldn't give a fuck about the rules, we'll just write new ones, we've got the means to do it, so we're going to go in". And all the people who have died and suffered so much as a result of it, such misery and despair, and still the politicians twisting and lying and justifying themselves. It can make you feel sick if you think about it too hard.'

She looks across at a Stop the War stall.

'I mean, not everybody holds the views you take the piss out of quite so crudely. It's easy to set up opinions that people don't actually hold and then knock them down. And I do think George Bush is evil and dangerous – I'm less bothered whether he's stupid or not.'

'OK,' Evan says. 'But you're being very charitable if you don't think that all or some of those three core beliefs lie at the heart of the so-called left these days. Bunch of sissies, can you imagine one of *them* having any control over your life?'

He glares across the road at the stall, where a couple of young men of indeterminate age and social origin, dressed in fading denim jackets, black jeans and a faint halo of humourless impatience, are distributing Respect and SWP literature, while handing out leaflets which show George Bush with dollars for eyes and misspell Blair as Bliar. They are accompanied by a silver-haired pensioner who is leaning heavily upon a stick of education and showing considerable tenacity as she accosts people heading towards Clissold Park with their kites, dogs and frisbees, demanding that they sign a petition.

'At least they're doing *something*,' Kerenza says. 'I just sit and feel bad about it all or dream of things being different somehow, but I never actually do anything.'

'My dad was a Communist Party member,' Evan says. 'Miserable diehard bigot who thought the Soviets were great and threw a party when they sent the tanks into Afghanistan.'

Kerenza glances at him, surprised that he is mentioning his dead father.

'When I was a kid we went on commie holidays. Stalinist tours to Romania, Hungary, the whole lot. My dad helped to organise housing for refugees from Chile. I had a penpal from Bulgaria who used to write to me about world peace, football and the need for justice for the Palestinian people. Sometimes festivals in France and Spain, where they had proper dancing and food from all the different regions. Not like *those* . . .' He indicates the Respect stall contemptuously. '. . . dreary fucking know-alls who probably opposed the Soviet presence in Afghanistan even though it meant that women could wear make-up and teach in universities without getting stoned to death or having their throats cut.'

'Yeah, but follow your own logic. There's no Soviet Union and there are no miners any more, your Bulgarian penpal's probably some fat cat capitalist . . .'

Your dad drove to the end of the road and poisoned himself with carbon monoxide.

'You don't need to tell *me*. That's why I do what I do rather than hand out stupid leaflets and pretend that Islam is a misunderstood religion for kind and progressive people in order to win an election in a Muslim constituency. Hold on a moment, though . . .'

She watches as Evan darts across the road to the Respect stall, where he chats for a second to the old woman with the stick, signs her petition demanding that Bush and Blair be tried as war criminals at The Hague and returns with a newspaper and some leaflets with pictures of George Galloway on them.

'OK,' he says. 'Few props never go amiss.'

They arrive at the café where Evan has arranged to meet Maggie Thompson. For a moment they are daunted by the sheer volume of mothers with prams inside.

'Millions of dem,' Evan murmurs thoughtfully.

Maggie Thompson is frighteningly skinny with thin lips and the faintest trace of a Geordie accent. She is wearing the Trotskyist shoes that annoy Evan so much – a pair of red campers – and has just come from a screening of a film about black-on-black gun crime.

'It's so difficult,' Evan sighs. ' 'Cos there's a tendency among the general public to think, "Well, who cares if a bunch of drug-dealing pimps are killing each other rather than decent hardworking people?" '

Kerenza gives him a warning glance. He shakes his head sorrowfully.

'But that's just ignoring so many issues of social exclusion and institutional racism.'

'Plus,' Maggie Thompson eats a tiny fragment of the lettuce surrounding her tahini burger, 'the five-year-old girl shot in the head in Clapton *wasn't* a drug-dealing pimp.'

'That's right,' Evan says. 'Not even a mule probably.'

Maggie stares at him.

'Which is the way the local press will probably present it,' he says.

'Actually,' Maggie says, 'the focus of the film was much more complex than that. It was linking the rise in violence to the decline in political and social organisations within the black community. There was a whole range of such groups in the 1970s and 1980s that just don't exist any longer.'

'That's true in general, though,' Kerenza says, noticing that Evan is staring sulkily at Maggie's red shoes and worrying how long he will tolerate her bid to rival him for argumentative didacticism. Things had got off to a bad start when he ordered a salmon and broccoli bake 'because I'm a vegetarian'. Unfortunately – and perhaps not unreasonably – Maggie did not accept this definition of vegetarianism. 'I don't care if you eat fish,' she had said crossly. 'I'm just saying you're not entitled to call yourself a vegetarian.' Kerenza took malicious revenge for Caro kiss kiss kiss by agreeing wholeheartedly with Maggie – putting Evan in the difficult position of having to swallow his irritation at being challenged when Kerenza was simply playing the part on which they had agreed.

Nor did Evan's George Galloway leaflets cut any ice with her as she regards the Respect MP as 'profoundly sexist, an apologist for Baathism, and, most seriously, an SWP stooge'. Evan had forgotten another golden rule – that the biggest enemy of the Judaean People's Front is not the Romans but the People's Front of Judaea. This then provoked an argument with Evan where he was put in the unusual position of mounting a spirited defence of Galloway in the face of sustained condescension and disdain from Maggie, whose lips – if possible – became even thinner during the encounter.

Now Maggie nods briskly at the waitress who is bringing their food and turns to Kerenza.

'You're right, though, about the general decline in political activity. The first film I ever made was about tenant cooperatives in Islington during the 1970s. Seems like another era.'

'Well, it was,' Evan says.

Kerenza kicks him under the table. She's not a big fan of Maggie either but she thinks that if he was able to hold it together with the posh druggies then he should be able to cope with an arts administrator with Trotskyist shoes.

'So tell me about your work in Latin America, Lizzie,' Maggie says.

'Well, I did the documentary on indigenous peoples in Central America and attempts to construct a new judicial process in the war-zones.'

'Didn't exactly have people swarming to the multiplexes,' Evan says.

'I think we've got to accept that not all worthwhile stuff is going to get a huge audience,' Kerenza replies tautly.

'Absolutely,' Evan agrees hurriedly. 'That's what I'm saying. We're not showing the stories of these people for entertainment.'

'What *are* we showing them for?' Maggie asks. 'It's still a question we have to ask ourselves.'

'Empowerment,' Kerenza replies, thinking that this is a bit like taking a driving test and having to show the examiner the brake fluid and the oil stick. 'I've been influenced in most of the stuff I do by the work of Paulo Freire.'

Maggie nods slowly.

'Long time since I've read him. Who else do you like? Outside documentaries.'

Kerenza studies Evan hard.

'We're both pretty big fans of Ken Loach, aren't we, Gareth?'

'Yes,' Evan says.

'I like the British films, but you prefer the ones with a Latin American angle, don't you?'

'Yes,' says Evan.

'Which is your favourite?' Kerenza is torn between her desire not to torment Evan so much that he snaps and her malicious enjoyment at his discomfort. One of the things that she has quickly realised is that Evan finds it easy enough to swallow his scruples and have a cocaine threesome with Caro and Internet Toby in Shoreditch or hang out with Hetty the Snackhead. Those things, however, that truly offend his delicate sensibilities, from running the marathon dressed as a chav to praising Ken Loach over a lefty platter, put his adopted persona under serious pressure and he would prefer others to do this kind of work for him.

'I remember you said you absolutely *loved* the one about the Glaswegian bus driver and the Nicaraguan girl.'

'That's right.'

Kerenza feels a faint passing breeze near her ankle, a suggestion of foot nearly connecting with shin.

'The film about the Spanish Civil War is my favourite,' Maggie says. '*Land and Freedom*. Asks some awkward questions about Stalinist complicity in fascist terror.'

A small vein is starting to throb worryingly in Evan's forehead.

'Especially the way the heroic militia were good-looking and dressed up just like Dexy's Midnight Runners,' he says. 'What's not to love?'

Maggie stares at him again, so Kerenza intervenes hastily.

'And I'm a *huge* fan of Iranian cinema.'

Kerenza has read Maggie's own article in *Sight and Sound* on the subject.

'Ah well, Kiarostami . . .' Maggie murmurs reverentially.

'Yes, Kiarostami,' Evan echoes and they all nod wisely.

As they start to eat, Maggie asks them about the project, and Kerenza produces a folder marked Spark Productions which outlines their mission statement, the basic pitch for the project and the amount they would need.

'The costs seem very reasonable,' Maggie says. 'And it is just the kind of project the diversity fund is for.'

Kerenza takes a couple of DVDs from her bag. 'We also have these,' she says. 'The first is the project I mentioned about local justice systems in Guatemalan indigenous villages. This other one is a sample by one of the project participants, Selma Romanovich. She'll be filming her own return to her village in Turkmenistan.'

Maggie studies the DVDs.

'I only live around the corner,' she says. 'We should go and watch them at my house.'

Kerenza glances at Evan.

'I can't,' he says. 'But Lizzie could go back with you, couldn't you, Liz?'

'Yes,' says Kerenza in a tight, small voice.

'Good. Just hold on while I go to the toilet,' Maggie says.

'What the fuck . . .' Kerenza turns furiously to Evan when Maggie is out of earshot.

'Sorry,' Evan says. 'But I can't stand her and I might forget myself, and then where will we be?'

'I don't want to go on my own with her.'

'Well, too bad – I've got stuff to do.'

'Like what?'

'I've got to explain to you?'

'You just don't like her. Off to see Caro?'

'Well, she's certainly easier on the eye.'

'You're just giving me the job you don't want.'

'And in our little hierarchy of two, that's one of the perks of being top dog. Besides, consider it payback.'

'What for?'

He regards her mockingly. 'What's your favourite Ken Loach film, Gareth?'

'Excuse me, I thought we were meant to be playing a part.'

'You're the actor. I use the term loosely.'

She glares at him.

'So, just another boss after all.'

'We wouldn't be here at all if it weren't for me. And you wouldn't be swanning around in those Marc Jacobs sandals.'

She glances down at the brightly coloured orange and red rope-lace wedge sandals she bought for herself the week before. Even now she can't help smiling at them. They are the nicest shoes she has ever had. They cost a small fortune.

'You shouldn't have worn them today, by the way. You're a fan of world cinema not a little fashionista, so let's see some appropriate footwear next time.'

Evan gets up and stretches – pats his stomach in his customary self-absorbed way.

'Maggie's coming back. Call me and let me know how it all goes. And remember: films don't have to be entertaining – that's tantamount to fascism.'

She glares at his departing back as he gives them a cheery goodbye wave.

My name is Selma Romanovich from Turkmenistan. My father was the local headmaster in the village school. He loved Britain and would always tell us that here was democracy and freedom and the mother of parliaments. I used to work in the light-bulb factory with my brothers and sisters, but then it was taken over by a Western company to make fizzy drinks, and most of the workers don't have job no more.

Kerenza glances at Maggie, who is watching this with rapt attention. They had filmed it with Ivo's friend Branka – an architecture graduate and radio comedian from Zagreb – a couple of days ago. This is the part of things about which Kerenza feels most uncomfortable. Branka had been paid £100 for making the video but had been told the whole thing was part of an experimental project to explore perceptions of asylum seekers rather than an attempt to defraud an arts funding body. And Branka had trusted her because she was a friend of Ivo's.

They had drunk a few beers and made the recording before Branka had shot off to a party which was being held for a friend returning to Zagreb because she had split up with her English boyfriend, using the £100 to buy a couple of grams of coke.

I came to this country in a van – we all paid five hundred US dollars. The journey seemed to take for ever and the conditions were terrible. I was very sick on the boat but I tried to look after my little brother and sister because I am the oldest, and they were crying because we thought we were all going to drown. When we arrived in Britain we were given some dry toast and water and then we were separated and taken to flat in a place called Hasting on Sea. I am asking where are the passports we were promised, but they tell us so many lies and they kick some of the men and then comes Mr Popovic from Serbia, who said we could only get our passports in exchange for a kidney or a lung. He said we had no choice in the matter – they would have our kidney or we would be taken out in a boat and thrown to the fishes or sold as slaves to the Chinese Triads. Then the house was raided by the immigration services, and, although we were scared, we thought we would be treated well because this is a civilised country and you have a democracy here – this is what believed at the time, this is what my father tell me. Now I know that it is all big lie and Houses of Parliament is just picture postcard.

Kerenza looks curiously across Maggie's large, comfortable tiled kitchen as a big ginger tom slides in through the cat-flap. The notice board is cluttered with invitations and old passes to foreign film festivals and women-in-film meetings and take-away menus. A poster for *Bread and Roses* signed by Ken Loach hangs on the wall, there are a few books on Iranian film-makers on the table, a vase with large blue hydrangeas stands above a fireplace with a couple of photos of Maggie in different parts of the world – standing in the snow somewhere smiling.

Because the men from immigration services laugh at our clothes and say we are asylum-seeking scum and terrorists and they will put us

*in prison and make us eat vouchers. We are all taken to big camp,
where we are thrown together with all the other people who are only
here because we are poor, and I want to ask Mr Tony Blair: is it a
crime to be poor? Is it a crime to try and improve your life? And one
day I escape from the camp and now I work cleaning lavatory in day
and making running shoes at night for one pound an hour so this is
why I say, yes, I will like to make this film and trace my journey back
to my village and show the world that we are not criminals, show
British people that we are only here to try and make a living and do
the jobs they do not want to do and send some money to our families
back at home . . .*

Branka breaks off and looks wistfully at her hands.

This is OK? I maybe get in trouble for saying all of this?

And Evan's voice from behind the camera.

It's fine, Selma. You've done really well, been incredibly brave.

'That's very moving,' Maggie says simply.

Kerenza shifts uncomfortably. She feels odd being alone without Evan – like taking a small boat out and finding the currents
are a little treacherous, the wind too high. She needs that rush of
amoral confidence that he imparts to all his business. Alone, she
might just crumple and confess.

'I think you've got a very interesting project here,' Maggie
says. 'Of course, it won't just be my decision. I'm having a few
people round to dinner on Saturday week – why don't you and
Gareth come?'

'That'll be great. I'll have to check with Gareth, of course.'

'Is he your significant other?' Maggie's thin lips almost smile –
she seems much less confrontational in her own home. Kerenza
shakes her head and runs smoothly through their agreed legend
about how they met at the Taormina film festival after she had
returned from filming in La Paz and Evan had finished a project

on the impact of heroin on teenagers in Welsh mining villages. And for a moment she starts to enjoy this vision of herself and Evan, heads together in the edit suite, planning interesting projects together, arriving in simple hotel rooms (a room which they share) with white sheets, drinking cool beers and eating seafood as they discuss the films they have seen together in the festival while Evan makes calls on his mobile to investors and is impatient with them in the arrogant and sexy way of one who knows his talent and what he is worth.

'What about you?' Kerenza asks. 'Do you live here with anybody?'

Maggie sinks the plunger slowly into the cafetière, watching intently the plug of coffee grains as it is forced to the bottom.

'Just Spoon,' she says. 'The cat.'

'I have a cat as well,' Kerenza says. 'Smut.'

Maggie smiles again.

'I used to live here with my husband. Michael Browne. You might have heard of him?'

'Michael Browne the film critic?' Kerenza is impressed, and Maggie nods.

'We're divorced now. Let me tell you something, Lizzie: there is nothing worse than a divorce. It's the most soul-destroying, joyless, nasty process in the world. There is something uniquely unpleasant about it, all the untangling . . .'

'You were able to keep the house, though . . .'

'Yes, I kept the house,' Maggie says flatly. 'Signed over to me like everything, decrees nisi and absolute, consent orders, your whole life with a person reduced to a series of exchanges between lawyers. Have you ever read *The Great Gatsby*?'

'I did it for A level.'

'You remember the big confrontation in the hotel room, Tom Buchanan tries to remind Daisy of times when she must have loved him, when he carried her home drunk to save her shoes. I used to want to write to Michael like that. Don't you remember? Can't you remember?'

She pours the coffee, hesitates with the milk over Kerenza's cup and then pours it in at her nod of assent. For a moment Maggie sits and stares at her mug of coffee, which has a picture of James Dean on it.

'I couldn't have babies,' she says.

'You were trying?'

'For a long time. There seemed to be no reason, they couldn't find anything wrong with either me or Michael. I wanted one so badly, I always imagined a little girl, I imagined I wouldn't make the same mistakes as my mother made with me, I would be able to help her to be happy and confident. But a boy as well, boys are funny, either would have been fine. It started to make me sick – every month the same rigmarole, the same excitement, the same horrible, crushing disappointment. It got so Michael didn't even need to ask me when my period had arrived, he could tell from my face . . .'

Suddenly Kerenza remembers Evan's mocking description of Maggie as being so thin she looked like she had never menstruated and the way she had laughed in response.

Maggie is sitting with her hands on her knees, still staring at her coffee, the toes of each red camper shoe turned inwards, as if her feet are seeking some kind of consolation from each other. Now her thinness makes her seem oddly windblown and vulnerable. She touches James Dean with her finger but does not drink her coffee.

'And it went on and on until I was nearly sick with it all. I hated the women outside with their bumps, I felt as if I would die of envy sometimes. How easy it seemed for them.'

'Especially around here,' Kerenza says.

Maggie laughs bitterly. 'Oh, especially around here. I felt cursed sometimes, I hated my body, I understood for the first time why people might want to cut themselves. I remember I was at a dinner party and this man made a joke about older women doing IVF and how it wasn't their *right* to have a baby, and I'd been drinking so I just went crazy and insulted him horribly, and it was so out of proportion to what he'd said, because there was a time when I might even have agreed with him, but I was shouting and crying and, well, I can some-times be a bit aggressive anyway, I don't really mean to be, it's just . . . it's almost a nervous thing . . . like with Gareth about George Galloway . . . I don't know why I can't just let things go sometimes.'

'Most people are a bit like that,' Kerenza says gently. 'Espe-cially when they've been drinking. And Gareth can be quite bloody-minded sometimes.'

'Well, the hosts of the dinner party seemed to think I'd done it once too often,' Maggie says. 'They said I wasn't welcome in their house any more.'

She holds her knees tightly, and Kerenza imagines the hosts indignantly discussing Maggie's behaviour as they are clearing away the plates, throwing out the remains of the salad, shaking the dregs from the wine glasses.

No, you have to tell her. It's not acceptable. She's done it too often.

'Well, I think I started to go a bit crazy. I used to go and sit in Clissold Park, by the lake. I used to watch the people going by, couples with prams, the children looking at the deer and the birds, all the mothers talking to each other, and I felt completely excluded. Sometimes I'd sit there and I'd think: nobody in the world can be as miserable as I am right now. Which is stupid, of course . . .'

'But understandable,' Kerenza says.

'So then we tried IVF, and it was terribly expensive and it didn't work either. Things got worse and worse, and Michael and I started to argue. One day we had a terrible fight, and he walked out and then he never came back. If you'd told me the night before: your marriage is going to end tomorrow, I would have told you not to be ridiculous, even though *now* I can see how bad things had got. He moved in with some friends and then he got himself a little flat. I still used to go and see him, but there was something just very artificial about it. We'd go to the cinema together, it was the one thing we still loved doing, and sometimes we would have a drink or a meal afterwards, but I used to find it all very strange, as if we were playing at being a couple, as if we couldn't bear to admit it was over, as if being alone was OK as long as you could *say*, "I'm still married." And I think then I just started to let go, like he was holding my arm over the ledge of a tall building but couldn't haul me back, and I wanted to say, "It's OK, I'll always love you but let me go now, just let me fall." Even so, I thought we'd always be friends, I thought I'd always have somebody to go on holiday with. Isn't it strange, that was my biggest fear – not the sex or loneliness, just that feeling when you're in a foreign city with somebody and it's just you and them. I thought – *who will I go away with*? But then Michael started seeing somebody else, a girl from the newspaper he worked at, and she didn't like him seeing me, so we stopped seeing each other and then . . . well . . . you can guess what happened next.'

'Oh no.'

Maggie nods – her two red shoes are virtually on top of each other now, her hands still clasping her knees, the coffee cooling in front of her. Outside, there is a sense of storm, the air shifting, sudden breezes moving in unpredictable ways, the tops of the trees in ominous movement. In the wind-tossed branches of the nearest tree, a pair of white-collared doves are snatching at berries, making a great disturbance among the flimsy branches.

'Mutual friends used to be very delicate about it, but of course I had to know, I had to know everything. They had a little girl. Called her Lauren. Which I have to say I found really quite surprising, because Michael had always said if we had a little girl he'd like to call her Lauren after Lauren Bacall, who was one of his favourite actors. He could at least have thought of a different name. And then you kind of think: are we interchangeable for them? Can they just move on like that? Is one woman just as good as another in the end?'

'Well . . .' Kerenza knows she has to be very careful what she says next. Maggie has opened up in this strange and unexpected way but she is still highly combustible. The hosts who banned her from their house had probably had a lot of provocation before they finally snapped. She remembers Grace Holding telling her about Arthur's apology before he died, how he had never meant to hurt her. Kerenza has always had a belief that men can be divided roughly fifty-fifty: those who adore women and want to spoil them and those who hate them and want to hurt them. Somehow, from the story, she doesn't think Michael belongs in the latter category, just as Arthur didn't. Evan is trickier for her crude category although she remembers him nosing playfully about in her room and spraying his wrist with her perfume. At all events, she suspects that Maggie wasn't the easiest person in the world, can imagine Michael both relieved to be away from her but consumed with guilt and pain at the idea of her suffering.

'Sometimes we just stumble into places and we're not quite sure how we got there,' Kerenza says. 'It sounds as if he cared for you, I'm sure the last thing on his mind was hurting you.'

Maggie nods slowly at this. 'But he did hurt me,' she says and she looks at Kerenza with slate-grey eyes. And for a moment there is silence; outside the window the pair of white-collared doves dance cooing around each other in the branches of a tree, flouncing and fluttering in courtship, while beneath them Maggie's cat Spoon moves in circles, soft, furry belly close to the damp grass, watching them through slit eyes.

'I should go,' Kerenza says.

Turtle Doves

INT. WAREHOUSE – DAY

Jamie Saunders is waiting with two of his henchmen. He is carrying a briefcase with him. One of his henchmen nudges him and he sees a figure walking slowly across the warehouse towards him. It is DC Kathleen McGuire. She approaches him and stands before him. A beat as they look at each other.

> SAUNDERS

Well, well.

> MCGUIRE

Let's make this quick.

> SAUNDERS

Wasn't sure if you'd come.

(Turns and laughs at one of his henchmen.)

> SAUNDERS (CONT'D)

Guess everybody has a price after all.

> MCGUIRE

It's all there?

> SAUNDERS

Fifty K. Count it if you want.

(She shakes her head.)

In return I want to know the name of the person who's setting me up.

MCGUIRE

It's Milena – the Colombian girl. She's working for us.

SAUNDERS

(bitter laugh)
Not any more.

(Regards McGuire puzzled and suspicious.)

SAUNDERS (CONT'D)
Just out of curiosity . . . why have you done this?

(beat)

MCGUIRE

I was up for promotion. They gave the job to a man instead. A laughing stock in the force but still . . . a man. What's the point in playing by the rules?

She takes the briefcase and starts to walk away. But behind her Saunders takes a gun from his pocket.

SAUNDERS

Stop.

(She pauses and turns round. Stares down the barrel of a gun.)

SAUNDERS (CONT'D)
You really think that I'm gonna just let you walk away with fifty thousand of my money now I've got the information I need, you stupid bitch?

(Releases the safety catch. McGuire is staring death in the face.)

MCGUIRE

This wasn't part of the deal.

SAUNDERS (CONT'D)
What's the point in playing by the rules?

(beat)
Your words.

Kerenza puts the script down and looks at Mark.
'McGuire's a traitor?'
'Bet you weren't expecting *that* twist.'
'No, I wasn't.'
They're sitting in Kerenza's kitchen, where Mark has arrived in a state of high excitement because not only has he got a date with the Australian waiter from Zetter but Superagent Emily Holt has arranged a meeting for him with the head of a major independent production company.

Kerenza regards him steadily. 'I mean, you never mentioned that you were thinking of doing that with her. She's replaceable, Hambleton's the star of the show.'
'I don't see what you gain by it.'
'It's about moral choices and consequences – that's what drama's all about in the end.'
'Maybe.'
'Maybe! What's maybe about it? From *Macbeth* to *Coronation Street*, you can't get away from it.'
'All right, I don't need a fucking writing masterclass. Anyway, who's to say she's made the wrong choice?'
'Betraying Milena? Betraying herself and everything she's believed in? Besides, she's placed her trust in a crook who's going to shoot her, so it wasn't even very sensible.'
'I suppose that death at least will release her from the terrible burden of her unrequited love for her prig of a partner.'
'Hambleton's not a prig.'
'A *gay* prig. You can't get much worse than that.'
'Well, at least he isn't a corrupt whore.'
'An expositional gay prig.'
'A self-pitying, corrupt whore.'
But suddenly a song comes on the radio, and Kerenza holds her hand up to shhh him as she hears a gentle lilting melody and picks out words with which she is suddenly familiar.

. . . a butcher boy I loved right well. He courted me my life away.
And now with me he will not stay . . .

It could be worse, love, Kerenza thinks. You could have disgraced yourself by climbing into bed with the butcher boy and have him lie limp and pretending to be asleep. At least he fancied you enough to shag you once, even if he did knock you up. You could be killed off as a corrupt traitor at the end of Episode One. And in spite of herself, Kerenza laughs and shrugs at her friend.

'What are you laughing at?' Mark demands but he is smiling as well.

'You, you transparent, expositional tart.'

He pats her hand.

'Actually, I'm not killing McGuire off at all. It's just a set-up to trap the criminal. That's the final twist – it was going to be a surprise for you.'

'She's in danger but will be saved by Hambleton?'

'Things go wrong, they go right again – it could all seem too simple . . .'

'. . . in the hands of a lesser talent, of course.'

Mark grins at her.

'Like the art of making love I make it all look very easy.'

She holds up a hand.

'Please don't.'

'He's got the biggest . . .'

'Please, I'm begging you, no detail, I want to listen to this song.'

. . . I wish I wish I wish in vain. I wish I was a maid again. But a
maid again I'll never be. 'Til cherries grow on the apple tree . . .

Kerenza hears the front door slam as Ivo comes in. He's been sleeping in Anna's room since her admission to hospital.

And that's 'The Butcher Boy' by the sorely missed Kirsty McColl
and a track from her excellent anthology . . .

Ivo comes into the kitchen and nods at them. He is sad and tired.

Kerenza raises her eyebrows questioningly at him, and he shrugs as he opens the fridge and takes out a bottle of wine, pours himself a large glass.

'The pain control is working better. She's sleeping at least.'

He pauses and looks at Kerenza.

'It's not going to be very long now.'

Kerenza feels a vague noise in her throat, a little spasm of protest.

'I'll go first thing tomorrow.'

Ivo nods and sits down.

'Text me if it's time.'

She nods.

'And you. I'll always have my mobile on.'

He takes Kerenza's hand and starts to weep.

Later, Kerenza sits in her room with her chin resting on her hand, looking out at the garden. She has downloaded Kirsty McColl from the internet and is listening again to 'The Butcher Boy' – her iPod connected to a Bose sound-dock – yet another ill-gotten gain for the self-pitying, corrupt whore to go with her Marc Jacobs sandals. The lights from the houses behind the garden allow her to see the dark mass of the willow tree stirring softly above the empty bench. She suddenly remembers the book *Tom's Midnight Garden*, which her mum used to read to her when she was small, after her bath, dressed in pyjamas and cradled in the crook of her arm on the sofa. And *The Silver Sword* and *Carrie's War* and *A Dog So Small* – always her favourite. Her little cat is sleeping on top of the wardrobe, tiny swishes of a black tail. The night is noisy; beyond the garden she can hear the thump of a car stereo, a shriek of drunken laughter. Her best friend is out there too, drifting away on her morphine cloud while a madman in a neighbouring war shrieks for the nurse. Chrome Rory and Hetty the Snackhead and Hug the Mad Lieutenant are listening to Masters At Work CDs and doing changy nose-ups on a roof terrace in Notting Hill – it will be dawn before they know it. Maggie Thompson is thinking about her missing husband and the child that never was. Grace Holding is dreaming of the back row of the cinema and the bluebells of Kew Gardens. And somewhere out there, perhaps Evan is lying plotting his next move; she very much doubts if he was ever lulled into sleep by the sound of his mother reading about midnight gardens or imaginary dogs.

That night Kerenza dreams that she walks barefoot through the dew to the bench under the willow where Anna is sitting in pyjamas reading about international law. She smiles when she sees Kerenza, squeezes her hand and unbuttons her pyjamas to reveal a pair of oranges.

'What are you reading?' Kerenza asks, and Anna shows her the book, which has a picture of a duck on it.

'I don't want you to die,' Kerenza says.

'We all die,' Anna, who is now a butcher boy called Tom, says to her. 'Even silly slips of girls. Into the foamy brine they go, into the foamy brine.' And he laughs.

Kerenza wakes suddenly, can't soothe herself, so she walks to the window again, but it is full moonless night now, dark and silent, and she can see neither the bench nor the willow tree.

Media Tarts

'How do I look?' Kerenza twirls round from the mirror. Evan is curled on her bed. She knows that she looks good – she's wearing a summer skirt with her Marc Jacobs sandals, can feel the fabric clinging to the lines of her body.

Evan considers her dispassionately.

'Probably a bit overdressed,' he says and returns to reading the magazine. She flinches as she sees that it's the article that she has already read about Kevin Marsh, the director of the *King Lear* in which she played her last significant part. He is tanned and jaunty, has been away in Hollywood, where he has made a couple of commercial flops, but has returned undaunted to direct a series of Chekhov plays at The Lyric. There is talk of Olivia Scott, talk of *The Seagull*. Kerenza looked at the smiling photo of the director sitting in his Sussex garden and felt angry, envious nostalgia flooding through her again. *Kerenza Penhaligon brings an admirable dimension to the character of Cordelia, investing her with both steel and pathos.*

What good is all that now?

She puts her hands on her hips and stares at Evan. He looks up again questioningly and then shrugs.

'You look fine.'

'Fine as in mighty fine or fine as in just about passable?'

He sighs. 'Fine as in the cars outside will explode as you go past. Hurry up, I've been ready for ages.'

This is hardly surprising, as he's wearing his customary jeans and black v-neck jumper. The jumper is cashmere because one of Evan's many dislikes is any material which irritates his skin.

He is so sensitive on this subject that Kerenza can almost drive him to distraction just by talking about having to get out of a bath and put on a coarse woollen jumper before getting dry. Kerenza feels so happy that they are going out to dinner together that she has almost forgotten the purpose of the dinner; it as if they are really going to pitch an exciting film project. She has opened a bottle of wine while they get ready, sprays some perfume onto her wrist and then a little onto Evan's wrist.

'Come on, then,' she says. 'Let's call a cab.'

Evan gets up. 'Oh, I nearly forgot,' he says. 'I think I've found that person you wanted.'

'Person?'

'The jeweller's daughter. Her name's not Sheldon any more, it's Susanna Carpenter. She lives near to Bath, but her father was the guy you're after. Here . . .'

He passes her a slip of paper with an address in a small Somerset village called Merryfield.

'That's brilliant,' Kerenza says. 'Thanks.'

'S'OK – let me see the ring.'

She goes to her jewellery box and takes out the sapphire ring that Grace gave to her. He whistles softly at it.

'If that's a real sapphire with the diamonds, that's worth a hell of a lot of money.'

'It is a real sapphire and it was worth at least a thousand pounds in 1941 so now it's worth . . .'

She looks at him.

'Taking a base compound multiple inflationary index? Millions of pounds.'

'Maths wasn't your strong point?'

They look at it in the light. Just a pretty stone really, hard and permanent.

'You sure you want to give it back?' Evan says.

'I promised,' Kerenza replies, putting it back in the box and ushering him out of the room while ringing the local cab number on her mobile.

As they wait for the cab, she tells him the story that Maggie related about being unable to get pregnant and splitting up with her husband.

'What did she tell you all that for?' Evan demands.

'I don't know,' Kerenza says.

'People are always blabbing away to you.' He says it like an accusation. 'Telling you stuff about their private lives, giving you rings. Even my bloody Uncle Tommy, and he doesn't talk to anybody except those stupid birds of his.'

He seems to be getting quite angry with her all of a sudden. He can do this, sudden unpredictable switches of mood. It is often when she tells him something about other people in her life – if she didn't know that he had so firmly renounced any kind of relationship that could allow him any claim upon her she might have put it down to jealousy. And it's not sexual, because of course he didn't bat an eyelid at her brief dalliance with Chrome Rory. Perhaps it is jealousy, but of a different type – he doesn't like the fact that she is capable of forming affective relationships. Except in so far as it helps them with their work by making people trust her.

'It made me feel quite uncomfortable,' she says now.

'Uncomfortable?'

'She's not a very happy person but she loves her job. We're going to attack the one side of her that lets her hold things together.'

Evan shrugs.

'A banker in the City presses a button and moves money around the globe. And probably each time he does that, somebody loses their job or even their life as a result. Virtually nobody can say what they do doesn't have some kind of bad consequence for somebody somewhere. That's just the way of the world.'

'Mmmm.'

'What's that supposed to mean? "Mmmmm".'

'Just that. It's complicated is all I'm saying.'

'No, it really isn't.'

'Where's that cab?' She looks at her watch while Evan folds his arms and glowers at her.

The journey is only a short one, but as they are heading down Green Lanes alongside Clissold Park, Kerenza's mobile bleep-bleeps a text message. It is from Ivo, who is on hospital duty: *COME NOW.*

She snaps her phone shut.

'I can't come to the dinner.'

'What?'

'I've just had a text message from Ivo at the hospital. I have to go there. I'll drop you in Church Street and take the cab on.'

Evan frowns.

'What are you talking about? I can't do this without you, you can't just walk out now.'

'Anna's dying.'

'Oh, she's been dying for ages.'

'Sorry?'

'I'm just saying, they always think it's gonna happen and it doesn't. You'll be sitting around in the hospital for ages. Whenever you get that call you're always waiting around a few days more. It'll be more upsetting for you just hanging about drinking rubbish coffee and getting stressed out.'

'You want me to go down Church Street?' the cabbie asks.

'No,' Evan says. 'We're still going to the same address.'

'My friend is dying. Jesus, Evan . . .'

'We're working. You can't just walk away when things are at this stage.'

'Can't I?'

'No. Come to this dinner and then I'll drop you at the hospital afterwards.'

'I'm going now.'

'No, you're not.'

'Watch me.'

The cab has stopped at some traffic lights and Kerenza opens the door and jumps out, starts running down Green Lanes towards a bus stop, looking out for a black cab. Evan thrusts a note at the cabbie and also jumps out of the cab, running after her. He has obviously told the cab to wait for them because it remains at the side of the road with its hazard lights on.

'Come back.'

'Leave me alone. I'm going to see Anna.'

'You walk away right now and we're finished.'

A couple passing in the street smile at each other, taking this for just another couple squabbling on a Friday night. Kerenza stumbles on her sandals, nearly twists her ankle and turns to face Evan.

'Do you really think I'm going to go and eat dinner with those people, try and rip money off them while my friend is asking for me?'

'You don't know she asked for you, he just told you to come.'

'I don't believe this.'

She flags for a cab, but it is more in desperation because she can already see that its yellow light is not on and that there are lucky shapes already sitting in the back. She hobbles down the road with Evan still following.

'I want to see Anna.'

'What does it even matter if you're there?' Evan shouts, running his hand through his hair in exasperation. 'She won't be conscious.'

Kerenza turns and stares at him. Tommy was right – there is something broken inside him, he doesn't get anything, care about anybody, his selfishness is ingrained. He genuinely cannot understand why she is doing this, why she should think that she has an obligation to her dying friend that surpasses their own arrangement.

And she thinks of Maggie in her kitchen, the James Dean mug, the hydrangeas, the ginger cat, perhaps she is tasting some of the food she had prepared, pouring herself a loosener, giving herself a stern lecture about not getting too drunk and starting arguments.

'You have to do it. We started this. Just come for an hour or so. Have a drink and then skip dessert or something.'

'I can't do it anyway. I feel sorry for her.'

'You should go and live in rags in a mud hut somewhere, then, because everything we have that is more than we need is bought at somebody's expense. Even a cup of instant coffee. Live with it.'

'Suicide bomber logic – everybody is guilty.'

'Don't try the moral high ground. You're greedy. You want all the perks and none of the consequences.'

She looks down at the sandals on her feet, bends down to unfasten the pretty red and orange laces around her ankles, takes them off and hurls them at him. He recoils slightly as one of the shoes hits him in the ribs and she stands barefoot and furious in Green Lanes, staring at him. He turns away from her.

'Fine. I'll find somebody else who isn't a weak-minded hypocrite.'

She looks at his broad back in its black cashmere jumper, remembers the first time she met him sitting in a bar in Shoreditch covered in petrol. And she shudders at the implications of what she has just said. Does she really never want to see him again, never want to drive down the M4 and over the Severn Bridge, smelling the woodfire of the Welsh mining cottage, watching the hawk swooping over the valley? Joke about Welsh bands and thick'eads and millions of dem. Go shopping and buy almost anything she chooses – an iPod for herself, a fan for her sick friend. Because it has been freedom, her life before Evan seems miserably cramped in comparison.

'I know about your dad,' she says.

He turns back to her, his eyes narrowing, and for a moment she glances nervously around to see if there are other people about.

'What do you know about him?'

'I know what happened at the end of the valley road. Your uncle told me.'

He turns his head to one side for a moment. Then he looks at her and laughs.

'And what? You think that explains everything? You think I'm damaged but I might be redeemed by the love of a good woman? Which you're not, by the way – you're a fucking loser who hangs out with old ladies and queer boys. That's partly why I chose you. Ever stopped to think that you're the only one who thinks your lack of acting options is some major injustice? Here's an alternative scenario: you're not fucking good or pretty enough.'

'Not like Caro?'

'Exactly. Not like Caro. Just like you weren't good or pretty enough to make me want to fuck you that night. I would have thought you would have got the message by now, but let me spell it out for you: I don't want any other kind of relationship with you but a working one. You don't want to work, then we have no relationship at all, and you can get back to waiting for your phone to ring with offers of work that will never come. Is it so difficult to get through your thick fucking head, you stupid, sentimental weakling?'

'My thick head,' she echoes. 'I do . . . yeah . . . I think I've got it now, Evan.'

'We'll see how long you can last with no money again. Maybe you'll go back to stealing from old ladies.'

'We're done here, Evan,' Kerenza says. 'I'm going to get in that cab and I'm going to see my friend.'

She starts walking towards the flashing hazard lights of the cab. He follows her quickly.

'That's my cab,' he says.

'Don't be so childish. You could even walk from here.'

'You're not getting that cab.'

They are almost level with the car now, she reaches for the door handle, he grabs her wrist very hard and she lets out a little yelp of pain. For an instant he is staring at her, his eyes black with hatred, and she realises that there is very little of which he is incapable. But even now she realises that she has made him very angry, and that is perhaps better than the cool indifference he showed when she met him, when the last people he conned were about to burn him alive. The couple who passed them earlier and smiled at what they thought was just a silly public row are returning from the off-licence with a bottle of wine. The girl notices Evan holding Kerenza's wrist and pauses.

'Are you OK, love?' she asks Kerenza. Her partner looks reluctant to intervene, tries to drag his girlfriend on, but the girl isn't giving up.

'Is he bothering you?' she asks again.

'Come on, Julie,' says the man, but then Evan makes a fatal mistake.

'Mind your own business, you silly slag,' he snarls.

The man drops Julie's hand.

'Say what, pal?'

He is a big man, has almost half a foot on Evan anyway but draws himself up even further as he walks quickly towards them, his intention clear, his arm drawing back. And Kerenza almost calls Evan's name in warning as, seeing what is coming, he drops her hand, but it is too late, because the punch has already landed, and he falls to the ground holding a nose already starting to drip blood. The man looks down at him but does not land another blow, the first was quite hard enough. He rubs his knuckles.

'Get in your cab, love,' he says to Kerenza, turning back to his girlfriend. Kerenza looks at Evan, whose jeans are already splashed with his blood, then at the cabbie, who is watching with a puzzled frown. Evan is making strange noises and then Kerenza realises that he is laughing.

She gets into the cab.

'Just drive,' she says.

'Where to?' the cabbie asks, still looking in his rear-view mirror.

'Homerton,' she says.

The cabbie pulls away, and she turns and looks out of the rear window. Evan is standing now, holding his nose and trying to stop it bleeding with one hand. In the other, hanging from red and orange laces, are Kerenza's sandals. His broad shoulders are shaking – with rage, with laughter, with grief, she cannot tell. He's shouting something she can't hear, it could be yes yes

yes yes yes yes. And for a moment, Kerenza feels a tremendous wave of love and pity for him, this broken person who was nearly killed by his own father, she almost wants to yell at the cabbie to stop and let her go and comfort him, put her shoes back on, wipe away the blood, take him to the dinner party, where they will play their roles perfectly, pull off the plan they hatched back in Pant-y-brastrap over bread and cheese and Sicilian wine. She will be hard and smart and unmoved by Maggie's stories because, after all, everybody has a sob story, a tale to tell. And Evan's quite right: nobody lives a blameless life, everybody is compromised one way or another. But the cab speeds on through the night, and Kerenza puts her head back on the seat, thinking of Anna's last laboured breathing in a hospital somewhere in East London, praying to a God in which she does not believe that she is not too late.

Legacies

My lovely brilliant friend,

I am writing this quite late at night while I still can. The loony is still shouting for the nurse, the person opposite is still shouting, 'Shut up, you selfish cunt.' I'm not sure how much I'll be able to write, so this letter might just stop suddenly.

Let's start with the most important thing. I've appointed my sister as executor to my will because she's more efficient, trustworthy and reliable than you. But I wanted you to know I'm leaving you the house and it's yours to do what you want with. I hope you'll carry on living in it – that idea makes me oddly happy – but if you want to sell it, then that's up to you. I'm leaving you the house because I want you to carry on acting and I know for that you need some basic security.

I don't know what's been really going on in your life the last few months. I have to admit that I've been a little hurt that you haven't told me, but maybe you thought that I had other things on my mind. I know it's a little to do with that Welsh rascal and it's on the margins of acceptability/legality, and I worry about you, sweetheart. Please, whatever you do, look after yourself properly and don't let him mess you about. He's handsome and out-of-the-ordinary but he's also a self-regarding, opinionated idiot, and there are plenty of other handsome boys out there for you.

I also wanted to thank you for all our years of friendship. Delicacy and good taste almost forbid me from saying this, but by the time you read this I'll be gone and maybe I won't have been in much of a condition to tell you how much I love you (pause for self-indulgent little snivel). Anyway, I wanted to say that you have loads and loads of great qualities, but the one I've always liked most about you is that you're always interested in stuff and especially people. I've sometimes noticed that you can't remember what something looks like at all, no sense of direction whatsoever (remember that time we got totally lost on holiday in France and ended up having a proper fight?) but you can always remember what somebody told you about themselves, what they like or don't like or what they think about something. That's really very unusual because most people don't really care about anything that isn't directly connected to them and it's your best quality. I just wanted you to know that!!!!

Please look after Ivo – he says he wants to go back to Croatia for a while, but I hope you'll remain friends, I'm sure you will. I'm getting tired now, so I'll stop. My heart is telling me to write all kinds of sentimental slush, my brain (which, modesty does not prevent me from saying, has been an exceptionally good one) is telling me to stop.

So I will stop, and anyway here comes the nurse to do my obs.

Goodnight, darling, take care of yourself and enjoy the house (although obviously not as much as when I was in it).

Anna X

Kerenza puts the letter down on her lap; reading it now no longer makes her sob as it did the first, second and third time she read it a few weeks ago. Evan had been right that Anna would not be conscious by the time she arrived at the hospital but quite wrong that it would be a drawn-out affair. She had died just half an hour after Kerenza arrived in the presence of Kerenza, Ivo and her mum and sister. Kerenza can remember very little about the succeeding days – she did not weep, it was as if a cold, dumb stone had settled on her chest. Then Anna's sister had been sorting out her personal possessions at the hospital, had discovered the letter and brought it for Kerenza. And she had taken it out to the garden to read – just as she is reading it again now – and the sterile membrane that had been holding back her grief had finally broken.

She stares at the house from the bench under the willow tree. Smut is staring back at her from behind the window of her bedroom – she's not allowed out since she had a narrow escape from a fox. Smut was not much of a going-out cat anyway – she would never normally stray much further than sniffing cautiously around the rosemary and lemon thyme that Anna planted.

Now it is Kerenza's garden.

Mark comes out of the back door carrying a tray with some tea and biscuits. He has visited a lot recently because Kerenza has been alone after Ivo returned to Croatia straight after Anna's death. He has had his customary lack of fortune with his love-life – the stupidity of the Australian waiter proving to be too high a price to pay for access to his over-pierced body. He has had, however, several meetings with TV executives who are considering commissioning a pilot of 'Gay Bergerac' and a couple of storylines after reading his treatment. Kerenza has no doubt now that Mark will succeed, but she feels no *Hardenbukentoft* or *Jassenheinkelbrot* about it now, she is pleased that things seem to be going well for him. Mark and Kerenza have sat around considering slightly more feasible titles – *Hambleton* was a front-runner for a while (too boring), followed by *Hambleton and McGuire* (too ITV), followed by the current favourite, *Street Life* (edgy and urban, and it allows Mark to prance around singing the song at every possible opportunity). Mark is also delighted at Evan's disappearance, although it means he gets no more pulled pork and mojitos in Bodeans, since Kerenza is now working for the cleaning agency again.

Mark rubs his eyes as he pours the tea and tells her that he got little sleep the night before because the Italian squatters upstairs were playing grime until the dawn. As they don't keep any regular hours they can erupt at any time, making it impossible to work. Even when they're quiet he is aware that they might wake up or come in at any moment and so lives in a state of almost perpetual nervous anxiety.

'Come and work here,' Kerenza says. 'It's always really quiet.'

She considers him.

'You could move in.'

He glances around at the peaceful garden and then up at her eagerly.

'You think we could? Live together?'

'Sure. Although I have power of veto over Aussie waiters, wall hangings and gay artefacts.'

'What about rent? I pay next to nothing for my flat.'

'You don't have to pay anything here.'

'But you could make money renting out that room.'

'We'll renegotiate all of that when *Street Life* is greenlit.'

'You think it will be? You really think so?'

'Well, it would be stupid for me to say and you can never predict these things. But all the signs are positive and a pilot script would be a good start. Especially as you've already written most of it.'

He nods slowly.

'You know, those Italian bastards sounded like they were gearing up for another big session tonight. Would it be OK . . .'

'Course. I'd like the company, actually. I'll be off tomorrow to Bath.'

'What are you going there for?'

So Kerenza tells him the story of the ring and how she is going to return it to Catherine Sheldon's daughter. She has photocopied the relevant pages of Arthur Holding's diary so that she can read about her amazing rescue when she was such a tiny baby. Susanna Carpenter had sounded surprised by it all but told Kerenza to come down one afternoon and stay for the night. Kerenza wanted to prepare her for the fact that Arthur Holding had hated her father enough to steal the ring but had been unsure how much to tell her on the phone and, in the end, had not mentioned the ring at all. She had been a little relieved, therefore, when Susanna had said that she had known very little of her father, as he had died when she was seven from prostate cancer, and that, following his death, she had been brought up by her mother's side of the family, an aunt from Bristol. Kerenza didn't point out that it sounded as if she may have had a lucky escape in this regard but was relieved that Susanna was quite pleasant and cheerful and said that it all had sounded very intriguing and that she would pick her up from Bath station.

'I'll go and get some stuff, then,' Mark says. 'And pick up some takeaway for us on the way over.'

'That'd be good,' Kerenza says, cradling her tea-cup in her hands.

Later in the evening, while Mark is away picking up some stuff from his flat, she wanders into Anna's room at the top of the house, where he will stay. It is completely empty now, her mother and sister had come and taken away her possessions. Kerenza checks under the bed, but there is nothing there except a kirby grip and a dusty one-day travelcard. She picks them up and turns them over in her hand for a moment as Smut wanders in and stares at her before jumping onto her lap. They sit together in the empty room with its curtainless windows, Smut crackling and purring as Kerenza strokes her, feeling the little heart beating fiercely under the rib-cage, hating the idea of a fox hurting her cat. Then the doorbell rings, and Kerenza throws Smut down as she goes to answer it.

'I hope you didn't get Indian,' she says as she opens the door.

Evan smiles at her.

'Why, what would you prefer?' he asks.

She stares at him.

'What are you doing here?'

'I came to give you these.' He holds out a carrier bag containing the sandals she had hurled at him in Green Lanes. She does not take it from him.

'And I wanted to talk to you,' he says. 'Can I come in?'

'No.'

'Come on,' he says. 'I'm sorry about what happened. Really sorry.'

She turns away from the door but leaves it open. She hears it shut behind him as he follows her into the kitchen, where he puts the bag with the shoes down on the table and sits down.

'How was the dinner party?' she asks. 'You manage to get through a whole evening with Maggie?'

He shakes his head.

'I didn't go. Might have been a bit tricky explaining a broken nose and no Lizzie.'

There is still a tiny mark on his nose where he was hit by a man in the street.

'She'll think we're very rude and strange. Hope I don't ever bump into her in Clissold Park.'

'Make up a story,' he says. 'You're good at that.'

He scrutinises her closely.

'What about your friend?'

'She died. But then, like you said, people do, don't they?'

'I've sometimes said things . . .' He shrugs helplessly. 'There were things I said to you in that row . . . I didn't . . .'

'It's OK,' she says. 'Let's not go there.'

He twists one of the rope-laces of the sandals miserably around his finger and then looks her full in the face.

'I didn't mean the things I said. Maybe I was just jealous of you 'cos you always have people around you.'

'Stop feeling sorry for yourself,' she says, but her heart is beating hard and she is almost shaking. He gives her a rueful half-smile.

'You answered me back,' he says. 'I wasn't used to it, but it was good for me. I've missed you.'

'Please,' she says. 'Next you'll be saying you've been redeemed through the love of a good woman.'

He raises one bushy eyebrow, laughing, and she blushes as she realises what she has just confessed to.

'So what's next for thick'ead?' she asks him.

'Well, I'm sorry about what I said to you, but I'm not sorry about what I do. That'll never change. We blew a great opportunity with the Film Diversity Fund, but I'm revisiting the IT for Refugees idea. I can't tempt you?'

She shakes her head.

'Sorry. You'll need a new accomplice.'

'Yeah.' He contemplates her sadly. 'Hard to find one like you, though.'

'What about Caro kiss kiss kiss?'

He shrugs vaguely.

'Probably got her nose stuck to a toilet seat somewhere. She didn't like making up nicknames.'

'But she had other qualities.'

'Short-term ones. I'm off to Pant-y-brastrap tomorrow, see my uncle, speak to Geraint about an urban regeneration web page.'

'Really? I'm going to Bath to that address you found for me.'

'Oh.'

They look at each other for a moment. Then, casually, he says, 'Give you a lift if you like?'

'I don't know, Evan.'

'You're a good road companion, and I owe you for the scene in the cab. Maybe I can stay here and we can get off first thing – I'll buy you lunch in Bath?'

She is startled by this but before she can respond, the doorbell rings, and she goes to answer it. Mark is standing there with several bags and a suitcase.

'Didn't get the takeaway yet,' he says. 'Thought we could phone for pizza. Or kebabs?'

But his face darkens when he sees Evan over her shoulder, sitting in the kitchen.

'What the fuck is *he* doing here?' he hisses, and in that moment Kerenza decides.

'He's staying here tonight, giving me a lift to Bath in the morning.'

'Staying where?'

'In with you, I thought. He's just been telling me that a lot of his problems were caused by repressed homosexuality.'

But Mark isn't in the mood for jokes.

'His problems are caused by the fact that he's a crook.'

He raises his voice.

'A fucking Welsh crook who can't get it up and doesn't deserve a further minute of your time.'

If Evan hears this he pretends not to. He's studying the soles of Kerenza's shoes.

'Don't be like that, Mark. He came to return my shoes and to apologise.'

Mark looks down at his bags and then back to Kerenza.

'You don't want me here right now.'

'Don't be silly. Of course I do.'

But she doesn't really, her face shows it. Mark shakes his head.

'I'll just dump my stuff and set up my computer and then I'll come back tomorrow.'

'I'll be in Bath tomorrow night, so I'll give you keys.'

He nods and she goes back into the kitchen, where Evan is turning her shoe round and round in his hand. Mark starts hauling his stuff up the stairs without saying hello to Evan.

'Who was that?' he asks. 'New boyfriend?'

Kerenza explains about Anna leaving her the house and Mark moving in. Evan nods slowly.

'That was nice of her.'

'Yeah, that's lefty academics for you.'

'*He* doesn't like me much.'

'One of the few times you've been guilty of understatement.'

'I've never had friends,' Evan says. 'After my dad . . .' He shrugs. '. . . I mean, I'm not using it as an excuse, I was never the most sociable . . . but I just used to sit in my room and read and listen to music.'

'Your uncle said.'

'He's a bigmouth.'

He regards her carefully.

'It's nice to see you again.'

'And you,' she says. There is a pause, and then she picks up her sandals. 'These too,' she says and laughs tightly.

'I mean it,' he says. 'I'm looking forward to spending the day with you tomorrow.'

'I'll have to make up a bed on the sofa,' she says.

Later, however, as she is lying awake in the dark alone, she hears footsteps outside her room. She tries to quell her thumping heart, he probably just wants to ask her something, perhaps he can't find the bathroom. Her bedroom door opens, and he stands there, she can just see the shape of him lit by the light outside.

'I can't sleep,' he says.

She blinks and props herself up on her forearm.

'What do you want to do?' she asks.

He comes into the room and sits on the edge of the bed.

'The thing is . . . I don't know if I can . . . you know . . .'

'That's OK,' she says. 'I don't mind about that. You want to sleep here anyway?'

He nods, and she holds up the duvet, and he gets in. It feels very strange being in the same bed with him, especially after the last disastrous attempt. She reaches out and holds his hand for a moment.

'Goodnight,' he says.

'Goodnight.'

They lie in the dark for a moment and then she sighs, rolls away from him and, after a little while, she lets herself fall asleep.

At some point in the night, she has no idea of the time, she wakes up to the tiniest of caresses on her back. She rolls back to face him, his face is very close to hers, his hands begin to move over her body in the dark, his lips are fluttering on hers, he moves on top of her, she can feel his satisfying weight, his mouth on her neck, his hands under her t-shirt and suddenly the hardness of him straining against her. Then he enters her, holding her very tightly, his head right down next to hers, no tricks, no throwing her about, just slow and deep movements, her arms pinned to her sides as if she is swaddled in him, his breath in her ear until she comes, crying out in the darkness, knowing that he is also coming inside her but not particularly caring as he whispers in her ear.

'I love you, thick'ead.'

In the morning, Kerenza wakes and stretches out an arm into the empty space where Evan has been sleeping next to her. Later, she will think that she knew in that instant, later she will think that perhaps she even knew when she was lying under him in her bed, later she will wonder a lot of things about what he said or did that night. She blinks and gets out of bed, calls out his name, but she knows. The house is very silent and the bag she has prepared for Bath is still in the same place, but it is unzipped and a t-shirt is half hanging from it. He probably looked in the jewellery box first and when he did not find what he was looking for, guessed that she must have already packed it in her overnight bag. She opens the bag anyway and searches rapidly through it, but the sapphire ring – used to purchase a young bride, slipped from a finger in a collapsing building, handed to a sweetheart in the bluebell woods – the hard blue stone on its band of gold has been stolen again and she knows it will never be returned.

Honey

INT. POLICE STATION – DAY

Hambleton and McGuire are drinking Scotch. The mood is one of quiet celebration.

> HAMBLETON
> Great job with Jamie Saunders. You even had me convinced you were a traitor.

> MCGUIRE
> Some of what I said was true.

> HAMBLETON
> About being passed over for promotion? Your time will come.

> MCGUIRE
> What about Milena? I think she may have fallen a little in love with you.

(He gives her a rueful grin.)

> HAMBLETON
> Well, she's only human but she's not my type. Technically, she should be deported back to Colombia.

> MCGUIRE
> You're joking! After putting her life at risk to help us.

> HAMBLETON
> I'll see what I can do.

(She looks at him with admiration.)

Suppose if I had been promoted . . .

HAMBLETON
We wouldn't have got to work together any longer. Ifs and maybes,
Kath . . .

(He studies her fondly.)

HAMBLETON (CONT'D)
Life has disappointments, the critical thing is how you overcome
them. Everybody has loneliness and insecurity and most of all
fear inside them. You've just got to believe in yourself.

(She nods.)

HAMBLETON (CONT'D)
We make a good team.

MCGUIRE
Yeah, yeah we do.

(She gets up to leave.)

MCGUIRE (CONT'D)
See you in the morning.

(She exits, leaving Hambleton studying his Scotch before downing it in one gulp.)

(Music cue: The Crusaders, Street Life.)

End of Epsiode

Kerenza puts the script down and then makes a star next
to 'Epsiode' and writes 'sp'. She then makes a star next to
Hambleton's little sermon to McGuire about overcoming life's
disappointments and writes, 'Expositional thematic dialogue.
Nobody would say this in real life.'
The 12.51 pulls out of Chippenham on its way towards Bath,
and Kerenza puts the last pages of Mark's script down and stares

out of the window at the soft countryside, the gentle western light. After discovering Evan's disappearance with the ring, she had considered cancelling her trip to see Susanna Carpenter and changed her mind several times about it. But in the end she knows it is still the right thing to do, she has a duty to Grace Holding, and also the idea of staying at home contemplating Evan's deception was just too miserable. Besides, she wants Susanna to know the part of the story that involves Arthur Holding crawling through the rubble and singing to the baby in his arms. So she decided that she should go and explain and tell the truth about what had happened. She was very tired from the night before and fell asleep almost as soon as the train left Paddington until she was woken by her mobile ringing and her agent telling her that Kevin Marsh the director just back from Hollywood had called to ask her to audition for the part of Masha in his forthcoming production of *The Three Sisters* at The Lyric.

'That's quite a story,' Susanna Carpenter says as they sit drinking tea in her sunny garden of apple trees and soft grey walls of Bath stone. The small baby with whom Arthur Holding struggled through the wreckage is now an elegant, softly spoken woman in her sixties who has just retired from her job at the University of Bristol, where she was a biologist. She had wept a little at the descriptions of her mother's death and Arthur's odyssey through the building carrying her in his arms. The descriptions of her father come as little surprise to her, as she remembers him as a stern and unloving man, although she has, still, upstairs the doll's house he gave her for her fifth birthday. 'My aunt Jane hated him, though,' she says. 'She said that he was cruel and petty, always wanting to punish my mother for being young and beautiful. Turning hoses on wounded men . . .' She looks in mock-helplessness at Kerenza. 'My son's a geneticist, but I do hope that I don't have too much of my father's DNA in me.'

'He loved your mother as well, though,' Kerenza says. 'That's what Arthur says.'

'Yes.' Susanna contemplates her carefully. 'Now, what about this ring. Did you call the police?'

Kerenza shakes her head. She knows that Evan would have been completely certain that she would not take this course of action.

'The person who took it, he's kind of a lost soul, I don't think it would help matters much. If you want to, of course, I can't stop you, the ring is yours after all.'

Susanna shields her eyes from the sun as she looks at Kerenza.

'You didn't need to come and explain,' she says. 'I would have been none the wiser. And my mother obviously hated the thing by the end, she described it as cursed . . .'

'You could have sold it.'

Susanna looks around her beautiful garden and shrugs as if to say, 'What more do I need?'

'Let him keep the ring; it doesn't sound as if it brought anybody much happiness, and besides – what better way to lay the ghost of my father than by renouncing the idea of punishment?'

Her face lights up as a large dog of indeterminate breed races across the garden. She holds her arms open.

'Saska, Saska,' she says as the dog enters them in a typically doggish frenzy of excitement, spinning around and falling on its back, tongue lolling happily. A good-looking young man with dark floppy hair, dressed in shabby but pleasing style – jeans, flip-flops and a corduroy jacket – twirling a lead follows Saska and sits down at his mother's feet, very clearly the indulged and beloved son.

'This is Jack.' She strokes his hair affectionately. 'He's driving back to London tomorrow morning – you could give Kerenza a lift, Jack.'

'Oh, it's OK,' Kerenza says. 'I've got a return.'

He laughs good-naturedly.

'So what? Save it for another time. Come on, I could do with some company.'

Yeah, but I couldn't, Kerenza thinks. She wants to read and

listen to music and zone out to the British countryside flashing past. She smiles at him, thinking that she will manage to get out of it somehow, but when Jack has read the diary he says that he would like to meet Grace Holding, they could stop in on the way back.

'After all,' he says, 'without her husband I wouldn't be here.'

And Kerenza suddenly thinks that she would like to demonstrate to Grace that she carried out her will and that Grace might also like to meet Jack – this flesh-and-blood outcome of Arthur Holding's desperate rescue. She sips her tea and smiles as Saska chews one of the loose laces of her sandal and the sun beats down on this curious little triumvirate sitting in an English garden.

Later that evening, they drink gin and tonics, and Jack helps his mother with supper, and they sit in the living room, chatting and half-watching the television. It is a comfortable house with beams and high ceilings and Kerenza nurses a fantasy of one day living out in the English countryside with a dog and apple trees, driving into town to stock up on supplies, maybe rent DVDs for evening excitement or read books, far away from Green Lanes and its dirt and poverty and selfish noise and kids scoring on the street corners.

Jack is a scientist like his mother who works in the field of genetics and makes similar good-natured jokes about escaping the DNA of his stern, punishing grandfather. His mother is an apiarist who both studies and keeps bees. She is also a member of the local Stop the War group, and Jack teases her gently about being a dangerous radical and asks her what she thinks would happen if the troops were pulled out, and she replies honestly that she doesn't know, she imagines the bloodshed and chaos will continue and even get worse, but that the invasion was an international crime of such tremendous proportion that it is unthinkable that the criminals should be the ones left to resolve the consequences of their actions.

'My mum wears her heart on her sleeve.' Jack grins at Kerenza.

'Don't be so patronising,' Susanna replies tartly. 'Besides, at least wearing your heart on your sleeve is evidence that you have one.'

Later that night, Susanna Carpenter shows Kerenza the spare room, asks her whether toast and honey would be OK for breakfast, whether she prefers tea or coffee, and gives her a towel for the morning.

'Thank you for coming,' she says. 'And for being honest about the ring. That must have been very difficult after what happened. You must be upset about it all if you were close to this boy.'

Kerenza nods dumbly. As Susanna leaves the room she can hear her singing:

I come from Alabama with a banjo on my knee . . .

Later in the night she gets up because she is thirsty from the alcohol she consumed earlier in the evening and makes her way across the guest room in the profound darkness. As she does so, she stumbles on something and curses as she almost falls. She gets to the door, finds the light and switches it on. As she blinks out of the darkness she realises that the obstacle was her favourite pair of sandals, orange and red rope-laces, the shoes she threw in fury at Evan, the shoes he has returned to her, all there is left of him now.

Jack Carpenter drives a VW Golf and talks with exuberance about his research on evolutionary psychology.

'What does that mean?' Kerenza asks.

'The degree to which differences between, say, individuals and ethnic groups are down to evolution. How much can we help the way we act, I suppose.'

'You mean like the scorpion stinging the frog: it's in my nature?'

He laughs.

'Yes, but what I'm interested in is the scorpion that gives the frog a lift and doesn't sting it. Why did that man risk his own life to save my mother? Why did he then steal the ring? How much can evolution tell us about the basis for morality?'

'Why does the hawk share its food with the falconer?' Kerenza says.

Jack almost crashes through the central reservation with excitement.

'Yes! Because obviously one of the crudest challenges to evolutionary psychology is that we're programmed to act in certain ways, and that could be used as a defence by all kinds of weirdos and freaks. But understanding why we might behave in certain ways also gives us the opportunity to intervene to change those factors, although obviously the hawk doesn't *love* the falconer – or think it does.'

'You don't really know what the hawk thinks,' Kerenza observes. 'Or anybody else for that matter.'

'Well, we might one day. But that's what makes human behaviour so much more interesting – we have these ideas of morality, love, duty, goodness, fidelity. Where the fuck did it all come from? If we start with Darwin . . .'

Kerenza smiles to herself, remembering Uncle Tommy explaining about bating and manning and creances. She resists the temptation to ask Jack the genetic reason for the male need to expound at huge length on stuff-I-know. The answer, she suspects, may have something to do with sexual rather than natural selection.

They stop at some services and drink coffee. Kerenza watches the cars flashing endlessly in and out of view – millions of dem, she thinks a little sadly.

'Don't you think sometimes,' she says, 'there has to be something more to it than just genes?'

Jack frowns.

'*Just* genes? That's an extraordinary statement. It's the most incredible, miraculous, weirdest story imaginable. That's like saying "just life" or "just human difference" or "just sex". There's an almost endless array of stuff to find out, to question, to wonder over. The thing that always baffles me is that there are still semi-intelligent people who would prefer the incredibly uninteresting answer: "just God".'

He pronounces the last sentence with utter contempt, and she remembers Arthur Holding's rage about the man killed by the falling church steeple.

'My friend died,' Kerenza says. 'She was only young but she died of breast cancer. I can't understand it . . . I can't . . . where is she . . . I miss her . . .'

She struggles for breath, struggles not to weep in front of this stranger.

'If it's all about survival, if it's all about genetics, then why did she think further than her own death, why do I still cry for her?'

'Tears are a puzzle,' Jack says, smiling gently at her. 'But then scientists like puzzles.'

Grace Holding now lives in a residential care centre in Hounslow, where she is very popular among staff and residents alike.

'Tell her you gave us the ring,' Jack says to Kerenza as they park the car. 'Don't tell her about it being stolen.'

'Why?' Kerenza asks.

'Just . . . it's a better end to the story for her, isn't it? What's the point in her knowing somebody nicked it from you? That just makes it sour and unsatisfactory.'

Kerenza considers and then she thinks that he is probably right and nods OK.

'She's a lovely girl,' Grace tells Jack as they sit drinking tea in her room, which still smells – as her house once did – faintly of lavender. 'I've always known that. But I don't even know what she looks like.'

'That's certainly your loss,' Jack says flirtatiously, and Grace crackles out her laugh.

'A charmer,' she says. 'You be careful, Kerenza.'

The afternoon is sliding away as they sit and talk; from outside there is a constant low, reassuring noise of suburban traffic. Grace says that she is glad that the ring has been returned to its rightful owner and that she is sorry that it has taken so many years. Jack replies that the grandfather he never knew was, by all accounts, an unpleasant individual, and that he would not be sitting here right now were it not for the bravery of her husband. And Kerenza looks at his dark eyes, his floppy hair, his long eyelashes, every tiny detail of him, and thinks how astonishing it all is – not just that he is alive but every accident, every possibility, every new channel down which life flows: if the shell had fallen a little closer to Arthur Holding, if the Prince had commanded a different military hospital, if the German bomb-aimer had flow a hundred yards further before releasing his deadly cargo, if her conscience had not impelled her to return to the house of the old woman from whom she had stolen money, if, if, if . . . millions of dem.

As they are leaving, Grace asks Jack to give her a second alone with Kerenza, and he says he'll wait downstairs.

'Thank you,' she says when he has gone. 'I didn't doubt you would do it for a moment. He sounds as if he's a good-looking boy. Is he?'

'Not bad,' Kerenza says. 'He's a bit of a show-off.'

But of course Kerenza has a soft-spot for irrepressible show-offs.

She goes over and kisses Grace lightly on her papery cheek, and the old woman squeezes her hand very tightly.

'My daughter hates me,' she says.

'Why?' Kerenza asks and Grace sighs.

'I wasn't a good mother.'

'I'm sure that's not true.'

'It is. I was cruel to her sometimes and I didn't like Richard, her fiancé.'

'Why didn't you like him?'

'He was boring and stupid and he was a Conservative councillor. I wanted more for her. But she loved him, and he wasn't a bad person, and I should have respected that. I thought I was being smart and funny but I was being a bully. I was really rotten to them, Kerenza, it wasn't right, I should have cared about whether she was happy or not. Anyway, now they live thousands of miles away, and I don't see my grandchildren. I'll always regret that. But I want you to keep coming to see me, do you promise? You're like a daughter to me now, you're all I have.'

'It's a deal,' Kerenza says. 'My mum and sister don't like me very much.'

'They must be mad,' Grace says and holds Kerenza's hand very tightly. 'Try and make things up with them, though. It's terrible when it's too late. Nothing should matter that much, you shouldn't allow things to get so bitter.'

Kerenza contemplates this piece of advice and suddenly she knows that the only way to really wipe the slate clean for the stolen money is to tell Grace everything.

'I haven't told you the truth,' she says.

'What do you mean?'

And so Kerenza tells her. About how she met Evan and saved his life, about their strange relationship, their trips to Pant-y-brastrap, the chavathon and the plan to rip off the British Film Diversity Fund – a plan which makes Grace cackle slightly and then stop herself, as if guilty for doing so – the final row in Green Lanes and his return when he slept with her, told her he loved her and then stole the ring and vanished. About her journey to Bath.

'So,' she says. 'I was lying. Susanna never got the ring back but she didn't care really.'

Grace says, 'She sounds like a good woman.'

Kerenza nods.

'She was. Is.'

'So you've been living life in the fast lane,' Grace says.

'I'm not very good at it.'

'No. Don't you think that this Evan chap, don't you think he might have known that? Why do you think he came back?'

'To steal the ring, of course.'

'He wasn't to know you still had it. He only found that out when he got there. From what you've told me he can't really have thought you had a future but he wanted to see you again anyway. Even that night he told you he'd always be a conman, so there was no real way you were going to be together after what you had decided. You *chose*, remember, you chose to feel sorry for that woman from the Film Fund, you chose to be with your friend at the end. Perhaps he just wanted a different kind of goodbye from the one you'd had. And the ring wasn't really yours, was it? That was just his little flourish for you. He liked showing off to you, perhaps in his own way he did love you.'

I love you, thick'ead.

And Kerenza suddenly starts to weep, her tears falling onto the old gnarled hand she is holding in her own.

'Are you crying?' Grace asks. 'Why are you crying? Don't cry.'

Why is she crying? A pair of pretty sandals, a kirby grip beneath a bed, a bird swinging upside down from a leash, the baby sucked from its cot by the bomb-blast, two detectives clinking glasses together at the end of a successful operation, a blind woman who can no longer see the fading light. She rests her head on Grace's shoulder, this woman who was cruel to her own daughter but has tried to make up for it by kindness to another, and Grace strokes her hair and soothes her and dabs her eyes with a tissue and tells her not to cry, silly thing, you poor silly girl, and murmurs the soft reassurances that mothers give to their wounded daughters.

Jack lives in Kentish Town and says that he will take Kerenza back to her house, so they drive across the Westway and through the traffic of the Euston Road and up past King's Cross and the Angel to Newington Green.

'You can drop me here,' Kerenza says to Jack when they are approaching Clissold Park.

'You sure?' he asks. 'I'll drop you at your door if you like.'

'It's a really nice evening. I'd like to walk for a bit.'

'OK.'

'Well, goodbye.'

'Yeah, bye.'

As she is unfastening her seatbelt he turns to her:

'You want to give me your mobile number? I might send Grace Holding a card so I'll need her address.'

'Sure,' she says, a little disappointed that that is the only reason.

They exchange numbers, and she watches as he drives off, waving in his rear-view mirror as he goes. Then she walks up Green Lanes to Clissold Park, where groups are still sitting having little barbecues and throwing frisbees and drinking wine and smoking spliffs, and kids in Arsenal shirts are running around chasing footballs, and it might be the lefty capital of Britain, but there are far worse things than that. She's quite tired by the time she arrives at the lake and so she sits down on a bench to think for a little. The day is coming to an end, and she allows herself the last luxury of wondering about a Welsh valley, a lone man swinging a bait lure for a faraway hawk, a stolen sapphire nobody else cares about weighing down a pocket.

She knows that she will never see the valley or Uncle Tommy or Evan again, that their memory will fade with time, and the thought is both strange but also oddly fascinating. She thinks about what Grace said to her about his motives. The incorrigible crook with something broken inside him, the man who lay still hard inside her and whispered, 'I love you.' Did he come to say goodbye, to release her somehow back into a world of normality, to ensure that the last image she had of him was not the spiteful figure of Green Lanes. And perhaps the ring *was* simply a final flourish, an audacious sign-off so that she should never forget the person with whom she had been dealing – a person who would never wear his heart on his sleeve, who knows that there is no such thing as a blameless life, that there are victims.

Perhaps.

Make up a story. You're good at that.

I love you, thick'ead.

A couple of other people are also sitting on the benches, staring at the water – an elderly couple with walking sticks, a man in shorts and flip-flops talking miserably into his mobile.

He is saying, 'I just wanted to go for a walk in the park like normal couples do, I can't stand the fucking drugs any more, I'll die of boredom.' And a young mother is kneeling next to a pram, pointing to a log in the lake where several terrapins sit absolutely motionless staring up at the dropping sun.

Kerenza's own mobile bleep-bleeps a text message. It's from Jack and it says: *I really want to see you again. Come for a drink with me next week?* And she smiles and shivers inside and hopes that Mark is home, because suddenly she can think of nothing she wants more than to sit under the willow tree in the garden with him, drinking some wine and listening to his agonising over whether there are too many concluding beats in his screenplay and his latest *amour fou* and – if she can get a word in edgeways – about her audition for *The Three Sisters* later in the week, about her possible date and how she will call him Genetic Jack to make Mark laugh. So she walks on around the lake, and, coming into view – as she approaches its far corner – is a man she has seen before in the park walking his dog. He turns and whistles and calls 'Rab!', and from far away she sees the dog running, its forelegs rising in manic glee as it belts towards its owner. Does it love him, Kerenza wonders idly as the man nods to Kerenza at the crossing of their paths.

'Lovely evening,' he says pleasantly, and she smiles at him as she walks out of the gate of the park. She is thinking about the tone she will use to accept Jack's invitation and about her audition for *The Three Sisters* and as she walks she hums Masha's song to herself.

By the sea strand an oak tree green, upon that oak a chain of gold

And a couple of kids on bikes career around her and they laugh at the red-haired girl in bright rope-lace sandals singing to herself as she walks down Green Lanes, past the Ockabasis and coffee shops on her way back home.

Acknowledgements

Three books were very useful for the sections on the Blitz years. These were: *An Underworld at War: Spivs, Deserters, Racketeers and Civilians* by Donald Thomas; *Voices from the Home Front* by Felicity Goodall and *The Longest Night* by Gavin Mortimer.

The letters in the book are real. The letter written from *HMS Bulwark* was from my Great Uncle Tosh who was killed when that ship was sunk. The work reference is also a real one although the names have been changed. It was written for my grandfather, Arthur Bradford, who at sixteen years old was badly injured fighting with the Middlesex regiment during the First Great War for Civilisation. I am grateful to my mum and to my (hugely missed) aunt for passing them on to me.

Although I have drawn on my grandparents' wartime histories, the characters of Grace and Arthur Holding are entirely fictional creations and the story of the ring is imaginary.

I would also like to thank Dory Renzi for her hospitality in Pont-y-rhyl, Wales.

For invaluable insights into the educational backgrounds and other habits of posh druggies I am grateful to Bewcolla Godfly.

And for her patience, tactful suggestions and support, thanks to my editor, Helen Garnons-Williams.

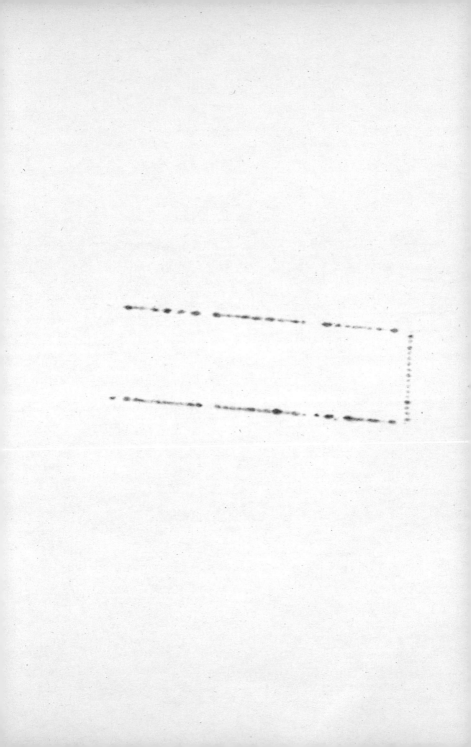